It's 1940...

ITALY'S DICTATOR BENITO MUSSOLINI sees his image as a world leader overshadowed by Adolf Hitler's European conquests. Determined to demonstrate Italy's strength, he invades neighboring Greece. When his army fails to subdue the Greeks, Hitler is forced to step in to aid the Italians. The invasion sparks a fierce resistance both against fascism and the Nazis.

A Country of Heroes follows the wartime lives of three university students in Thessaloniki—a German and two Greeks, one of them a Jew. With conflict intensifying, the German returns home to fulfill his duty; the Greeks become leaders of resistance groups.

As war rages the young men encounter one another from time to time as allies in the struggle against their invaders and as enemies when the German army moves across the country. Meanwhile Mussolini, Hitler, the Soviet Union's Joseph Stalin, and Great Britain's Winston Churchill are making strategic decisions that will have significant impacts on the war effort and its outcome.

In the fall of 1943, losing badly, Italy withdraws its forces from Greece. Soon Germany follows suit. Now the resistance leaders and fighters must turn to helping shape Greece's future. As WWII winds down in Europe, the student survivors seek out each other before turning to their own futures.

ALSO BY MICHAEL J. BAKALIS

In Search of Yannelli
A Son's Journey to Know His Father

The Achilles Heel
A Citizen's Guide to Understanding
and Closing the Black-White Academic
Achievement Gap in Our Schools

Trial and Triumph
Critical Episodes in the Lives
of American Leaders

A Long Hard Journey
Debating Issues in
African-American History

Times of Crisis
Case Studies of Presidential Decisions
That Have Shaped Our History

The History Detective
Solving Problems in American History

A COUNTRY OF
HEROES

A COUNTRY OF
HEROES

A NOVEL OF THE
GREEK RESISTANCE
IN WW II

MICHAEL J. BAKALIS

Harbridge Press
Woodridge, Illinois

A Country of Heroes: A Novel of the Greek Resistance in WW II
Copyright © 2015 by Michael J. Bakalis

International Standard Book Number: 978-0-9863190-0-6
Library of Congress Control Number: 2014958497

PUBLISHER'S CATALOGING-IN-PUBLICATION DATA

Bakalis, Michael John, 1938-
    A country of heroes : a novel of the Greek resistance in WW II / Michael J. Bakalis.
    pages ; cm
    ISBN: 978-0-9863190-0-6
    1. World War, 1939-1945—Underground movements—Greece--Fiction.
        2. Greece—History—Occupation, 1941-1944—Fiction. 3. Fascism—Greece—
        History—20th century. 4. National socialism—Greece—History—20th century.
        5. Historical fiction. I. Title.
    PS3602.A435 C68 2015
    813/.6   2014958497

Production by Adams Press, Chicago, Illinois

PRINTED IN THE UNITED STATES OF AMERICA

1 3 5 7 9 10 8 6 4 2

COVER: German troops raising the swastika over the Acropolis, 1941.
Bundesarchiv, Bild 1011-164-0389-23A/photo: Scheerer

Harbridge Press
Woodridge, Illinois

THIS BOOK IS DEDICATED TO THE men, women, and children of the World War II generation in Greece, who suffered greatly, fought valiantly against tyranny and evil, and demonstrated to the world the true meaning of courage.

Author's Note

A Country of Heroes is a book of historical fiction. Almost all of the events presented actually happened, but some episodes I have created. The main characters in the book, Nikos and Vasili Gantos, Mordecai ben Nathan, and Klaus Schreiber are fictional and are not based on any historical figures.

Much, but not all, of the dialogue attributed to Adolf Hitler, Benito Mussolini, Galeazzo Ciano, Claretta Petacci, Edda Ciano, Ioannis Metaxas, Joseph Stalin, and Winston Churchill, as well as other minor figures, is taken from historical sources and memoirs.

CONTENTS

PROLOGUE
ATHENS, GREECE
2011

CHAPTER ONE

THE OLD MAN SAT QUIETLY ON the bench in the park area directly across from the Parliament building, the section of Athens called Syntagma. He was dressed in a suit jacket, shirt, and tie and had a straw hat tilted slightly on his head. The cane that he used to steady himself when he walked was placed vertically against the bench. For those walking by him, he was a somewhat strange sight, if they noticed him at all. Old people, especially people as old as Nicholaos Gantos who had just had his ninety-first birthday, were seldom seen in downtown Athens. And the fact that his attire was so formal—suit, tie, hat—also seemed out of place since it was early June and the temperature in the city had reached eighty-eight degrees. The old man had slowly walked to the park bench from his apartment in the Plaka section of the city because he wanted to see firsthand the demonstrations and the activity of the large number of people he had seen on television the night before who were protesting the latest actions of his government.

While he sat silently, absorbing the sights and sounds around him, activity and loud shouting seemed to be present on every inch of the grounds that made up the park area. Young people and those not so young, were marching with handmade signs protesting the government decisions to reduce the number of government employees. Others were loudly chanting in a rhythmic fashion words conveying the message that the government was a den of thieves, robbing them of early retirement pensions that had been a benefit offered to Greek society for decades. Still others marched with signs accusing the government of selling key assets to private corporations, mostly non-Greek corporations, and calling the politicians "traitors to the people." Along with the protestors who occupied the plaza were the police, standing quietly in groups while they scanned the crowd looking for any sign of potential or actual violence. They were young men, mostly in their twenties, who appeared to be very physically fit and who were armed with tear gas and threatening automatic weapons in full view of all the assembled crowd. There were also others, those with little concern for Greek politics but quick to take advantage of the commercial and business opportunities. There were ice cream vendors and sellers of a round sesame-covered bread called a "kouloudi." Still others, mostly African black men, East Indians, or Pakistanis, were spreading sheets on the ground and displaying their counterfeit merchandise of Gucci, Louis Vuitton, and Coach purses and wallets as well as a selection of equally fake Rolex and Movado watches. A Gypsy woman sat huddled against a tree, holding a frail, sickly-looking small child in her arms, while she extended an outstretched hand with a cup that she begged passersby to fill with coins or Euro paper bills.

Nicholaos Gantos absorbed the sights, sounds, and activity around him with feelings he could not quite understand and sought to sort through his head. As he looked around, he quickly concluded that of the thousands assembled he was, as far as he could see, the oldest person here. It was a feeling that, by now, he was used to. Almost anywhere he went, to a store, to a coffee house, to church, to the park, he was now always the oldest person in the place. All these thousands of people assembled at this demonstration, Gantos thought to himself, were all born after him. He had seen things they may have read about but never actually seen, experienced life in a way none of them could imagine, and witnessed changes in this country that he loved that he could never have imagined when he was the age of those holding those signs and marching around him. They were oblivious to the fact that he was even there, but he had been here before any of them and wished that he had the strength to stand straight, walk along with them, and talk to them about the past, the country, and the future that was in their hands. Yes, Greece faced an economic crisis now, he thought, but this crisis, as serious as it was, seemed almost mild as he thought of the national crises he had seen and in which he had lived and somehow survived.

The current economic crisis was real enough, he believed. Greece had gotten itself into enormous debt, it couldn't pay its bills, it possibly would have to default on its loans and obligations. In effect, the nation might have to declare bankruptcy if any nation could even do that. And now the European Union, led by Germany, was telling Greece that it would provide no further financial help for his country unless widespread and severe austerity measures were put in place. Failing to take these drastic measures would probably mean Greece would exit the European Union and become an outcast, no better in the eyes of the world than those underdeveloped third world nations in Africa and Asia.

As the old man reviewed these thoughts in his mind, he suddenly was brought back to the present by another group of protestors chanting slogans directly against Germany and especially against German Chancellor Angela Merkel. "Germany will not strangle Greece," they shouted. "We will never surrender our history, our country, our pride, to Angela Merkel—we owe Germany nothing, Germany owes us everything!"

Germany was now the major player in the crises that had overcome Ireland, Italy, Spain, Portugal, and Greece. After the worldwide economic collapse of 2008, Germany was the big economy of Europe that had basically survived the economic collapse and now was the key to any hope of European economic recovery. And because the Greek economic fiasco was the worst of all of these other countries, the German response to the Greek crisis was now especially crucial. The anti-German signs and demonstrators brought forth especially conflicting feelings in the old man. What he had seen, what he had lived through, and what the Germans had done to his family were experiences and thoughts that he had never erased from his mind. Even now, so many decades later in his ninety-first year, he would periodically wake abruptly from his sleep at two or three in the morning as thoughts of those bygone days returned to his subconscious. The truth was he still hated the Germans. What he had seen as a young man convinced him that they were barbarians—cruel, vicious, thieving murderers who had raped his country and killed thousands of his friends, family, and fellow countrymen. As he looked at the words crudely written on the protestors' signs, he knew he agreed with them—Greece owes Germany nothing. Germany owes Greece for the economic resources they stole and pillaged during the last World War as well as for the more than half million Greeks they had murdered. It was right that these young people were resisting this latest attempt of Germany to break Greece, to make it an economic slave subject to German direction. He and his generation had resisted Germany, too, for many different reasons and in different ways. The Nazi pigs, he felt, even after all the destruction they brought to the nation, had never broken the Greek spirit or the Greek nation, and they now, in a different way, could not be allowed to try to break and subdue Greece again.

But as the sign-holding marchers passed him, the anger within Nicholaos Gantos began to subside, and more rational and realistic thoughts came into his head. After all, he thought, Angela Merkel and the German people were not the same Germans that continued to trouble his mind. They were not Nazis. They were not even born when he had experienced what that previous generation of Germans had done to his nation. In fact, after having been a defeated country in physical and economic ruin, the postwar generation of Germans had brought back their nation to the point of economic prominence and dominance in Europe. And what had Greeks done in those same years? Greeks had killed each other in a civil war, given control of the country over to a military dictatorship, and allowed corrupt politicians to buy off the country with social policies that eroded Greek incentives to achieve and created a society addicted to government but unwilling to pay for government services through any system of fair and collectable taxes. No, thought the old man, again watching the protestors as they marched and chanted their anti-government and anti-German slogans, the problems of his country today were really not caused by Germany but rather by his fellow Greeks who keep electing corrupt politicians as long as they load the public sector with jobs and then keep tolerating the continued use of family connections, bribes, and political patronage as the standard mode of operation. Now this unholy alliance between politicians and people had brought the country to its knees. Nicholaos turned these thoughts over and over in his mind trying to sort out his feelings about Germany and about his own countrymen. He rubbed his forehead as if that gesture might make things make sense but finally could not escape the conclusion that the Greeks had only themselves to blame for the crisis the country now faced.

As he continued to observe the activity around him, the protestors now increased the level of their vocal protests with different messages coming from across the large open area. Immediately in front of Nicholaos, a bearded man, probably in his forties, repeatedly chanted his message as he raised and lowered his placard on which was written the same message as his repeated vocal refrain: "We don't need Austerity—We just need jobs!" "We don't need Austerity—We just need jobs!" "We don't need Austerity—We just need jobs!" Fifty feet to the left of the old man another, younger protestor held signs with a different message: "Jobs for the people—No Jobs for the politicians." Another sign read, "Pasok and New Democracy—Different Parties, Same Crooks."

Nicholaos continued to sit quietly attempting to absorb and understand who these people were, and what his country had become. It was a very different country now, he thought, and old men like him seemed like museum relics from a bygone era. Looking around he saw that he was the only person among the thousands that had gathered who was actually wearing a suit jacket and a shirt and tie. But that was how people were supposed to dress when they came to the center of the city when he was young, and now shorts, jeans, and gym shoes were the uniform of choice. Continuing to scan the crowd and activity, his eyes and ears absorbed other new aspects of twenty-first century Greece. The language of the assembled crowd was no longer just Greek. He heard people speaking English, German, Polish, Arabic, Albanian, and various dialects of two or three African countries. Ten or twenty years ago, Gantos thought, they probably would have been tourists, but today these people lived here and they were part of Greece. Even a decade earlier he had seldom seen a black face; now those faces filled Parliament Square along with many from India, Pakistan, and Bangladesh. The country was changing, and who were the Greeks today? And, he thought, how can one even define what it means to be Greek today? And what was happening to his Christian nation with the cross boldly displayed in the blue and white national flag? Already he had heard there were more than 100,000 Muslims living in the city. These questions consumed Nicholaos as he sat on his bench and thought that probably when all those questions were answered he would not be around. Maybe, he concluded, there was some value in being old with only a very limited time left. Maybe there was a time to die.

Gantos' thoughts were interrupted by the voice of a young man, probably eighteen or nineteen years old, who approached the bench where the old man was seated. "Papou," the boy said, " mind if I sit down?"

The old man looked at the young man who had addressed him with the Greek word for "grandfather."

"You must be mistaken, young man," Gantos said, "I'm not your Papou. My name is Nicholaos Gantos, Mr. Gantos to you."

The boy was momentarily taken aback, not quite knowing how to respond. He obviously had offended the old man for some reason although he had not intended to be disrespectful. "I'm sorry, sir," he finally said, as he placed his placard, on which was depicted a strange symbol, on the ground. "I meant no disrespect, did you say sir your name was Gantos?"

" That's what I said," Nicholaos replied, "and who are you? And why are you here?"

" My name is Lakis, Mr. Gantos, Lakis Stamatis, and I am here to express my anger at what these politician thieves and foreigner immigrants are doing to destroy our country."

Gantos looked at the boy. He was a tall, thin, rather handsome young man, dressed in his jeans, gym shoes, and a shirt with a slogan printed across the front that read, "Wake up Greece! Look forward to a Golden Dawn!"

Golden Dawn. Nicholaos had read about this rather new political party in Greece and seen their demonstrations covered on television but for the sake of conversation acted as though he had never before heard the term before. "Golden Dawn?" he asked with a quizzical expression on his face. "What is this Golden Dawn?"

The boy thought for a moment, ran his fingers through his uncombed thick brown hair, and settled himself as though he was preparing to educate the old man about what he believed was the answer to the current Greek crisis.

"The party," Lakis began," has some clear and basic beliefs. We are strongly nationalistic, we want Greece to remain a country for real Greeks. We want to throw out these crooks who control both of our political parties, and we want to stop this invasion of foreigners who are taking our jobs, changing our country, and even eventually threatening the religious foundation of our Greek Orthodoxy. And finally, we will not submit to the demand of the European Union that we drastically cut, in fact, almost eliminate government programs and employment. Greece must chart her own destiny, Mr. Gantos, we must determine our own future and fate."

Gantos actually knew a great deal about the political party known as Golden Dawn. He still lived alone even though his daughter Penelope had virtually begged him to come and live with her and her husband. Nicholaos was an independent man who still, at ninety-one, was able to move around and even cook for himself. He no longer drove his car but considered that to be almost a blessing when he saw what traffic chaos the streets of Athens had become. When his wife died five years ago, he vowed that he would not depend on his two children or his now adult grandchildren. He had lived through difficult times in his youth, so being old and living alone didn't seem like some undue hardship. He had his small apartment, his television set, his stack of books, and his two or three daily newspapers, so he had plenty to do to pass his time and learn what was happening in the Greek political world. And about once or twice a month, he would meet up with the few old-timers who were still around and they would have coffee and some sweets and in an hour or two seem to solve all the problems of the world. So he believed he knew much more about Golden Dawn than he conveyed to his new young acquaintance.

The Golden Dawn party had grown out of the foundation established by a man named Nikolaos Michaloliakos around 1980. It formally became a political party in 1993, was somewhat dormant for a number of years, and then surfaced again in 2007. The media began to notice the party in 2010 when it received 5.3 percent of the vote in local elections in Athens, winning a seat on the city council. In 2011 it seemed to be gaining in popularity and support among certain segments of the Greek population who were attracted to the party's emphasis on extreme Greek nationalism, anti-foreign rhetoric, and its call to attack the serious unemployment issues. The party strongly denounced the severe austerity demands forced on the nation by the European Union. By 2011 the Golden Dawn seem poised, thought many, to make major political inroads in the Parliamentary elections that were scheduled for 2012. The party had achieved a level of support in Greek society through activities such as delivering low-cost or sometimes free food to some to some of the poorest Greeks and offering citizens protection from crimes perpetrated on native Greeks by the new immigrant influx. In return, the party wanted allegiance from those they had served or protected.

There was also another darker side to the party and its mode of operation exposed by the media that troubled the old man. Often party members spoke positively of Nazi Germany, spoke against homosexuality, advocated the use of violence to achieve their aims, and displayed symbols and acted in ways that seemed to emulate those of Germany's Third Reich. The party followers even appeared to use some variation of the Nazi outstretched arm salute and displayed a flag that seemed to be a variation of the Nazi swastika. The Greek media had labeled them Neo-Nazis and accused them of being fascists, racists, and anti-Semites who were responsible for an increase in anti-Jewish graffiti on buildings throughout Athens. The party had, of course, denied these allegations and repeated that its sole program was to rid corruption from Greek politics, stop immigration, and stand firm against the austerity program forced on Greece by the European Union. Their party slogan troubled the old man and brought back too many difficult memories. Golden Dawn planned to campaign for the 2012 election on the slogan and platform of, "So we can rid this land of filth." So, contrary to his façade of ignorance, Gantos knew a great deal about Golden Dawn, but he was curious about the young man sitting next to him and wanted to know how he felt about the message of the party whose support he now proudly announced by wearing his Golden Dawn tee shirt for all to see.

"So, Lakis, tell me about Golden Dawn. What does the party really stand for, and why are you so attracted to it?" asked Gantos as he moved to retrieve his cane that had fallen to the ground.

The young man thought for a few seconds and then, with a somewhat quiet voice, said, " I'm young. I would like a future in our country, but I see no future. It's people my age and in their 30s who are suffering most. Mr. Gantos, we have more than a 50 percent unemployment rate for young Greeks. Fifty percent! I want to finish my studies, go into some profession, but when? Here? In Greece? There's nothing here. The politicians have raped us, the immigrants are bringing crime to our country and destroying our identity and eventually polluting our very blood, and the EU, led by Germany, is killing us economically. Golden Dawn, for me, offers hope, common sense, and an agenda to reform all of Greece. That's why, Mr. Gantos, that's why I am willing to stand out here, sing protest songs, and hold up signs until my arms feel like they will fall off my body. That's why, Mr. Gantos, can't you see? If you were my age I bet you would feel the same way." Lakis seemed exhausted with emotion as he finally finished answering the old man's questions. He put his hands together, and his head seemed to drop into them in a final act of mental fatigue. Gantos noticed a wetness in the boy's eyes. He had started to cry.

Nicholaos waited before he spoke, and as the young man put his arms down and lifted his head the old man said, "I understand what you are thinking, Lakis, but doesn't it bother you that some people think Golden Dawn resembles the ideas, symbols, and operation of fascists and even Neo-Nazis?"

The young man quickly perked up and was quick to respond, "Those opinions are the conservative elements of Greece, paid off by the established political parties. They live off graft, corruption, and outright theft of public money. They will never want change of any kind. I don't buy that media propaganda that we are Nazis, and, you know, even if we are, what they stood for wasn't all bad."

"It wasn't?" fired back Gantos, not waiting one second to respond. "What do you know about the Nazis, Lakis? What did they teach you in school?"

"Well," he responded. " I know they did some bad things, but overall I think they did many things to help the German people. They restored their pride, and they let the world know that though they had been defeated in the First War they would not as a proud nation tolerate being humiliated by the so-called victors. Maybe things didn't turn out well in the end, but in just a decade they got people jobs, reduced inflation, and obtained the lands they believed were historically and rightfully theirs, and we should have done the same thing."

"Really?" said Gantos softly. "And I assume you mean what was rightfully theirs was Austria, Poland, Czechoslovakia, France, the Netherlands, Norway, Yugoslavia, Britain, and Greece? And they tried for Russia as well?"

"I don't know about all that," said Lakis, sensing that the old man was telling him things he should have known. "But I think in Greece, Germany at least brought some order," he said with little confidence and conviction in his voice. "You know, Mr. Gantos, we Greeks need a strong leader like Hitler or at least one like Metaxas. Yes, someone like Metaxas, a strong person to lead us out of this crisis."

The old man hesitated before he spoke. He had been a young man when Ioannis Metaxas had led Greece as a virtual dictator. Metaxas had been a military man to whom the Greek King George II had given virtual dictatorial powers, and this Greek leader had ruled with a grand vision of leading Greece into a third epoch of greatness following the glory of ancient Greece and the splendor of the Byzantine period. Metaxas had also tried, with considerable embarrassment and failure, to institute symbolic salutes and flags that the Greek people not only rejected but also ridiculed.

"You do know, I hope," said the old man, "that we did invent democracy here. Metaxas, later the Greek colonels, Hitler, Stalin, Mussolini, were all megalomaniacs who were failed deniers and destroyers of a basic human desire—freedom, Lakis, freedom." Gantos' tone was sarcastic, almost letting the boy know that he had wasted his time in school, that he had learned nothing, or perhaps that his teachers had taught him nothing.

The young man quickly got up from the bench, took his protest sign in his hand, and prepared to walk off. "I don't need your lectures, old man. It's your generation and those that followed that have brought us to where we are. You went along with corruption. You benefited from the devil's compact in which you supported corrupt politicians as long as they gave you all free this and free that, and you all lived off the public, feeding like gluttonous pigs. This country will never be saved except by radical, even violent, change. Your days are over, old man, and mine are just beginning. Call us radicals, call us fascists, call us Nazis, Greece might be finally saved by a Nazi leader like Hitler!" Turning his back on the old man, the young man took his protest sign, refused to say anything more, and quickly walked away.

Nicholaos silently watched the boy walk quickly into a crowd of vendors and protestors who were still there and who planned to camp at the site throughout the night. He sat on the bench and seemed to be starring into nowhere. He stood up and looked across the plaza toward the Grand Bretagne Hotel, one of Athen's oldest and finest establishments. Protestors stood outside there as well, but as he stared at the building, in his mind he saw other, different images, those he had seen when he was the age of the young boy who had just left him. In his mind's eye he saw helmeted Nazi troops parading by on motorcycles and on foot and Nazi officers moving into the Grand Bretagne Hotel to establish the Greek headquarters of the Third Reich. And as he began the slow walk back to his small apartment he once again thought of those days and times, so many years ago, when he was so young and so hopeful about his future and when everything around him seemed to be falling apart and he was about to begin the most tragic and most important years of his life.

Thessaloniki, Greece
1938-1939

CHAPTER TWO

THE THREE MEN, BOYS REALLY, sitting at the coffee shop smoking their cigarettes were an unlikely trio. Any passerby who would have wagered that he could identify their nationality or ethnic origin would have soon parted with his money. The tallest one was fair-skinned with blue eyes and light brown, almost blonde, hair. The second young man was a bit shorter and had hazel-colored eyes, very fair skin, and dark brown hair that he wore in a stylishly longer fashion. The third companion was the smallest of the three with darker features, and eyes that appeared as dark as the olives that were on the salad placed before him at the table. His hair was black and combed straight back from his high and pronounced forehead.

The tallest and fairest of the three was eighteen-year-old Nicholaos Gantos and a native Greek. The one with the fair skin and longer hair was nineteen-year-old Mordechai ben Nathan, a Greek Jew. And the third of the group was twenty-year-old Klaus Schreiber, a German. Gantos was born in Kalavryta, Greece; ben Nathan was from Thessaloniki, Greece; and Schreiber was born in Munich, Germany. They had met about a year ago when each enrolled at the Aristotle University in Thessaloniki; each was now at a common location but pursuing different hopes for their futures. That the three men had become close friends could hardly have been due to similar personalities or interests. Nikos, having been raised in a small village, was an individual who loved the outdoors. He understood the rugged mountainous terrain of rural Greece. From the age of ten he had gone hunting with his father and had shown, even at that young age, an unusual ability to use firearms. By the time he was fifteen he was already known in his village as the best marksman of all, including all of the adult men. His precision in hitting targets, whether they were birds or small objects used for practice, had already created for Nikos a reputation that went beyond his immediate village. Now at the university, Nikos hoped someday to be an academic, teaching and writing in the field of German literature in Greece or perhaps in some other part of Europe. Much of his time at the university was studying the German language since he needed fluency in that language if he was to do scholarly work in his field.

Mordecai was an artist. He seldom traveled without his sketchbook, always finding something, large or small, that he was moved to draw on paper. He had shown this talent from a young age and had, as a teenager, done landscapes in oil and many pencil sketches of his rabbi and friends of the family. He wanted to use his creative talents to create works of art but knew that he needed to have a more secure way to make a living. It was this necessity that had brought him to the university to study art history and specifically the art of the Italian Renaissance. His days were spent in class learning the Italian language, studying art history, and doing his own artwork.

Klaus was the most reserved of the three young men. He had been attracted to Greek history when, as a young boy, he had been introduced to Greek mythology and in his mind would imagine the exploits of these gods and heroes. He spent much of his teenage years studying; his one nonintellectual diversion was futbol, and he followed the German team as an avid fan. The more he learned about ancient Greece, and particularly the works of the Greek philosophers, the more certain he became that teaching Greek studies was what his life's vocation would be. He spent hour after hour becoming literate in both ancient and modern Greek so that he could understand the ancient source material as well as be able to do his studies at the university. The three had met during the first week of the beginning of the school year; they seemed to be instantly compatible and decided to room together and share expenses of their small four-room apartment.

The three friends sat sipping their coffee and drew heavily on their cigarettes as they enjoyed the cool breeze that blew in from the seashore. The café location was a popular one for citizens of Thessaloniki, and each evening old people, teenagers, families with children, and young lovers took strolls on the cement pathways that hugged the Aegean seashore. Periodically two young girls would walk by hand in hand, and Nikos, Klaus, and Mordecai, or Mortis as he was known, would make admiring or sarcastic comments to each other about the physical attributes of the young women they inspected from afar.

But just as often their conversation would center on each other's families, their own lives, their aspirations, and the places they had been born and raised.

"I was worried about coming to Thessaloniki," Klaus said, in the best Greek he could manage, "but I really like this city now." The three boys spoke Greek most of the time, but periodically Nikos would try the German he was studying on Klaus and Klaus would speak in his evolving Greek to both Nikos and Mortis. Mortis knew no German and spoke only Greek with a particular dialect called Ladino that the

Sephardic Jews who had come to Thessaloniki centuries before spoke.

"It is a good place," said Nikos, "and I think I like it even more than Athens." Nikos had lived in Athens for the year before coming to Thessaloniki, having left the village of Kalavryta so that he could have a head start learning the German language by attending a special language school in Athens where he had lived with an aunt and uncle.

"I like it, too," offered Mortis, "but you know I don't have much to compare it to since I was born here and have lived here all my life."

Klaus flicked the ashes from his cigarette to the ground, lifted his cup to sip the coffee, and with a somewhat quizzical look on his face turned to Mortis, "Mortis, why is this such a Jewish city? How did so many Jews settle in Thessaloniki?"

Mortis snuffed out his cigarette on the ashtray, ran his fingers through his hair, and prepared to educate Klaus about the Jews of Thessaloniki.

"Well, Klaus," he began, "Jews have been in Greece since ancient times. When Paul came to Greece to convert the pagan Greeks to Christianity he made reference to Hellenized Jews. But the real influx of Jews here came after 1492, when the Spanish rulers, Ferdinand and Isabella, enacted the Alhambra Decree that expelled Sephardic Jews from Spain. Many of those Jews settled here in Thessaloniki. In fact, by

1519 the Jews were more than 50 percent of the population and by the seventeenth century the percentage of Jews living here was about 70 percent of the population. That's why you see so many synagogues here, and today there are about 70,000 Jews in the city. My family came here many generations ago, I really don't know how far back, but my father thinks it was sometime in the 1600s."

"There are Jews in Athens, too," added Nikos, "but the percentage isn't nearly as high as it is here."

"But, Klaus," said Mortis, "everything I read tells me that perhaps my people are having some difficulty in your country. Is that right?"

"I've heard that, too," answered Klaus, "but I don't know how true that is or if it's just anti-German propaganda. I don't pay much attention to all that political gossip."

Nikos looked at Klaus and hesitated before he spoke. Finally he said, "Klaus, something is definitely going on about the Jews. Certainly you must hear that when you go home. Just three years ago laws were passed in Germany taking citizenship away from the Jews and making it illegal for them to marry non-Jews."

Klaus inhaled from his cigarette, now only a small stub between his fingers, in a slow and deliberate fashion. "I guess I did hear something about that," he conceded, "but it's all politics and I'm just not that interested. Let's talk about something else. Tell me about your village of Kalavryta and about your family, Niko, and when are you going to invite us there?"

Nikos loved the village of his birth. His mother, father, one of his older brothers Vasili, and his sister Eleni still lived there. His other brother Petros had married and moved to the island of Crete with his wife. His mother had been born and raised in another village, one named Dorvitsa, in the western part of Greece. Nikos told his two friends that he had heard that his mother had hoped to marry a boy named Dimitri Papandreou from that village, but he had decided to enter the priesthood with aspirations to someday move up the Church hierarchy, which meant that he could never marry. A mutual friend of both his father's and mother's families had arranged for introductions that eventually led to his parent's marriage and his mother's moving to Kalavryta.

"The village is actually a place of great historical importance," Nikos said. "It's about forty miles northwest of Tripoli and is the end of the Diakopto-Kalavryta Railway that was built at the end of the nineteenth century. There's a great deal of snow in the mountains, and for many in Greece it's a great skiing location today. Over the centuries the village was controlled by the Venetians and the Turks, but its real importance to Greek history is that the revolt against the Ottoman Turk's control of Greece really began in my village. In March, 1821, the flag of the revolt was raised at the Agia Lavra monastery by Bishop Germanos III. The banner of that revolution is still kept at the monastery. This is where it all began, Klaus, the Greek call to the country to fight for either freedom or death. They made the choice and won. It's part of the Greek character, you know, to refuse to be dominated by any outsiders."

"Well, I'm not so sure of that," responded Klaus. "Don't forget your own king is not even a Greek."

"That's because I forgot to tell you about another Greek character trait, Klaus," Nikos said smiling. "It's called 'ego,' and its simplest translation is the word 'me,' an intense, almost destructive individualism that too often prevents cooperation and teamwork. Your point is a good one, Klaus, but I do want you and Mortis to come and visit my village and meet my family. But enough about me and Mortis. What about your family, Klaus?"

Klaus Schreiber was not one who was comfortable talking about himself or his family. Not that there was anything to hide or something that would bring on shame; he simply was basically a very private person.

"Not much to tell," he said, "I have one older sister who is married and lives in Berlin. My father works in one of the new munitions factories, and my mother cares for our home. I spent some time when I was sixteen going with my father to some National Socialist rallies, and I even heard Hitler speak in person once. I was a member of the Hitler youth organization, like most people my age, but I left when I finished school and decided to come here for university studies. That's about all. Not too exciting, just the life of a regular German family, I guess."

Mortis seemed especially interested in Klaus' brief family summary. "Klaus, tell me more about Hitler. What do you and your family think about him and how he is leading Germany?"

"Well, as you know," said Klaus, almost eager to answer Mortis, "he came to power in a totally legal way about five years ago. And in that short time I think it's accurate to say he has revitalized my country and focused people's attention on how Germany was wronged and humiliated after the war. He has put people, like my father, to work, reduced inflation, rekindled national pride, and has an agenda to unite Germans, wherever they may live under one flag. That's why he peacefully annexed Austria to Germany just last year. I can tell you this, I have never heard a more powerful speaker than Adolf Hitler. When he speaks, the audiences are almost hypnotized."

"But what does all that have to do with what his party did just last April when they basically eliminated Jews from the German economy and seized many Jewish assets?" asked Mortis.

"I can't answer that, Mortis," Klaus softly responded. "I don't know the party thinking on that issue, and whatever it is I'm not in agreement with it. And don't get nervous, Mortis." Klaus smiled, put his arm on Mortis' shoulder, "You're still my friend, and none of this political crap can ever get between the three of us."

"I'll drink to that," said Nikos loudly as he raised his virtually empty coffee cup and gently tapped it against the cups held by Klaus and Mortis. "Now forget this politics stuff, and let's focus our eyes on those girls across the way."

The three friends passed weekend after weekend at coffee houses and bars throughout Thessaloniki, which they preferred to call by its shortened, popular name "Salonika." As the months of 1938 quickly slipped by, the political landscape in Europe seemed to be deteriorating. In September France and Great Britain, seeking to avoid war with an increasingly aggressive Germany, agreed to the German annexation of Sudeten Czechoslovakia, and in November the violence against the Jews in Germany increased as Nazis violently attacked Jews and destroyed Jewish property. During a two-week period ninety Jews were killed, and dozens more were beaten. But the three friends whose bond of brotherhood was becoming ever stronger, deliberately avoided discussing European politics for fear that their deepening friendship would be strained.

Klaus and Mortis finally accepted Nikos' invitation to visit his home village during the Easter holiday. They met Nikos' mother, brother Vasili, and his eleven-year-old sister Eleni. Nikos' father had not been there, since he was in Athens looking after his ailing brother who was suffering from some disease that the doctors were unable as yet to correctly identify. It had been a pleasant visit with everyone, even for Mortis, who participated in all the traditional customs that were part of Greek life during the Easter season. Mortis, whose commitment to the religious side of being a Jew was minimal, had no problem even going to the village church with Nikos' family although the church rituals, prayers, or the whole congregation singing a hymn celebrating. "Christ is Risen" had no real meaning for him. His major contribution to the conversation at the Easter dinner was to remind everyone, "Let's not forget, Christ was a Jew."

As the months of 1939 passed, the situation in Europe became even more troublesome, and the tensions that seemed to be leading to war were evident throughout the continent. In March Germany annexed the remainder of Czechoslovakia, and the British government pledged to support Poland if that nation were attacked. In August the Nazis signed a nonaggression pact with the Soviet Union, thus eliminating any potential conflict with the Russians in the east and paving the way for the Soviets to participate in any acquisition of Polish territory. That was accomplished when the Germans invaded Poland from the west on September 1, 1939, and the Russians did the same from the east on September 17. By October Warsaw had surrendered, and the Nazis began gathering the Jews in Poland and moving them into designated ghettos. In that same month Germany began air strikes against the British Isles.

As November began Thessaloniki was experiencing an unusual wave of cold weather. The events of the past months had been followed closely by the three young students, and the news they were receiving was causing them to deliberately not spend too much time discussing the possibility of all-out European war because of what impact such discussions might have on their friendship. The three had grown close, studying together when they could, socializing together, and developing a genuine affection for one another. If any three individuals with such different backgrounds could forge a bond in which they felt as though they were "brothers," these three had done so. But now events were moving so quickly that Nikos felt he needed to talk.

In their apartment they could feel a chill through the poorly ventilated windows as they sat around the one common room. Mortis was sprawled on the dark brown sofa with his shoes off, while Klaus sat in an old padded rocking chair that they had bought at a local flea market when they had first met. The German seemed not to be bothered by the chill that filled the room, while Nikos wore a large green sweater and sat on a large pillow placed on the floor. For Klaus the temperature was still mild compared to what he was used to in Munich, but to Nikos it was simply a cold temperature that rarely affected his village in southern Greece.

"I think we need to talk," began Nikos, "because what's happening around us will, I think, affect each of us."

Rubbing his eyes and adjusting his position as he lay on the brown sofa, Mortis at first said nothing. Then, as if carefully deciding how to respond, he said, "You mean about the Jews and all that?"

"About the Jews, yes," answered Nikos, "but much more than that. I'm talking about everything, you know, what are we going to do?"

Klaus continued rocking in his chair and then added, "I don't think you have to decide anything, Niko. I don't see how Greece is affected by any of what's happening in the rest of Europe, but I think I have a lot to think about. My country is at war, and I am sitting here in the comfort of Greece. I'm not sure I can continue to stay here."

"What do you mean, Klaus?" asked Mortis, "you mean you're going back home to Germany?"

"I think I have to. My country is at war, and I have to be there. I don't think I can just stay here and watch it from a distance—like some journalist or, in some people's eyes, like some coward."

"Coward!" burst out Nikos. "That's ridiculous. I know it's your country, Klaus, and I know you have admired what Hitler may have done for Germany, but don't you think it's gone too far? Austria? Czecho-slovakia? Poland? France? And now Britain? What's next, Klaus, the United States? China?"

Klaus' expression was one of mild irritation. "There must be a reason Hitler has moved into those areas, I don't know. Maybe he has been provoked into do-ing it. Maybe it's payment for what happened to my country after the last war. I just don't know, Niko, but I don't think you have to worry. I'm sure Greece is not on Hitler's list."

Nikos raised himself from his sitting position on the floor and began pacing the small room. "Well, I hope not," he said, "we have enough troubles without getting involved in a war. But even though I'm not crazy about Metaxas, I think he's smart enough to keep Greece neutral in whatever happens."

"All I know," injected Mortis, "is that the farther we Jews can distance ourselves from Hitler, the better off we'll be. Don't you agree, Klaus?"

Klaus slowly got up from the rocking chair, went over to the window, and simply starred out for a minute or two.

Now Mortis seemed upset. "Klaus, did you hear me? I asked you a question?"

Klaus turned abruptly away from the window and snapped back, "Yes Mortis, I heard you. I hear you loud and clear. I have told you if not once, then twenty times over, the position of the National Socialist party is not my position. Not mine! If I go home to fight, it will be against the enemies of the Reich, not against Jews. Have I not always treated you with respect? As an equal? As I would my own brother? Tell me Mortis, have I not?" Klaus returned to the rocker, his face displaying stress that the others had not seen before.

Mordecai kept silent, rose from the sofa, walked slowly over to Klaus, and put his arm around the German's shoulder. "Yes you have, Klaus," he said softly, "yes you have, and I am sorry if it sounded like I felt otherwise."

"Mortis," said Nikos, "if I were you, I'd make sure I stayed in Greece. I'm going to do the same thing. I do believe we can stay out of these troubles. I can't see what interest Hitler and Germany would want with Greece. We are a poor country, and we manufacture virtually nothing unless Hitler has some secret passion for olives. I think he and the English will leave

Greece alone. So are you really going back, Klaus? Going back to join the army?"

Klaus once again got up from the chair, walked over to Nikos and Mortis, and brought them together in the center of the room. As the three men stood together, Klaus put his arm around each of the other's shoulders and began to speak, "We really are like brothers," he said, "I love you both as I would my own family. I think I have to go back, but I'm not totally sure. I need a few days to think it through, and even if I do, I'll be back and we can pick up where we are today. Maybe we'll all get married, have kids, and visit each other's homes, and our wives and our kids will be friends, too. Maybe all that can happen. Give me a few days, I'll let you know."

Within a week Klaus had made his decision. He brought Nikos and Mortis together and told them that he was going home to join the army to fight for his beloved nation and the building of a new, strong Germany. The three shook hands, hugged one another, and Klaus took his baggage and left through the door.

Miles from Thessaloniki, other decisions were being discussed: decisions, which if acted on, would alter the plans and lives of the three young friends forever.

War With Italy
1940-1941

CHAPTER THREE

THE DOMESTIC HELP TALKED about it all the time, wondering how the man who resided in the Palazzo Venezia ever had time to attend to his official duties as head of state. Day after day, there was a constant stream of women entering the building who would be officially recorded as "fascist visitors," but the man's valet, Quinto Navarra, and the rest of the help knew better. Their leader, Benito Mussolini, all five feet six inches of him, was either one of enormous sexual appetites or the magnetic object of hundreds of adoring Italian women whose desire for him he could not resist. Mussolini, or Il Duce, The Leader, as he was known to the nation, received hundreds of letters from women throughout Italy every month, some merely paying him compliments on his leadership, some asking for favors or help, and some simply expressing their love and devotion to him, conveying both implicit and explicit messages as to how they desired to share his bed.

Il Duce, of course, was married, but that small fact never seemed in the past or present to inconvenience him with other women. Although the records had been destroyed, those close to him assumed that as a young man Mussolini had been married, or virtually married, to a woman named Ida Dalser, and together they had a son. The situation was complicated by the fact that at the same time he fathered Ida's child he was also living with another woman, Rachele Guidi, whom he did officially marry in 1915. Rachele and Benito remained married and together had five childen: Edda, Anna Maria, Vittorio, Bruno, and Romano.

Over the years there had continued to be many women, as even now in 1940 there continued to be, but in 1936 a young girl of nineteen became his mistress and held a special place in Mussolini's life. Claretta Petacci had been writing the Italian leader letters and poems since her early teens and in her young mind fantasized about Il Duce. Driving with her parents one day, she noticed a red Alfa Romeo car speed past her father's automobile. Claretta recognized that a passenger in that red car was Mussolini, and she shouted out her window, "Il Duce, Il Duce!" Mussolini stopped his car to meet the young woman, was immediately attracted to her, and invited her to his office. From that chance meeting soon developed a physical and emotional relationship that overcame their almost thirty years age difference. By 1940 Claretta had become one of the very few people that Mussolini could speak with to convey his true ambitions, fears, frustrations, and anger. Claretta had become so special to Mussolini that she was now assigned bodyguards, a chauffeur, and even living space at Palazzo Venezia. So comfortable and natural was their relationship that he confided his most innermost personal information to Claretta, and she encouraged such trust and candor by continuously telling her Benito, whom she called "Ben," how great he was and how much of a towering historical figure he would be not only for Italy but for all of Europe and beyond.

Sitting on the flowered patterned sofa in one of the sitting rooms of the Palazzo Venezia, Mussolini was relaxed. His shoes were off, his shirt was open at the top, and his arm was placed around Claretta. Her mood seemed to have quickly changed. She was not smiling and seemed to be trying now to distance herself from her lover's embrace.

"Clara," Mussolini said, "what's wrong with you? Why such a long face? Where's that beautiful smile that first drew me to you? Talk to me, Clara, talk to me."

Claretta at first said nothing, trying again to disengage from Benito's arm that was around her shoulder. In her mind she was thinking and rehearsing what she wanted to say. Finally she slowly got up from the sofa, walked over to the table on which there was a pitcher of water, and poured some water into a small glass. "Ben," she said, then hesitated, as if she were still not sure she wanted to continue, "we need to talk about something." She continued to walk nervously around the room, periodically sipping water in an almost nervous movement.

"Of course," said Benito, "of course, we can talk. Don't we talk about everything? Don't I tell you things no other ears ever hear? Come, sit down again, what's bothering you?"

Clara returned to the sofa but not to Benito's embrace. "It's these other women, Ben, it drives me crazy. You know I love you, you know I adore you, you know I'd do anything for you. Why, Ben, why, why do you do it? And why, Benito, why with that Pallotielli woman?"

Clara was not in tears as yet, but it was only a matter of time. Once again she rose from the sofa and nervously crossed back and forth in the room.

"Bambina," Mussolini said quietly, "we have talked about these matters before. These women mean nothing to me. You need to understand men, you need to understand me. There was one time I had fourteen women and took three or four of them at a time, every afternoon and evening, one after another. And, yes, I don't lie to you. I was with Pallotielli, I did it. I hadn't seen her since before Christmas. I felt like seeing her. I don't think I committed a crime, I spent about twelve minutes with her."

Claretta stared intently at Mussolini, "Twelve minutes! It was probably twenty-four!" she yelled back.

"All right, twenty-four then, it was a quick thing, who cares? She is past, there was no enthusiasm, it's like when I take my wife," he said in a matter of fact tone.

Claretta's eyes were now moist. She said nothing, turned from Mussolini, and quickly left the room, saying, "But it's different for me, isn't it, Ben, isn't it? You are crazed if another man simply looks at me, aren't you?"

Claretta's jealousy was surpassed only by that of her lover. He had people reporting to him his bambina's every move. The reports to him, however, were invariably the same. Clara spent her time away from Mussolini waiting for him in her apartment listening to Chopin recordings, writing letters or poems, faithfully recording things in her diary, and eating sweets while her Ben was dealing with state matters or, as likely, spending time with other women like Cornelia Tangi or Giulia Caminati or Romilda Ruspi or others on a list that seemed to go on and on. But in spite of his physical liaisons with other women, Claretta did hold a special place in Mussolini's life. It was she that he wanted near him not only for his physical desires but as much for her companionship. With Claretta he could reveal his most private thoughts, while she, in turn, continually reinforced his constant need for approval and adoration.

When he and Claretta were not discussing each other's jealous tantrums, they spoke often of a topic that seemed to dominate Mussolini's thinking: what he perceived to be his diminishing importance in relation to Adolf Hitler. They talked as well about his own frustration with his own Italian people whom he viewed as a nationality more concerned with the "good life" rather than with the possibility of following him in the creation of a twentieth century Roman Empire.

Mussolini had first met Hitler in 1934 shortly after the German leader had assumed power. Il Duce had already been in power for more than a decade, so out of respect for Mussolini's stature and seniority as a head of state, Hitler traveled to Rome for this initial meeting. Hitler came to the meeting in civilian clothes, wearing a wrinkled coat and a hat more floppy than stylish. Mussolini met him in full military attire, which left the German embarrassed by the comparison of how the two leaders appeared to the public. Hitler had learned a lesson and vowed that he would never again allow himself to be in such a position to be humiliated.

In 1937 Mussolini reciprocated the visit by going to Berlin, and what he saw shocked the visiting dictator. Hitler had put on a military and civilian display that was filled with pageantry, huge crowds of more than 800,000 people, and an impressive show of military troops and equipment. Hitler, presiding over this display of intense nationalism and strength, was, this time, in full-dress Nazi uniform.

"Why was that so surprising?" asked Clara now after Mussolini had related the story as they sat at the dinner table. The servants, after having served chicken, salad, pasta, and crusty bread, had left the room. Mussolini was suffering from an ulcer and tried to be careful about what he ate, though periodically he abandoned caution and ate whatever he wanted at that particular moment. The servants knew to serve no alcohol, only milk and water, and tried to be careful not to prepare certain meals that would tempt their leader but also would inevitably cause him to suffer severe stomach pains. Claretta's desire to smoke a cigarette was met after dinner when she and Il Duce moved to another room.

"I hadn't fully realized what Hitler had accomplished since he took power," responded Benito. "He seemed to have ignited a German renaissance. The crowds he assembled were incredible, and their response to him was something to see. But I'm glad I went because when we invited Hitler back here a year later we put on a show I know surprised and impressed him. We hosted the Germans for six days, and they saw cheering crowds and Nazi swastika banners everywhere. We had military reviews and naval demonstrations that I know truly impressed Hitler."

"That's wonderful, Ben," said Claretta, "and I hope they saw the new marching steps of our soldiers."

"Of course, and I explained to them that the origin was from the Piedmont region, so that they understood that we did not simply copy the goose-step movements of their army. When they saw our soldiers executing the precise marching moves, their eyes were transfixed. The Germans said to me, 'It took us years to teach our soldiers this march, and you got it perfectly in a few months. It's wonderful.' And when they saw our long guns and tanks, it was something they hadn't expected. They were terrified by the power of our army."

Claretta rose from her seat at the table and approached Mussolini. As he sat in his chair, she wrapped her arms around him from the back of his neck and gently kissed the top of his head. "You will show them all, Ben, you will show Hitler, Italy, Europe, the world that you are truly The Leader. Your greatness will overpower them all. But, Benito, tell me, what is your impression of Hitler?"

Mussolini smiled. "Thank you, Bambina, thank you always for what you see in me." Il Duce motioned Claretta to join him on the two large cushioned chairs facing each other in front of the large bay window. "Ah, Hitler, here's how I see him. He's really not much more than a boy at heart. When he came here, we laughed a great deal and told jokes. He is respectful of me and a bit intimidated. You know, those Germans are nice people, and Hitler is like a big child when he is with me. He said to me when he was ready to leave for Berlin, 'These have been the most beautiful days of my life. I will never forget them.' You know, Clara, deep down Hitler is a real sentimental person. When he left, he had tears in his eyes. He really loves me, Hitler adores me."

"I'm not surprised, my love, I'm not surprised. I'm sure he looks up to you and sees a real leader."

As the months passed by quickly in 1940, Mussolini's exuberance for Hitler and the Nazis became more muted. The admiration for Hitler remained, but for Il Duce there was growing concern that his own position in the eyes of Italy and Europe was changing from one of preeminence to one of supporting actor to Hitler who was becoming the main attraction. He viewed the lightning speed success of Hitler's armies with awe and concern. The Nazi victories were quick and decisive, and by the end of the year Hitler would control not only Austria, Czechoslovakia, and Poland but also Finland, Denmark, Norway, the Netherlands, and France; and the attacks on Britain would have begun. Hitler was doing what Mussolini only spoke and dreamed of doing. Hitler was taking risks and showing bold defiance to all who would dare stand in his way, and his army displayed a discipline and focus of purpose that Mussolini had tried, with little success, to create in the Italian military.

"The German people are formidable and dangerous," he now confided to Claretta. "If that mass sets itself in motion, it is a terrifying future." But if Claretta was one to whom he voiced his concerns, she was not the one with whom he discussed his future military plans and strategies. The only other person in which Mussolini could have total confidence in discussing matters of state was Galeazzo Ciano, his Foreign Minister, who was married to his daughter Edda.

Galeazzo Ciano had held a number of diplomatic posts in Brazil, Argentina, and China before he married Mussolini's daughter in 1930. He flew some missions in a bomber squadron in the 1935 war against Ethiopia and then became Minister of Popular Culture and finally Minister of Foreign Affairs in 1935. He was thought by many to be the eventual successor to Mussolini and had some of the same traits as his father-in-law. He was more handsome, with slick black hair combed straight back from his forehead, but he was also viewed, by many with justification, as a playboy who liked to stay at plush resorts, visit fashionable bars and restaurants, and spend much time away from official duties on the golf course and with a variety of women. At times he even tried to act like his father-in-law, striking poses for his photographs that emulated the serious, chin-jutting profiles of Il Duce.

Ciano had been instrumental in the negotiations between Italy and Germany that resulted in the 1939 Pact of Steel. In that pact both countries agreed to be in permanent contact with each other so that they could jointly answer any questions that threatened their national interests and to come to the aid of the other if either one were at war. Finally, they agreed that neither would negotiate any armistice without the consent of the other. Though the two countries had signed the agreement for mutual assistance in the event of war, Hitler had assured the Italians that he had no plans to enter into a war for at least three more years. Yet within hours after the pact was signed, without consulting Mussolini, he ordered German troops to begin the invasion of Poland.

Because of his closeness to Mussolini, Ciano could understand his words and sense his moods better than all the others who surrounded their leader. As Hitler seemed to be succeeding in victory over country after country in Europe, Mussolini's foreign minister witnessed his leader's growing frustration with being pushed aside by Hitler and his Germany. Ciano became determined to equalize, or at least alter, Mussolini's image vis-à-vis Hitler and assist his leader in carrying out his grand vision for Italy, which was to instill national pride in his countrymen and to create a new Roman Empire. But Ciano knew that talk and speeches were not enough. Il Duce needed action, he needed conquest, and he needed something concrete, like taking over a country, to show everyone that he was on an equal footing with the German leader. In Ciano's mind, Greece was the perfect target.

Originally Ciano had felt that Greece was not an appropriate target because, as he told one of his aides, "Greece is too poor for us to covet," implying that even victory over that country would not be viewed as a major accomplishment in the eyes of Europe in general and Hitler in particular. But after the Italian takeover of Albania in 1938, he changed his mind and began to plant the seeds to convince his leader that an attack on Greece would be the way for Mussolini to move. In order to keep the Greeks off guard, he instructed the Italian ambassador to Greece, Emanuele Grazzi, to assure the Greek leader, Ioannis Metaxas, that any rumors that might be circulating about an Italian invasion of Greece were totally false. In April 1940 Ciano scheduled a meeting with Grazzi in Rome. He welcomed the ambassador to his spacious office and invited him to sit in the chair in front of his desk, while Ciano remained in his chair behind the desk. The room was decorated with replicas of classical Italian paintings and photographs of Mussolini with Ciano himself and other foreign leaders. "Mr. Ambassador," Ciano started, "I'm glad you could come here. How are things in Athens?"

Grazzi responded," I'm glad to be here, Mr. Minister. Things are generally calm in Athens, but General Metaxas has expressed some concerns about our moves in Albania. I think we should be careful in whatever posture we take toward the Greeks."

Ciano was quick to respond as he reached for a cigarette and lit it, inhaled, and slowly exhaled puffs of white smoke. "Mr. Grazzi, Il Duce is actually very interested in Greece and believes it is in our national interest to take action there and establish our presence in the country. I think we could set the stage by causing some chaos. Do you think it would be possible to find someone, maybe some Albanian, to do away with the Greek king?"

Grazzi's face conveyed a message of disbelief; he was stunned by the suggestion. "Surely you're joking, Mr. Minister," he said, suspecting that the statement was actually not a joke. Grazzi wanted no part in such an outrageously stupid suggestion.

Ciano said nothing. He had not been joking but immediately realized that he had spoken foolishly and that such a plot would not only be difficult to

53

execute successfully but also probably would not be conducive to Italy's long-range plans. "Of course, I was joking," he lied, "we have more serious plans."

Weeks later Ciano traveled to Albania and instructed General Carlo Geloso to move five Italian divisions to the Greek border to prepare for an invasion.

"Five divisions!" exclaimed Geloso, shocked by the directive. "To succeed we would need twenty to twenty-five divisions."

"General, please be serious," Ciano said, smiling, "an invasion of Greece will be the easiest mission you have ever led. The conflict will be over not in months but in days."

Geloso hesitated, thought carefully about his response, and finally said, "Mr. Minister, the rumors of our intentions are rampant throughout Greece. They will resist and resist fiercely. Don't be fooled by anyone who tells you otherwise."

When Ciano returned to Rome, he rewarded Geloso's forthrightness by relieving him of his command and replacing him with another general. Mussolini himself was at first not totally committed to going into Greece but debated in his mind whether Greece or Yugoslavia should be Italy's target. Ciano was convinced that Greece was the easier target and initiated a media propaganda campaign in Italy to promote anti-Greek sentiment. Mussolini began to think that his foreign minister son-in-law was making sense.

On October 15 Mussolini met with Ciano and the chief of the general staff, Marshall Badoglio. Il Duce was now totally committed to the invasion of Greece. He was particularly incensed by what he considered yet another example of German disrespect for him and Hitler's ignoring of him. Days earlier German troops had entered Romania, and once again Il Duce was never consulted or told of the action beforehand.

"Hitler always faces me with a fait accompli," Mussolini said loudly, as he paced the room, "and this time I will pay him back with the same coin. He will learn from the papers that I have occupied Greece. Thus, the balance will be re-established."

Ciano smiled and nodded his head. "Mark my words," the foreign minister said, "a few bombs on Athens, and it will be over. And besides we have bought off the key Greek political and military leadership with five million lira and they will give us no trouble. Our people in Athens have told us that the Greeks on the border will not fight and, in fact, will most likely rise up in a popular revolt against Greece."

Marshall Badoglio was not impressed, "The heads of the general staff are all, Il Duce, unanimously opposed to the planned attack," he said. "We are not ready, we definitely are not ready, and the rainy season will not be conducive to the easy victory of which the foreign minister is so confident. We need more time to organize the number of divisions we will need. And I want to stress that it is a mistake to think that Metaxas and the Greeks will not offer the fiercest resistance."

"Nonsense," said Ciano, "this operation will be easy. I guarantee it, Il Duce."

Badoglio saw that he was presenting a losing argument but remained strong in his convictions. "I must state again," he said, "that we are not ready. I do not want our nation to be humiliated in the eyes of Europe. If the decision is made to move ahead, I must consider offering my resignation."

Mussolini looked at Badoglio with a look of both surprise and disgust. "I will also give my resignation, Marshall," he said with a rising tone in his voice, "yes, I will give my resignation as an Italian if anyone finds difficulty in fighting Greeks! In fact, I will go personally to Greece to be present at the incredible shame of Italians who are afraid of Greeks!"

As the meeting ended, Badoglio saluted Mussolini, said nothing, and left the room. Ciano remained with Mussolini and made the decision that action would commence around the end of October. Contrary to the lack of information Mussolini received from Hitler prior to the Nazi dictator's military moves, Il Duce informed the German leader of his plans to invade Greece but without identifying the specific date the invasion would be launched. Hitler had cautioned Mussolini earlier about the danger of opening too many military fronts at once, as well as the danger of the United States' possibly entering the war. What Hitler did not reveal to Mussolini were his own plans to move against the Soviets, which he did not want disrupted by any distractive actions.

Foreign Minister Ciano believed he had all the information he needed to assure Mussolini that everything would go smoothly with the plan that they labeled "Contingency G." On October 24 he wrote in his diary, "I examined the plan of attack on Greece. It is good because it is energetic and decisive. With a hard blow at the beginning, it is likely that everything will collapse within a few hours." He told his undersecretary Giuseppe Bastianini, "It will be a military walkover." Referring to the alleged bribes paid to the Greek military to offer little resistance, he continued, "Everything is arranged. It will go very well."

Bastianini's expression conveyed doubt.

"Why the face, Giuseppe? You have doubts?" questioned Ciano.

"I think you underestimate the Greeks, Mr. Minister. They will resist like lions."

"Then a few bombs dropped on Athens will quickly tame the lions," answered Ciano in a tone that revealed his annoyance that his undersecretary would question his judgment.

57

"With all respect, Mr. Minister," Bastianini started slowly, "dropping bombs on Athens, killing hundreds, destroying the city and perhaps the Parthenon itself would be a most serious mistake. It would bring on the whole wrath of the civilized world and force us to fight still others, which we could not and should not do."

Ciano said nothing and dismissed Bastianini from the room, telling him he would meet with him later. Sitting at his desk he reached for a piece of paper, took a pen from his pocket, and hesitated as he thought about the words he would write to his ambassador to Greece, Emanule Grazzi. Grazzi had cabled Rome days earlier reporting that the Greek leader, Ioannis Metaxas, had told him that Greece desired to remain neutral in any European conflicts but that his country was determined to resist if it were attacked and that he had deployed troops to the Albanian border as a precautionary measure. Ignoring Grazzi's concerns, Ciano wrote out his ultimatum statement to Greece that was later cabled to Grazzi with orders to deliver the statement to Metaxas.

On October 27 Grazzi attended a reception at the Grand Bretagne Hotel. Grazzi mingled with the crowd and spoke with various Greek officials and their elegantly dressed wives, giving no hint of the ultimatum document he held in his pocket. Sipping what he knew was Italian wine, since he thought little of the inferior liquids the Greeks considered wine, he became preoccupied with what his mission would be later in the evening. As the music and dancing continued, Grazzi periodically looked at his watch as the reception began to wind down well past midnight. At 2:30 a.m. Ambassador Emanuele Grazzi excused himself from the reception, left the hotel, stepped into the car driven by his military attaché and headed for the residence of the Greek prime minister. The Greek guard at Metaxas' home recognized Grazzi and allowed him entrance to the grounds. The ambassador rang the bell at Metaxas' home, but there was no answer. Grazzi waited, but there continued to be no response. Finally a phone call was placed to the house, and Metaxas came to the door wearing a dressing gown obviously just awakened from sleep.

"Mr. Ambassador," he greeted Grazzi, "I assume this is of great importance for you to come to my home in the middle of the night. Please come in." Metaxas asked the Italian to be seated, but Grazzi continued to stand.

"It is of utmost importance, Mr. Prime Minister. I have been instructed by my government to present the following document to you and your government."

Grazzi, still standing, reached for a sheet in his pocket and began to read:

"The Italian Government as a guarantee of Greece's neutrality, and the security of Italy, has the right to occupy with her armed forces, and for the duration of war with Great Britain, a number of strategic points on Greek territory. The Italian Government demands that the Hellenic Government shall not offer any resistance to this occupation. Should the Italian forces meet with resistance, the resistance will be crushed by the force of arms, and, in that case, the Hellenic Government will bear the responsibility for whatever may ensue."

When Grazzi concluded, he looked to Metaxas for some response. Metaxas took a moment to digest what he had just heard. His response to Grazzi was succinct: "Ochi," the Greek word for "No." Pausing for a moment, he then looked directly at Grazzi as he ushered him to the door. "Then, Mr. Ambassador, it is war."

Grazzi returned to the Italian embassy office hoping that Metaxas would reconsider after the initial shock of reading the document brought to him at 3:00 a.m. He waited for a call from the prime minister, but none came. After Grazzi had departed from his home, Metaxas then sat at his desk and wrote in his diary, "I shall place the problem of Greek dignity over and above everything else. I shall not bow my head to the Italians."

Within hours, Italy invaded Greece from Albania.

In the early morning of October 28, Athens radio announced, "Since 05:30 this morning the enemy is attacking our vanguard on the Greek-Albanian border. Italy has declared war. The Italian Ambassador, having awakened the Prime Minister at 3:00 a.m. this morning, delivered an infamous ultimatum. The Prime Minister rejected it. Hostilities began at 5:30 a.m. The frontier troops are defending our freedom and defending our fatherland."

Metaxas, having alerted his key military and government leaders, as well as King George, drove to the radio station to address the Greek nation. "The time has come," he began somberly, "for Greece to fight for her independence. Greeks, now we must prove ourselves worthy of our forefathers and the freedom they bestowed upon us. Greeks, now fight for your fatherland, for your wives, your children, and the sacred traditions. The struggle now is for everything we value."

Immediately the citizens of Athens responded, leaving their homes and coming to the streets, congregating before the Parliament building chanting words of defiance to the "macaronades," the "macaroni eaters," and singing the Greek national anthem. Metaxas, the previously less than beloved leader, had struck the right Greek chords of defiance, patriotism, and a glorious tradition. Metaxas, with the radio address, had unified and rallied the nation.

On that same day Mussolini was meeting with Hitler in Florence where he told the Nazi leader what was happening in Greece. Hitler showed little emotion, but in his mind he was furious with what the Italian was telling him—that Mussolini was informing him of the military action taking place at the very time they were meeting. Hitler contained his anger but thought that the action was egocentric stupidity on the part of Mussolini. Hitler's generals had little regard or respect for the Italian army and had told that to their Führer. And Hitler saw Mussolini's move on Greece as potentially harmful to his own plans to attack Russia because now Britain and the United States might enter the war, creating another war front in Greece, which he had always cautioned against. And, he thought, what if the Soviets themselves had designs on Greece for strategic reasons? Hitler was upset but said nothing, knowing that Italy alone was his only ally in all of Europe. He needed Mussolini.

On that same day of October 28, 1940, others were hearing the news at different places and with different reactions. Nicholaos Gantos and Mordecai ben Nathan were in their apartment in Thessaloniki, listening to the local radio broadcasting of the outbreak of war.

"Are you surprised, Niko?" Mordecai asked Nicholaos they sat in the room while they viewed the heavy rain falling outside their window.

"Yes and no, I guess," answered Nikos, "because I thought it might happen, but I didn't think it would happen now. I just can't stay here, Mortis, I need to go to Athens, probably join the army or else help out in any way I can. What about you? What are you going to do?"

"My parents are older, Niko. I need to be with them for as long as I can. Let's see what happens. I know I'll do something, maybe join the army, too."

In the next two days Nikos packed his belongings and left, he hoped temporarily, his college life and headed for Athens. Mortis left to meet his parents at the synagogue where his father served as cantor.

To the north in Yugoslavia Private Klaus Schreiber learned of the Italian invasion from a fellow soldier. Klaus' division had been part of the Nazi movement into that country north of Greece. Thus far he had seen no real combat action; the move into Yugoslavia had been easy, with no real resistance. He offered no opinion of the Italian attack on Greece to his fellow soldier comrades but privately hoped it would end quickly with little impact in terms of Greek casualties or Greek property. He wondered what his friends Nikos and Mortis would do and where they would go. And he very much wanted the Italian action to end quickly so that there would be no need for German troops to even consider going to Greece. He prayed that he could remain where he was.

In the early days of the Greek conflict, Ciano and his group of friends and government officials were based in Bari, Italy, all of them residing in a plush villa. Arrangements had been made to bring twenty girls to the villa for the parties and pleasures of Ciano's entourage. Juvenile games were played: the men and women divided into two teams that would squirt streams of water at each other's genitals and then attack each other's clothes with scissors as the girls targeted the men's ties while the men aimed at the women's bra straps. The entire scenario was observed by the local residents since the windows were left open for all to see and hear, a disturbing sight to those whose sons were already in combat on the Albanian-Greek frontier.

As the party progressed Ciano drank from his glass, the alcohol quickly clouding his head, as he joined in the games chasing after an attractive dark-haired girl with scissors in his hand. He stopped, raised his glass, and shouted out, "To Italy! To Il Duce!" After finishing what remained in his glass, he laughed and shouted again, "Aren't you all glad we're not in Athens!"

In Rome an even stranger scenario was taking place. Mussolini and Claretta had just returned from the bedroom where they had been engaged in love-making for the past two hours. They had moved to the kitchen where they sat at the table sipping their small cups of espresso and munching on flavored biscotti. Mussolini was holding a recent portrait of himself, admiring what he saw. Showing the picture to Claretta, he said, "You know, I understand why women are attracted to me, Claretta, look at that nose, that perfect mouth, that strong powerful chin."

"Of course, they love you, Ben, but you know who loves you most, don't you," she said, while her hand gently caressed the hairless head of her lover. "But, Ben, what has begun now in Greece will have both women and men, all Italians, in love with you. You will not fail; this is your moment for greatness, my love." Mussolini took Claretta's hand in his, while he gently kissed her on the cheek. "Of course, you are right, my Bambina. In a few hours I will be drinking my coffee at the Acropolis."

CHAPTER FOUR

WITHIN TWO DAYS OF THE invasion Nikos returned to Athens and to the home of his uncle. He was joined a day later by his brother, Vasili, who had left their home village of Kalavryta. Both immediately joined the Greek army and, though little prepared for combat duty, were given a much abbreviated one-week training session with orders that they were to be moved to the northern front in another three days. Because of their lack of training, they were told that they would be involved in support and logistical roles and only be called on for combat duty in an emergency. Sitting in their uncle's home, the brothers discussed the situation and what it might mean for their family.

"Vasili," asked his brother, "do you think Mamma and Patera and Eleni will be safe in the village?" Vasili had grown a mustache and a full beard since Nikos had last seen him. He sat with his legs crossed and puffed on a small cigar exhaling smoke that filled the room with a bitter and stale odor.

"I think they will be fine. The village is too far away from anything the Italians want. They probably want control of Thessaloniki, Athens, Tripoli, Patras, and maybe a few other points. I'm sure they will be safe. And besides, I have confidence that Metaxas will get us through this."

"Metaxas?" questioned Nikos, "I can't understand why you support that man. He's no better than Mussolini or Hitler. He's just a smaller and inferior version of them. I'm surprised he just didn't just invite Mussolini in. He's a dictator, Vasili, and you know it."

Vasili flicked the ashes from his cigar into a small cup that he held in his free hand. "Well, you know, Niko, you can call him what you want, but sometimes I think that's what we Greeks need, a dictator to get things done while we sit around and philosophize about what should be done. We have an incompetent, not even a Greek, king, and a dysfunctional Parliament. You may not like Metaxas, but he's done some good things."

Ioannis Metaxas was a polarizing figure for all the Greeks. His career had been a military one; he had been trained in the premier military academy in Germany, which had given him a particular fondness for Germany and the German people. In his political philosophy he was a staunch supporter of the king and of authoritarian rule. When he was given virtual dictatorial powers by King George II in 1936 because of the fear of growing Communist strength in the country, he announced, "Our model is Sparta, not Athens," the obvious reference to a nondemocratic, military-based society. A man small in height, he was the target of jokes and ridicule as people mocked the shoes with high heels he customarily wore and his attempts to copy many of the symbols of his contemporary fascist state leaders. If Adolf Hitler was the *Führer* and Mussolini was *Il Duce*, Metaxas assumed the title of *Arkhigos*, the Greek word for "leader." He also utilized other titles in an attempt to be accepted by the Greek people, calling himself, "First Peasant," "First Worker," and "National Father." He even tried to institute a form of salute that closely resembled that of the Nazis and had designed a flag with a symbol that seemed to most to be some altered configuration of the Nazi swastika. His vision was to build a new and glorious Third Hellenic Civilization, which would be a worthy successor to fifth-century classical Greece and the succeeding Byzantine era. He believed the prescription to achieve that vision was to restore the key values of classical Greece, those of order, moderation, organization, and a passion for excellence. And Metaxas had introduced some popular reform measures such as an eight-hour work day, improved working conditions, a social security system, and laws to reduce the debts of the peasant farmers. But unlike Mussolini and Hitler, Metaxas was not a charismatic leader who could verbally inspire the nation; and he had no real base of popular support or any kind of strong, viable political party. Yet for all of these shortcomings, his dramatic response to Ambassador Grazzi's ultimatum and his subsequent patriotic radio addresses to the Greek people accomplished what he previously had been unable to do: unify and inspire the nation behind him to join in the fight for freedom.

"Well, I will say this," conceded Nikos, "I think what Metaxas did at the moment of the invasion and since has made me respect him a little more. It's good that he is really a soldier and has personally taken command of the army and our defense operation."

"And you will see what a difference that will make," said Vasili as he finally crushed the cigar to extinguish the burning and the smoke. "I have confidence in him. We'll see soon. I don't know if we can stop these 'macaronades,' but with Metaxas at the lead, we've got a damn good chance." Two days later both brothers were sent to the northern front.

Miles away, in London, Prime Minister Winston Churchill was following his usual routine. He awoke from sleep at 7:30 a.m. and remained in bed while he ate his usual breakfast of eggs, bacon, ham, and chipped beef. Often he would also have a small piece of sole, but had no taste for it on this day. And, as was his habit, alcohol of some kind was a part of every Churchill meal, often what his daughter called the "papa cocktail," which consisted of a small dose of Johnnie Walker Red Label Scotch poured into a tumbler filled with water that he would slowly sip throughout the morning hours.

Staying in bed until around 10:00 a.m., he would dictate letters to one of his four secretaries who would sit at the bedside and record his words. After that he would rise from bed to bathe, and his valet would then help him dress. He would resume his work until he would join his family around 1:00 p.m. for lunch. On October 28, 1940, his dictation to his secretaries was interrupted by his wife, Clementine.

"Winston, I have news, and it's not good. The Italians have invaded Greece."

Churchill adjusted himself to a more attentive position in his bed and conveyed an expression on his face that signaled both surprise and anger. "Kat," he said, using the name that he always called his wife, "that is not good at all. I have always thought Mussolini was just a crafty, cold-blooded, black-hearted Italian. Both he and Hitler are the same except that Mussolini is a bogus mimic of ancient Rome who is manipulated by Hitler who is the real manipulator. Both deserve the fate of all gangsters, the electric chair."

Immediately upon receiving an official intelligence report on the situation, Churchill sent a cable to Metaxas, saying, "We will give you all the help in our power." He then called in his chief advisors, including Foreign Secretary Anthony Eden, who spoke first.

"Mr. Prime Minister," he started, "we must not act precipitously. We have troops in Egypt and the Middle East that we should not, and cannot, divert to Greece."

"I fully understand that," answered Churchill as he lit up one of his favorite Romeo y Julieta cigars, one of the 3,000 to 4,000 Cuban cigars he stocked for his use, smoking between eight to ten cigars each day. All of those cigars were not technically "smoked." He often allowed them to burn out and began to chew them, which left most of his cigars badly chewed up and frayed.

Eden continued to make his case that aid to Greece was not wise, but Churchill was adamant in his position. Churchill did not readily accept the ideas or arguments of others when his mind was set. "I don't argue with Winston," Clementine said, "he shouts me down. So when I have anything important to say, I write a note to him." American General George

C. Marshall's evaluation of Churchill after meeting him was that, "when Winston is taken up with his own ideas, he is not interested in what other people think."

Anthony Eden was now the observer of that same trait of the Prime Minister. Churchill told Eden that the reports he was receiving were that the Greeks were resisting vigorously and that, with aid from British troops in Egypt and elsewhere, the invaders might be checked. "The Greek situation must be held to dominate others now though we are well aware of our slender resources," he told Eden.

Having faced Churchill's stubbornness or determination, Eden accepted Churchill's directive but later that evening wrote in his diary, "It seems that Greece is now to dominate the scene." He then added two more words meant for his eyes alone: "Strategic Folly."

Back in Greece the tone Metaxas had set was bringing surprising results. He told the local press, "Greece has firmly decided to defend her territory, even if she has to fall." The country responded, with every man and woman eager to contribute to the war effort both on the battlefield and in noncombat support operations.

The weather in the north was cold and rainy, and as the conflict went from days to weeks and as the casualties mounted, the battleground was covered with an early deep snow. *Time* magazine reported,

"Snow laid a white blanket over thousands of stiff dead Italian soldiers on bleak slopes and in forested ravines where Italian commanders strove to make a stand against the relentless, amazing Greeks." Badoglio's warning to Mussolini and Ciano was beginning to look valid.

The Greek army doggedly pushed on with a fierce offensive against the Italians. Greek women, with their bodies covered with shawls, used large snow shovels to clear mountain passes so as to allow passage of the Greek infantry. Other women brought supplies and ammunition up the steep mountains, carrying eighty-pound packs on their backs, and dragged cannons behind them as they slowly worked their way, climbing mountain peaks that were more than 3,000 feet above. Nikos and Vasili loaded the supplies and along with other teams of men and women led draft animals and food to the front lines. Sitting on a rock in the middle of a cold, slow drizzling rain, Nikos stopped to rest, took small pieces of bread and cheese from his pack, and began to consume what would be his main meal for the day. Turning to speak to a fellow soldier, he said, "You know, from what I see, I think we're going to do it, I think we're going to push them back."

His comrade, standing in the rain with his rifle strapped across his shoulder, simply replied, "I hope you're right, I really hope and pray that you are right."

Thrust into this conflict, Metaxas once again assumed the role of military strategist and leader. He now was the driving force behind the increasingly successful Greek resistance. He planned carefully and strategically and seemed to have the ability to anticipate the enemy's next move. He placed the right man, General Papagos, in charge of the execution of the war plan. From the beginning Metaxas' plan had been one of not simply defending the Greek border but of rather aggressively attacking the Italians at every opportunity and in multiple locations. The fighting was fierce, and the casualties on both sides continued to mount. Within three weeks from the outbreak of hostilities, the Greeks had pushed the Italians out of Greek territory and back into Albania.

In Rome, Mussolini panicked. Calling in Ciano and his generals, he was enraged. He paced the room, his arms moving in a wild-like motion as he vented his frustration and anger. "If anybody had predicted on October 15 what actually happened later, I would have had him shot," he shouted. "I cannot tolerate it if the conviction that we are incapable of defeating the Greeks should be spread around the world."

Marshall Badoglio then spoke while the others sat silently through Mussolini's tirade. "Did I not declare that twenty divisions were necessary?" he said, directing the question at Mussolini. "And you," he continued, "took the decision to attack. I take no responsibility for this fiasco." Badoglio had said his piece, stopped speaking, walked toward his chair, wiped his moist brow, and sat down.

The unrelenting Greek offensive continued, confronting no effective Italian resistance. Reports of Greek soldiers to their commanders were odd. Italians captured as prisoners of war seemed happy to have been taken so that they would no longer be exposed to the possibility of death in combat on the rainy, frozen battlefields. "They almost seem relieved," reported one Greek soldier. "They almost seem friendly. When they surrender to us, they smile, throw up their hands, and greet us saying, '*Buono Greco, buono Greco*' and '*una facia, una rasa.*'" By which they meant that Greeks and Italians were really racial and ethnic brothers: "one face, one race." When reports of these welcomed surrenders reached Mussolini, it stroked is outrage even further.

Mussolini gave irrational orders to his armies, now trapped on frozen mountains by the Greeks. He insisted that they die in their positions. "This is more than an order from me," he exclaimed, "it is an order from our country." And when reports of the activity of his chief commander, General Soddu, reached him, his temper surpassed the boiling point. "He did what?" he shouted at Ciano. "The stupid idiot did what?"

Ciano put his head down, reluctant to repeat to Il Duce what he had been told. Reports had come to him, which he now had to relate to his leader, that while Italian troops were in an increasingly dire situation with the Greeks pushing them into constant retreat into the frozen ground of Albania, Soddu seemed oblivious to the unfolding tragedy and sat in his tent every night composing music for a film he hoped to create.

"Get rid of this fool!" yelled Mussolini. "Get rid of this idiotic fool!"

Ciano responded by replacing Soddu with General Ugo Cavalero who, in turn, began telling Mussolini what he believed his leader wanted to hear—that events were turning around, that in weeks the tide would turn and the Greeks would be in retreat. But as the weeks passed, none of this happened, and the prospect of 70,000 Italian troops being humiliated became increasing real.

Sitting at his desk, Il Duce seemed paralyzed to act. What could he do? he asked himself. Why did he listen to Ciano? Could this disaster be checked? Would he be forced to do what every instinct told him he never wanted to do: ask Hitler for help? Moments later Claretta entered the room, walked over to the desk, placed Mussolini's head between her hands, kissed him on the lips, and looked caringly into his eyes, "What's the matter, my Ben? Why so sad?"

Once again Mussolini revealed his inner thoughts to the woman he knew would never judge him as weak, indecisive, or accepting of defeat. For Mussolini, what was happening in the Greek war verified thoughts that he had long held. His vision had been to transform the Italians into disciplined and fearless warriors who would be fascist "new men," but the continued reports he received from the battlefield convinced him that it might be hopeless in the country he led. He put down the cables he had received from his commanders at the front and turned to Claretta, who had seated herself in the large chair at the front of the desk.

"Yes," he said, "I am bad tempered because I feel ill from what is happening and could break everything, smash everything! Yes, even you! As I just told Ciano about an hour ago, Italians are a race of sheep. I hate these riffraff Italians. While the Germans are tearing their enemies apart, here Italians are living in calm and serenity. This is beginning to make me sick!"

"But, Ben," interrupted Claretta, but she was quickly silenced by Mussolini's outrage.

"Don't 'Ben' me, Claretta, I am not finished! These Italians nauseate me. They think when they are attacked by cannons it's better to have a quiet time in the café. It's disappointing and soul destroying to see that I've failed to change these people into a people of steel and courage! These Italians only want their creature comforts, their coffee, their women, their theatres. Yes, my dear, I'm worried and disgusted."

Claretta said nothing, not wanting to again start Il Duce's flow of anger and complaint. Mussolini's secretary walked into the room, handed him new cables from the front, and quickly left the room. He picked them up and read each in silence. They continued to bring him news he did not believe could happen and desperately did not want to hear. By November 10, barely three weeks after the invasion had begun, the battle Ciano had assured everyone would be over in weeks, if not days or hours, was being lost, and the Italian armies were in full retreat. Mussolini threw the cables on the floor and instructed his secretary to bring Ciano to his office immediately. He then ordered Claretta to leave, telling her he would see her at dinner.

Within twenty minutes Ciano entered his father-in-law's office and sat in the chair placed before the desk. "What is it?" he quietly asked, as if he was unaware of what was troubling Mussolini. "Galeazzo," Mussolini started, "we cannot allow this to happen. We will be the laughing stock of Europe. We cannot be humiliated."

Ciano slowly nodded his head and nervously searched for cigarettes in his pocket. He took one from the package, lit it, slowly inhaled, then displayed to his leader copies of Italian newspapers that were now reporting the retreat and possible defeat. The stories reported increasing discontent of the Italian citizens who had shown no real support or enthusiasm for the war and were now questioning why their sons were being sacrificed for no apparent reason or cause. "It is serious," Ciano said. "We cannot keep public support if this continues. I think the problem is our generals, Il Duce. They are not up to the task and obviously needed more men, equipment, and time to launch this campaign."

"So now you tell me, Galeazzo! Now you tell me! Where were you last summer when you ridiculed Badoglio when he insisted we needed twenty divisions to succeed and not the five you so confidently told me and everyone were more than enough? And what has happened to the money you told us we gave to the Greek leadership to buy them off and pave the way for instant victory? That was supposed to eliminate resistance? The Greeks made you, me, Italy look like fools! You know what they did with that money, Galeazzo? You know what they did? They used it to buy equipment, train their army, and then kick us in the ass! That's what they did with your grand strategy! It's not just our worthless generals, Ciano, no, it's also advisors such as you who have put Italy, and me personally, on the verge of defeat. Hitler is probably looking at this and wondering what kind of paper tiger have I aligned myself with?"

Ciano said nothing. There was little he could say. He knew Il Duce was right; he had stupidly and arrogantly ignored the counsel of his generals and pushed Mussolini to a war they were losing. "Perhaps the tide will turn, Il Duce," he said with a voice that was barely audible. "As much as I do not want to say this, the only way to salvage this is to go to Hitler. We need the Germans."

The potential for humiliation now began to affect Mussolini physically. The image he sought to project to the Italian people was that of a strong leader who was never ill, never tired, and who was free of all addictions and vices. The reality was very different. With his added stress, he could not sleep at night and became a sleep walker. He deluded himself in those early morning sleepless hours into believing that the war could go on and he could prevail, but in his more rested and realistic moments, he knew the real truth. His ulcer condition worsened, and for weeks he ate only milk and crackers and found that the only relief he could obtain for the condition was to drink gallons of milk. He found that even that extreme approach did not work, and his doctor attempted to gradually wean him of milk as if it had become a narcotic. Finally he accepted the fact that he needed to meet with Hitler to ask for his help. He told Claretta, "I can give no further orders to our military. I can't give orders anymore. There comes a time when you can only be a spectator." He bowed his head, placed his hands around his temples, and then sat silently.

Things continued to deteriorate for the Italians. Greek forces converged from all over northern Greece into Albania and continued their relentless assault. They monitored Italian troop movement from high in the mountains and then launched vigorous attacks from all sides. The Italian invasion went nowhere. The Greek army trapped the Third Alpine Division high in the mountains and totally decimated most of the unit, taking 5,000 prisoners. Italian public opinion now turned swiftly against Ciano, since he had been the most visible, forceful voice for war from the beginning. More than blaming Mussolini, the public labeled the conflict "Ciano's war," and there were calls for his ouster. Mussolini refused to part with his son-in-law. As the cold and snow increased in November, he continued his posture of defeatism and disgust for his countrymen. He told Ciano," The snow and the cold are very good. In this way the runts will die, and the mediocre Italian race will improve." When one of his advisors suggested that perhaps he ought to ask the Greeks for an armistice, Mussolini replied that it would be better if all his troops retreated and then were killed. But he knew what he had to do, and he dispatched Ciano to meet with Hitler to seek German intervention.

CHAPTER FIVE

On November 18, 1940, Ciano went to Germany to meet with Hitler. He was ushered into the waiting room where he sat for more than half an hour. Finally the doors opened, and Hitler entered. His clothing was not distinctive; in fact, to the Italian eye, his suit was a poor fit. Hitler walked in very slowly, a technique he had deliberately developed that he had found made people uncertain and nervous. Hitler had seen that the technique served as a method of control, making those in his presence uneasy, unsure of why he was acting in such an unusual manner. The Führer took a seat, motioned Ciano who had stood to greet him to be seated, and at first said nothing beyond, "Greetings, Mr. Minister," as he shook Ciano's hand. He then took a moment to simply look at the Italian, staring at him directly in the eye yet still saying nothing. He slowly began to gently scratch his mustache, which further made Ciano nervous. Those who knew Hitler well, and Ciano was not one of them, always recognized that gesture as one for concern, since it usually meant that the German leader was angry or troubled by something. As Ciano sat silently waiting for Hitler to speak, the Führer finally did. "Mr. Minister, you and your government have made a serious and stupid mistake. The defeat you are suffering has very grave psychological and strategic consequences."

"But, Führer," interrupted Ciano, and he was quickly shut off by Hitler.

"I am not finished, Mr. Minister. Perhaps your leader did not tell you that when we met in Florence the very day your invasion began, I took Il Duce into a private room, away from all of our aides, I clasped his hand and said simply to him that the whole outcome will be a military disaster. But it was too late, since you had already begun. And now we have come to this, and you have come to Germany to save yourself from disaster."

Ciano searched for something to say but could only begin, "Führer, clearly we should have heeded your advice and caution. But our mistake, as serious as it is, cannot allow the world to see that we have, in fact, failed as partners in this great endeavor to create a new order in our countries and in Europe. Il Duce is counting on his personal friendship and admiration of you for your help. He knows you will not fail him."

The meeting ended within a half-hour with Hitler making no verbal commitment but telling Ciano he would contact Mussolini within days about what direction he would take. Hitler knew immediately what had to be done but wanted Ciano to be on edge with no decision to return to Mussolini. He also wanted to confer with his Nazi military leadership. He spent the evening contemplating his moves. At first, he sat alone in his study while his phonograph played music from Wagner. As he often told those around him, Wagner was "the man who reawakened German culture for the spirit of the masses. The music is like a divine manifestation." He would spend hours at a time listening to his Wagner records.

Leaving his study, he proceeded to the dining room where he was greeted by his secretary, Christa Schroeder, his mistress companion, Eva Braun, and a number of key aides and military personnel. His rule, which he insisted be followed, was that no business of government or state was to be discussed at the dinner hour. A routine had also been established from which Hitler seldom deviated. He feared food poisoning and always had his food and water checked, insisting on a special monitored water supply. He had constant stomach problems so was careful to eat only those foods he had found would not trouble him.

Occasionally he would order wine or beer, and he repeatedly lectured those he dined with on the physiological reasons for not eating meat, believing that abstinence from meat prolonged life. After dinner he enjoyed sweets and drank tea in which he mixed exactly seven teaspoons of sugar. At the table he insisted on a fixed seating order, from which there could be no deviation, and he would be visibly angered if that order were changed. Prior to eating he always washed his hands multiple times, repeating an action he engaged in many times during the day. As he ate his dinner, those with him could not fail to see the brownish-yellow color of his teeth that contained fillings. Hitler seldom displayed a sense of humor, but when something did amuse him he would cover his mouth to hide his teeth as he laughed.

Yet all at the table were transfixed by what they called his "compelling light blue eyes," which he often used to "stare-down" an individual. During and after the dinner, Hitler dominated the conversation, giving his views about diet and the evils of smoking that he believed caused cancer, as well as commenting on art, music, theatre, or the latest movies. Those attending these dinners were perplexed by Hitler's peculiar observation of people's hands. When he first met someone, he would carefully, but discreetly, examine the person's hands. He was always preoccupied with the length of his own fingers and would show his hands to his dinner guests and tell them how closely they resembled the hands of one of Hitler's heroes, Frederic the Great. After dinner the usual activity would be for Hitler to join his guests to view a movie, but often his guests had trouble staying awake later because after the movie concluded he continued to dominate animated conversation.

His guests were often struck by the difference between the public and private Führer. As this evening ended, his private driver and valet approached Christa Schroeder.

"Christa," he started, " I find him an interesting and complex man. You know, one evening I found him standing barefoot on a stool, changing a light bulb and I asked him why he did not call me. He looked at me with those magnetic eyes and simply said, 'Should I wake you up just to change a light bulb? I can do it as you can see.' The very next day the Old Reich Chancellery flooded, and the Führer asked if it could be fixed. The architect he called said it was unlikely a repair could be made. Hitler stood directly in front of the man and shouted directly at him, 'If you have not rid us of this problem within the shortest time, I shall have you sent forthcoming to a concentration camp. I hope you understand me.' Needless to say, the place never flooded again."

Christa slowly nodded her head in agreement. "He is always compassionate to both of us and others," she said, "but then he dictates orders for me to type where he tells his military to, and I am quoting his exact words here, 'close your hearts to pity. Act brutally. Eighty million Germans must obtain what is their right. The stronger man is the man in the right.' It is strange, but in person I seldom see that other side of him, Heinz. All I see and know is that to me and to others here he is a kind, thoughtful gentleman who has never used his title, position, or power in any way to be intimidating to us. My only complaints are about the sometimes long and tedious dinner evenings that keep me up far past the time I need to sleep."

The next morning Hitler prepared to meet with his military leaders to discuss Mussolini and the Italian war with Greece. He liked to work after his long dinners late into the early hours of the morning and usually awoke from sleep at around 10:00 a.m. He began the day with his usual breakfast, tea, a biscuit, and an apple, and when he finished he sat at his desk making notes before he met with his generals. He wrote with different colored pencils—red when he made a note about an enemy, green when dealing with a person he liked, and blue when he considered a situation a potential danger and and wanted to warn himself to be cautious. When his secretaries typed from his notes, they were amused but attributed the practice to another of Hitler's eccentricities.

Finishing his notes Hitler walked into the large conference room and sat at the mahogany table that was surrounded by swastika banners placed on each wall.

"Good morning, gentlemen," Hitler began as he arranged his notes and sat in his chair. "Good morning, *Mein Führer*," those assembled said virtually in unison.

Hitler wasted no time in getting to the heart of the matter. "The Italians are disloyal partners," he began. "They are ungrateful and unreliable friends and what they have done in regard to Greece was irresponsible and stupid. And now, as they sit on the verge of defeat and humiliation, they come begging for our help. I have met with Ciano, and he implores that we intervene."

"*Mein Führer*," spoke up Joseph Goebbels, Hitler's minister of propaganda. "Ciano is a fool. He is nothing but a social climber who now has lost all respect in Italy. He is also stupid, without manners, tasteless, and insolent."

Another military man at the table then added, "And, *Mein Führer*, besides Ciano being the idiot the minister has correctly described, as we have advised you before, the Italian army is a totally worthless entity. I'm not surprised the Greeks are walking all over them."

Hitler listened, looked down at his notes briefly, and then spoke again. "You are both correct, of course, but we are confronted with a difficult situation. To let Mussolini lose would be a blow to us as well. He is, however flawed, officially our ally, our only ally I must remind all of you. If he fails, it means that we have failed to act, that we have been weakened or are afraid of some negative consequences."

"But, *Mein Führer*," said Admiral Eric Raeder, "intervention will delay and drain our resources that are needed for our Balkan campaign against Yugoslavia and then the major effort against the Soviet Union."

General Franz Haider then added, "And we don't know what the Soviets will do if we go into Greece. They too may have designs there for strategic reasons. It may precipitate a conflict with them before we are ready, and our troops will be diverted to a front we should care little about."

"Your points are good, General, but I see no real alternative," responded Hitler.

"One other thing, *Mein Führer*," broke in General Walther von Brauchitsch, "it will also mean we will have to confront Churchill and the British who have already been involved in the present conflict as part of their guarantee of Greece's neutrality."

Hitler quickly answered the general's concerns. "I have little regard for Churchill. He is not and will not be a historical leader. In fact, if it were not for the war, who would even speak of Churchill?"

Goebbels sat smiling and as Hitler stopped speaking simply added, "Churchill, Churchill is a drunkard whose blood has been transfused with alcohol. Churchill will be no problem."

Goebbels' remark brought a smile to Hitler's face and to those around the table. Hitler then continued, "I'm afraid gentlemen, while all we have said is true, we must act. Greece is at war with our ally, however weak and unreliable the Italians might be. Greece has accepted the British guarantee to help, and we cannot allow that to stand. We cannot execute a successful action against the Soviet Union while at the same time fighting on another front in Greece. It is intolerable to us to allow the British to establish a foothold and presence on the continent. Even if the Italians had not initiated this stupid fiasco, we would still have to act if only to dispel the British of the idea that they would ever be allowed on the European continent. Thank you, gentleman, I will soon issue the order to act." Hitler signaled that the meeting had ended, all at the table stood, in unison said, "Heil Hitler," and their leader left the room. He proceeded back to his desk and wrote the order to move German troops into Greece sometime in early April 1941. He labeled the action, "Operation Marita."

From November 1940 into the new year, it was clear to the world that Greece had accomplished a stunning and unexpected victory. Because of the

1939 agreement, Britain, whose sole ally in Europe was Greece, had given some support, but the deciding factor in the Greek victory was the superior performance of the Greek army. Metaxas was offered even more extensive support by Churchill but declined the Englishman's offer, fearing that a wholesale involvement by Britain would certainly move Hitler to intervene.

In January 1941 the unexpected happened. A German medical doctor was placed on a Greek military plane in Belgrade and headed toward Athens, while the chief surgeon of the British Mediterranean fleet moved quickly to the same destination: the bedside of critically ill Ionannis Metaxas. The prime minister had received a tonsillectomy on January 18, and that procedure was followed by blood poisoning. Three blood transfusions failed to improve his condition. A Greek destroyer was then dispatched to the island of Tinos to secure what was purported to be a miracle working icon, The Holy Icon of the Virgin Mary, but that hope was also dashed, and Metaxas died on January 29.

For Greece, it was a stunning blow. Nikos and his brother had been ordered back to Athens as the victory over the Italians seemed certain, and both listened intently to the radio broadcast announcing Metaxas' death. "I was always skeptical of him and his dictatorial ways," said Nikos to Vasili, "but I have to admit, in this struggle he really rose to the occasion. I don't know that we really have anyone who can replace him."

"He knew what he was doing against the Italians, that's for sure," added Vasili. "I had heard he personally planned in detail every move we made against them, and his experience and knowledge of mountain combat took the Italians totally by surprise. Finally, a little late, I guess, we Greeks might appreciate him."

The two brothers, in full military uniform, joined the large crowd that had gathered for their wartime leader. Women wept as his body was placed in an unpretentious tomb at the foot of the Acropolis. The man presiding at the occasion was a tall man who had served as governor of the National Bank of Greece, Alexander Koryzis, a man better known for his stylish suits than for his governmental leadership or his ability as a military strategist. Koryzis closed the funeral ritual as if he were addressing Metaxas personally, saying, "You have opened the road to victory. We shall march along inflexible and determined. We shall reach the end."

Nikos and Vasili walked away from the burial site as the crowd dispersed. "I'm not sure about Koryzis," said Vasili. "He seems weak, uncertain. I don't know if he's really up to it."

"You're probably right, and you know I heard rumors that Metaxas was actually poisoned."

"Poisoned!" Vasili said. "More conspiracies? Is that all we Greeks can do is create mythical conspiracies?"

"No, I'm serious, Vasili, the word is that British operatives did him in because of his reluctance to really allow them to come into Greece in full force, and you know the British desperately want to establish a front in the Balkans as a diversion to Hitler."

"I don't believe it, Niko, I think it's ridiculous. The man was about seventy years old and just got sick, that's it, and he died. Forget that nonsense, and if you really need something to worry about I suggest two things—watch for what the Germans do now in Greece and see if Korizis is up to the job."

On the border before entering Yugoslavia Private Klaus Schreiber and his unit were idle. They were told that soon, within two months at the most, they would receive orders from Berlin for a planned move into Yugoslavia. "I'm not sure we're really going into Yugoslavia," said Schreiber to his colleague, "I think it's really going to be Greece."

The other soldier, Herman Herringer, sat on the bed shining his boots. "Maybe not," he said, "We're right here almost in Yugoslavia and ready to move. Doesn't that make more sense?"

"Maybe," said Klaus. "I hope you are right. I don't really want to go to Greece. You know, I studied there, I lived there, I have friends there, and I just know too many people there."

Klaus' tall, lanky colleague looked up from his boot shining and said, "But if you're ordered, Klaus, you will go just like the rest of us. And besides I think those Greek girls are pretty good looking. After all, we can't be shooting guns all day, can we?"

"Very good, Herman, should I ask the Führer about his opinions of Greek girls?"

"You know, Klaus, there are lots of rumors about Hitler, that he's kind of strange, does weird things with women. But then I've even heard he's homo-sexual."

Klaus seemed surprised. "Who told you that? What about that woman people say lives with him? Braun or something? I forget her name."

"Well, I don't know, Klaus, it's just what I've heard."

"Let's just hope its Yugoslavia, not Greece," Klaus repeated.

In Thessaloniki, Mordecai ben Nathan tried to sort out his feelings about the recent Greek success. He felt proud as a Greek Jew that his countrymen had done what most thought impossible, but he worried about what he believed would come next. The reports of the Nazi actions against the Jews in the countries they already occupied made him extremely nervous, and the rumors increased daily that Germany would, to save face for Mussolini, move its troops into Greece. He knew he could not move his aging and ill parents away from Salonika and he knew he could not leave them, but he thought about his older sister, Sarah, who was twenty-four. Mortis contacted Nikos in Athens, explained his concerns, and asked if his sister could possibly go to Nikos' home village of Kalavryta where, in a rural area, it was likely she would be safe if the Germans did come to Thessaloniki. Nikos quickly agreed, and within a week Mordecai's sister Sarah was living with Nikos' parents, and the locals were told that she was Greek and a Christian cousin. Sarah assumed the more Greek name of "Erini," and Mordecai felt a sense of comfort and relief.

In London Prime Minister Churchill received news of the Greek campaign with astonishment and jubilation. At dinner he turned to Clementine and to his daughter and complained about the food, while he drank is usual dinner champagne. "Why are we getting all of these boiled vegetables every day. Meals should please you, fill you, sustain you, not bore you. Kat, tell the chef to do something different."

"You know, Winston. those vegetables are actually good for you, they're healthy, and you might benefit from some health protection."

Churchill sipped his champagne again, wiped the wetness from his mouth, and smiled. "It's just another fad, Kat, just a fad. Almost all food faddists I have ever known, nut eaters and the like, have died young after a period of senile decay."

"Well," his wife responded, "I don't think you will develop senility, but I can't guarantee you won't decay," she laughed.

"But what about those Greeks!" exclaimed Churchill, quickly bored with the subject of good nutrition. "It is truly amazing. They turned back the pompous fool Mussolini and his fantasy 'Roman' legions! Those Greeks are tough, very tough, they are warriors, they are outstanding fighters. They have shown the world that these evil people, Mussolini and Hitler, and all the others like them can be checked. They truly are amazing! After dinner I must publicly make a short statement to all of Europe as to how important it is to acknowledge what they have done."

Later that evening when he had completed dinner, Churchill poured himself some brandy and sat down to write his public statement about the Greek resistance. It took only a few moments, and he wrote only a few sentences. He called in his valet Frank Sawyer and instructed him to have one of the secretaries type it and distribute it over the wire. Later, after another brandy and conversation with his wife, he then poured a glass of wine, drank it, and prepared for bed.

The reaction throughout the world to what the Greeks had done was electric. No other country had yet successfully turned back an invasion of an Axis power. Hope became alive again, even in those nations that had already fallen to the fascist aggressors. If tiny, poor Greece could do it, then it was possible anywhere. Throughout the globe, leaders of the free nations praised the Greeks.

The tension in Athens was real. It was only a matter of time most thought, maybe weeks, maybe days, before the Germans would make their move. The general population still hoped to avoid involvement in the European war, but the Greek government and military held no such hopes or illusions. Nikos and his brother were among those who believed the German involvement was only a matter of time and probably not much time. They were ordered to remain in Athens as part of the Greek forces preparing for any further action. Resting for lunch and a break from their posts located on the edge of the Greek Parliament building, they sat on the grass looking at the local newspapers.

"Niko," started Vasili, "listen to this, listen to what Churchill said about what we have done."

"What did he say?" asked Nikos.

Vasili smiled, lifted the paper with a sense of pride as if the paper were some kind of important historical document. "Here it is, Niko, it's short, it's simple, and it thrills me." Vasili then slowly read Churchill's words:

"Until now we used to say that the Greeks
Fight like Heroes. Now we shall say
That heroes fight like Greeks."

Nikos listened to the words, thought about what he had just heard, and was surprisingly overcome with emotion.

NAZI GREECE
1941-1943

CHAPTER SIX

IN BERLIN, HITLER WAS NOT FEEL-ing well. The cold temperature in December of 1940 may have had something to do with it, he thought, but it was not just the cold weather. The Führer called his personal physician, Dr. Theodor Morell, for some relief.

Morell, Hitler's closest allies thought, was a strange man. He seemed to be unsanitary in his personal hygiene, had disgusting eating habits, and many, except for Hitler himself, considered him to be a "quack" doctor. Eva Braun, Hitler's mistress, in particular disliked Morell but felt it was of no use to tell Hitler because the Führer seemed to trust him completely. She had told one of her friends, when asked about the doctor, that she didn't "trust him and I hate him." Morell recognized that Hitler tended to be a hypochondriac, always talking about his "weak heart" and constantly complaining of pains in his stomach, but Morell had found nothing seriously wrong with either Hitler's heart or stomach. But now, even though he disliked the process, Hitler ordered a complete physical examination. The examination found that Hitler had developed edema in his calves and shins. The drugs Morell prescribed for the Führer aggravated his heart, and other medications did nothing to clear Hitler's self-described stomach issues.

Hitler knew, however, that at least part of his ill health was due to another problem: Benito Mussolini. At the very moment the Führer and his generals were planning for what could be the key operation of the German march to the East—the invasion of Russia—Mussolini had forced him to take an action he did not want to take. Now, as he attempted to deal with increasing stress, Hitler had to send troops into Greece to rescue Mussolini from a complete public debacle. During this same month the Greek army had not only stopped the Italian offensive invasion but had also so dominated the Italians that they had retreated back out of Greece into Albania where even there they were forced to retreat even further.

After his examination by Morell, Hitler slowly sipped tea and carefully inspected a tray of cookies that had been served by his housekeeper for the benefit of the Führer and his guest, Albert Speer, his minister of armaments and war production.

"Herr Speer," Hitler started, "have one of these fine cookies, made personally by Mrs. Schultz, perhaps the finest baker in the whole country."

Speer looked longingly at the tray, inhaled their tempting aroma, but regretfully shook his head from side to side. "*Mein Führer,*" he answered, "the temptation is great, but I'm afraid the size of my waist is growing even greater. I must decline, but please don't let me hold you back."

"Maybe later," said Hitler as he once again paused to drink his tea, "but right now I have too much on my mind, like Mussolini and like Greece."

"Greece?" asked Speer. "Are we going in?"

"I have no desire to go into Greece, Herr Speer, We have no quarrel with the Greek people. In fact, I have always been an admirer of Greek civilization and culture. What the ancients did and their legacy to us are truly phenomenal. And, you know, even as a race they are far superior to the Slavic peoples. You know, Speer, the ancient Greeks had excelled in and perfected a variety of disciplines and fields. And that is what I want our Hitler youth groups to do—to match through sports the ideal bodies that the Greeks strove to achieve." Speer nodded in agreement as Hitler continued, "And what has been lost in history about the Greeks is that in their very veins flowed Germanic blood. The Dorians, Speer, who invaded and settled in Greece were of the Germanic race. But Mussolini has made it impossible for us to stay out. And Speer, as an architect, I know you personally must have admired what those ancients did. What could be more perfect than the Parthenon?"

"Of course, *Mein Führer*," responded Speer, "we must take care not to destroy not only that magnificent structure but others as well. We don't need the whole world thinking that we are some kind of uncultured barbarians. But what will be our rationale for going into Greece?"

"We will announce the invasion based on what I think the world community will accept. That is, Greece is at war with our ally, Italy, and we are obligated to come to Italy's aid. Secondly, we will argue that Greece has accepted the British guarantee to help them and that it is against our national interest to allow the English to establish a foothold on the continent. What we will not state publicly is that we can never be secure when we make our move against Russia if the British are in the Balkans." Hitler poured more tea into his cup, took a moment to stare again at the cookies, and then reached for one. After taking just one bite of the cookie, he rose from the chair, patted Speer on the back, and escorted him to the front door where a chauffeured car awaited the minister.

On December 13, 1940, Hitler issued Confidential Directive Number 20, now named Operation

Marita, which outlined a plan for the invasion and occupation of Greece. He set the date for the action to commence on April 6, 1941.

On that morning of April 6 in Athens, Nikos Gantos carefully and skillfully moved the straight razor over his friend's face, shaving off the heavy growth on the face of Apostolos Santas as he leaned back in the old chair that constituted most of the furniture in Santas' small apartment. Another friend, Manolis Glezos, sat watching Nikos demonstrate his skill with the straight razor as he waited for his turn to be shaved. Santas and Glezos were friends of Nikos, both nineteen years old and students at the University of Athens. The three men had known each other since Nikos had moved to Athens from Kalavryta and before he had gone to Thessaloniki to begin college. The three young men had spent time together talking, listening to music, having midday coffee, and frequenting the bars that catered to the young in Athens, often not leaving those establishments until the early morning hours after midnight. Nikos had become skilled with the razor and had, even in his early teenage years, become known as the person who gave the fastest, smoothest, and most nick-free shaves of anyone in Kalavryta. And when he had moved to Athens he continued practicing that skill, sometimes for a small fee but usually at no charge. He simply liked doing it and often thought that if for some reason he did not succeed in his field of German language and literature, he could always fall back on this skill and perhaps be a barber.

Earlier on that same morning, miles to the north across the border in Bulgaria, the German army had been given the order to activate Operation Marita. At 5:15 a.m. Nazi troops, in overwhelming numbers, entered Greece and faced fierce resistance from Greek troops. Greek radio broadcasts interrupted the shaving sessions that Nikos was conducting:

"Prime Minister Koryzis has announced that since 0515 hours," the broadcast began, "the German army that was in Bulgaria all of a sudden attacked our troops on the Greek-Bulgarian frontier. Our troops are defending the Fatherland."

Nikos finished his work on Apostolos, wiped off the remaining soap with a warm, wet towel, and said to both Apostolos and Manolis, "I've got to go. I must report immediately to the base. I don't know what we will do here in Athens, but I must go." His two friends said nothing but nodded their heads, as Nikos quickly gathered his belongings and left the apartment. What was unsaid among the three was the recognition that the fight against the Germans would be much different than the confrontation with the Italians.

For the next three weeks the Greeks fought the Nazi invasion with fierce and courageous resistance.

But the huge numbers of German troops and their superior equipment could not be matched by the Greeks. On April 21 the Greek commander General Georgios Tsolakoglou surrendered to the German army in Thessaloniki. The Greek general insisted that he surrender only to the Germans and refused to acknowledge any Italian surrender saying that the Italians had earned nothing. Hearing of the Greek position, Mussolini was furious. "We will not allow the Greeks to laugh in our faces," he insisted to Ciano and instructed his foreign minister to send an envoy to Berlin to insist that a second surrender ceremony that included the Italians be held. While awaiting a response from Hitler regarding this unusual request, Mussolini foolishly accelerated his attacks against the Greek forces and was rewarded by the Greeks with 6,000 more Italian casualties after the Greeks and Germans had already ceased hostilities.

In Berlin Hitler considered Mussolini's request for a second surrender idiotic; but once again realizing that, however flawed, Mussolini was his only real ally, he arranged for what was viewed by the Nazi generals as an absurd and embarrassing second official Greek surrender ceremony. Winston Churchill, hearing about this second surrender, sat with his wife and slowly smiled as he heard of Mussolini's demand for recognition. "Here surely," he commented to Clementine, "is the world's record in the domain of the ridiculous and the contemptible. This whipped jackal, Mussolini, who to save his own skin has made Italy a vassal state of Hitler's empire, comes frisking up to the side of the German tiger with yelpings not only of appetite—that could be understood—but even of triumph."

In Athens Prime Minister Koryzis met with King George and the government ministers and planned for the king and the government to evacuate Athens and establish headquarters in Crete. Clearly upset and nervous, Koryzis left the meeting and seemed unsettled and unable to think clearly, let alone lead a nation in this crisis. Alone, he returned to his home, went to his upstairs bedroom, and closed and locked the door. Moments later a shot was fired, and when Koryzis' bodyguards ran to the room and broke down the door, they found the prime minister's body on the bed with his hand holding the pistol with which he had ended his life. As Koryzis' lifeless body was removed, King George fled the country, leaving a message to the people he had abandoned: "Greeks," he said, "do not be discouraged, even at this painful moment of our history. I shall always be with you… Be courageous, the good days are to come. Long live the nation." But for many Greeks, and Vasili Gantos was one of them, the King was a disgraceful coward, who abandoned the country to others who were left to fight and to die. Vasili vowed he would not forget.

Small crowds gathered on the streets of Athens on April 27, but most Athenians chose to remain in their homes and watch what was happening on the streets of their city from their windows as Nazi troops moved through the city. Earlier that morning Adolf Hitler had received a message from Commander von Stumme in Athens. It read, "*Mein Führer*, on the 27 of April, 1941, at 8:00 a.m. and 10:00 a.m. we arrived in Athens."

Nicholaos Gantos, his brother Vasili, Apostolos Santas, and Manolis Glezos were among the small crowds lining the streets as German troops marched into the city, followed by two armored car divisions, a long line of tanks, and motorbikes, all making their way down Vassilessas Sofias Avenue. That morning the mayors of Athens and Piraeus and the commander of the Greek army in Athens drove to the Parthenon coffee shop in a northern suburb and officially handed over the city to the German commander. On Greek radio the playing of the Greek national anthem was stopped as a German military officer announced the official Nazi occupation of Greece.

Watching the impressive display of German military strength marching through the streets of Athens, the Gantos brothers and their two friends were not quite sure how to assess what they were witnessing. "What will happen now?" asked Vasili.

"I'm not sure," answered Nikos, "did you hear that German Field Marshall von List made a statement that the Greeks had defended the country so valiantly that he ordered his troops to treat the Greek prisoners, and these are his words, 'as befits brave soldiers.' In fact, he actually let our men return to their homes with their weapons."

"I did hear that," said Manolis, "but I still don't trust them."

"Niko!" interrupted Vasili, "Look at that soldier, the second one to the left of that first tank. Is that your roommate? It's hard to tell in those uniforms and those helmets, but is that Klaus? Your friend Klaus Schreiber?"

Nikos looked shocked but then strained to look more closely. Nikos felt an urge to shout out at the soldier but knew better than to make such a foolish move. He wasn't absolutely sure, but it did look like someone who resembled Klaus. But perhaps he was mistaken, he thought. But what if it was him? As the soldiers they were watching marched passed them and out of their view, the four young men then moved toward a location in which they could have a clear view of the German troops who had made their way up to the Parthenon.

Nikos, Vasili, Apostolos, and Manolis stationed themselves where there was no obstructed view, and they could see the drama that was unfolding at the base of the Parthenon. Watching from below they could see clearly but, of course, could hear nothing that was transpiring on the famous site that Hitler so admired. The Greek flag flew high on the pole as the young Greek soldier, one of the elite Evzone troops, stood tall and erect as the guardian of the symbol of the nation.

For those who were uninformed, the dress of the Evzone units could be deceiving. They wore what appeared to be skirts covering tight long white stockings, shirt tops with colors, shoes with what appeared to be feminine puffs on them, and headgear that sat on their heads with a rather long dangling cord that some might equate with a woman's braid. But the Evzones' external appearance clearly did not reflect reality. These units were an elite fighting force, carefully selected and rigorously trained. To the uninformed eye they might appear as quaint wearers of colorful costumes of a past era when in reality they were hardened tough warriors and killers, not afraid to fight and die for their country. The young Evzone on guard this evening was Konstantine Koukidis, and as he stood at attention at the base of the flagpole that flew the Greek colors, he was approached by another soldier, one wearing the uniform of the German Third Reich.

The German officer ordered the Evzone to "retire" the Greek flag. Watching the flag being lowered, the four friends were silent, but tears began to fall down the face of Vasili Gantos and Manolis Glezos. The Germans then raised their flag, and the symbol of the German swastika now flew over the most historic and recognizable symbol of the glory of ancient Greece. Then suddenly, there seemed to be confusion as persons on that elevated spot began breaking ranks and running toward the young Evzone.

"What's he doing?" asked Nikos in an excited and perplexed manner as he tried to make sense of what he was witnessing from a far-off vantage point.

Vasili, who had brought a pair of binoculars, focused intently on the scene, trying to discover why, suddenly, military order seemed to have broken down. "The Germans are running after him," Vasili reported, "but, but he's wrapping our flag around his body and he's running! He's running! He's running toward the edge! Oh, my God! He just jumped off the edge! He's falling! There's no way he can survive!"

The four young men watched in horror as the Germans ran to the edge of the high elevation on which the Parthenon sat and looked over the edge as the young Evzone's body crashed into the ground, a mass of broken bones and severed limbs, lying in a pool of blood-soaked dirt. Nikos and Vasili were speechless. Manolis and Apostolos closed their eyes, bowed their heads, and instinctively made the sign of the cross.

"Now maybe those Nazis will understand what they're up against in Greece," Manolis said. "That Evzone just made the first act of resistance to these invaders of our land. We cannot let his death mean nothing. We have to do something! That flag! That damn German flag! I can't stand to see it there! Looking at it disgusts me."

In Berlin Hitler was feeling satisfied and even almost admired the Greeks. He was pleased with the speed and efficiency with which, once again, German troops had overwhelmed those who sought to stop his drive for European hegemony. Speaking to a cheering audience in the Reichstag, Hitler did his best to cover for the pitiful performance of his ally Mussolini and continued to show uncharacteristic respect and appreciation for the Greeks. He told his fellow Nazis, "I must state categorically that this action was not directed against Greece. Il Duce did not even request me to place one single German division at his disposal for this purpose... The concentration of German forces was therefore not made for the purpose of assisting the Italians against Greece. It was a precautionary measure against the British attempt to entrench themselves in the Balkans."

The Führer's audience clapped enthusiastically, but all knew their leader was simply making a statement to help his bungling ally, Mussolini. In fact, it was widely known that Mussolini had directly asked Hitler for intervention and had exploded in rage when he had heard that the Greeks had surrendered to the Germans alone, while totally ignoring the Italians. But then Hitler continued his address with comments he had never made about any of the multiple nations the German army had already invaded, conquered, and occupied. Standing at the podium he began to speak with a swaying motion of his body, which those who had witnessed the Führer speak many times before knew was a sign that what he was saying was a genuinely felt emotion in their leader.

"For the sake of historical truth," began Hitler, "I must verify that of all the adversaries we have confronted, it was the Greek soldier in particular who fought with the greatest heroism, self-sacrifice, bold courage, and the highest disregard for death. Only when the continuation of resistance was no longer possible and no longer had any meaning did he capitulate."

When the speech was reported in the Greek press, Nikos read it to his brother and then put the paper down and said, " You know, Vasili, the story also reports that Hitler's chief of staff, Field Marshall Wilhelm Keitel, said that Hitler had ordered the release and repatriation of Greek war prisoners because, and here he quotes Hitler, 'because of their gallant bearing.' Keitel goes on to say that Hitler insisted on giving us an honorable settlement because of the Greeks' 'brave struggle' and because we did not start this war, he said, the Italians did. Maybe things won't be as bad with the Germans here as we thought."

"Don't be so gullible, Niko," Vasili said, "Hitler would say anything to get what he wants. I don't believe anything that crazy man says. But I'm glad he recognized a spirit of resistance here, Niko, and that spirit has not been killed by Nazi troops marching in our streets. The Germans haven't seen anything yet, you'll see. Now let's go. Manolis and Apostolos are waiting for us. They say it's important, and they want our help."

Nikos and Vasili met Apostolos and Manolis at the Zappion Promenade, a popular drinking establishment for students from the University of Athens. It was an old place, rather dreary in appearance with no real decorations or artworks that one might associate with a younger generation. The place was busy but not overflowing with students who usually began arriving after 10:00 in the evening. The four friends sat at a table deliberately chosen by Manolis to be away from the ears of the other patrons. After they had ordered drinks, Manolis began speaking softly and deliberately, careful that none close by could overhear what he was saying. "Apostolos and I have decided to do something, something you may believe to be crazy, but we feel we must do it anyhow."

Nikos listened intently while Vasili twirled the drink in his glass. "So tell us," said Nikos impatiently, "just forget all the mystery and just tell us."

Apostolos got right to the point. "Manolis and I are going to take the swastika flag down from the Acropolis."

Vasili's face seemed frozen. "You are going to do what?"exclaimed Nikos in a voice louder than his friends would have liked. "Are you both crazy, suicidal, or just plain stupid?"

"We're serious," said Manolis. "We're going to do it. None of us can stand to see that foreign flag flying on that symbol of our civilization. We can't. We built that structure while those German tribes were still living in caves and trees. We can't let that flag fly over our country! We can't, and we need your help, both of you!"

Vasili spoke next. "How can you ever get close? There are German guards everywhere. They will spot you the moment you begin to climb the Acropolis to even get to the top where the flagpole is located. They won't let you get close. You two, my friends, are courting some strange death wish. And, besides, what do you want Nikos and me to do besides probably getting ourselves killed?"

"It's not as crazy as you think, Vasili," said Apostolos. "Manolis and I went to the Acropolis yesterday as visitors on the pretense of wanting to take pictures of the Parthenon, but we really wanted to see how many guards were stationed there and where they were positioned. We think at the right time, on the right night when there is little moonlight, we can do it. We discovered some scaffolding left by French archeologists a few years ago that will allow us to climb up the Acropolis from the back end where it is unlikely the Germans will expect anything. We just need you two to be at the base of the Acropolis to see if any help might arrive to help the guards at the top. We can communicate with some equipment we got from the Greek army base. Will you do it?"

Nikos and Vasili listened carefully, looked at each other, and asked for five minutes of privacy to discuss their decision. In less than the five minutes, both returned to Apostolos and Manolis. "We think you're both crazy," said Nikos, "but we are crazy Greeks, too, just like you. We're in. When? Where? And what time? We're ready."

It had been a month since the German swastika had first been raised on the Acropolis. Over the following days the four young men waited and watched for weather and political conditions to set an action date. The news Nikos and Vasili received from their brother in Crete further fired their patriotism and enthusiasm for the bold plan to lower the German flag. The Germans had launched a daring paratrooper invasion of the island, sending thousands down by parachutes into a fierce resistance by the Greeks of Crete. Paratroopers were killed in mid-air, and others were killed by shovels and pitchforks as they attempted to land on the ground. Men, women, and children all joined to stop the invaders. When the Germans did finally land, they had lost thousands of men and rounded up Greeks to retaliate for their losses. In their jail cells awaiting execution the Greeks wrote on their prison walls, "Long live Greece, Long live Crete," and they sang patriotic songs as bullets from German firing squads dropped them lifeless to the ground.

The events in Crete now inspired Manolis Glezos and Apostolos Santas with even greater determination to execute their plan. On the evening of May 30, 1941, Manolis and Apostolos both climbed the scaffold the French archeologists had left behind and reached the top of the Acropolis as Nikos and Vasili remained at the bottom, their eyes searching left and right for any sign that additional troops were being directed to the site. They saw none. At the top Manolis and Apostolos had unknowingly chosen a lucky night to strike. The German guards, having heard the news of the final victory of their comrades in Crete, were celebrating, sitting off to the side singing and drinking heavily as they groped and fondled some Greek prostitutes who had chosen to work their trade that evening with the German soldiers. The guards were in no condition to "guard" anything.

"God must be watching us," whispered Manolis. "Let's go. Let's do it."

Apostolos lay silently on the ground, taking no chances that even drunken soldiers might still see him. He nodded agreement to Manolis, and both moved together toward the flagpole. They carefully untied the swastika flag and slowly began lowering it, but at half-point it would not move any further. For some reason it was stuck. Manolis looked at Apostolos and shrugged his shoulders, signifying that he didn't know what the problem was or what to do about it. Taking their time, which they knew consisted of only moments, they both untied the flag from where it had snagged, and suddenly the entire large flag fell over them, covering their bodies and completely blocking their vision. Unable to see but still listening for any movement by the guards, they felt relieved as they continued to hear the singing and laughing of the Nazi guards and their evening women companions.

Finally both men freed themselves from the covering of the flag, quickly rolled it into a bundle, and cut two small pieces as souvenirs of their daring deed. They deliberately left their fingerprints on the flagpole so that other innocent people would not be charged and punished for what had occurred. They then threw the now cut flag into a sinkhole. Manolis and Apostolos, the swastika now removed from flying over the Acropolis, began their descent from the top. They had vowed to each other that if they were about to be apprehended, they, like the courageous Evzone in the weeks before, would jump to their certain deaths. Fortunately, the drunken guards knew nothing about what had happened and continued their drinking and laughing with the Greek women of the night. Reaching the base of the Acropolis, Manolis and Apostolos joined Nikos and Vasili, took deep breaths, smiled, and slowly walked away as if they had simply been out for an evening stroll.

CHAPTER SEVEN

THE STORY WAS WIDELY COVered in the next morning's papers. In their homes Athenians smiled with pride and amusement at the bold act that had embarrassed the Germans. At the Nazi command center at the Grand Bretagne Hotel none were amused. Of all the countries that had thus far fallen before Germany like lifeless dominoes, none had dared such an audacious, openly defiant act. None had so publicly embarrassed the army of the Third Reich. Orders were given to search the city for clues, any kind of clues, to bring the perpetrators of this act to justice, a justice that would mean death.

Nikos and Vasili said nothing of the plot or of their small part in it to anyone, knowing well that no one could be trusted to keep such a secret and knowing what the consequences of even their minor involvement would be. Manolis and Apostolos could not contain their pride in what they had done and returned home on the night of their daring act and told their parents what they had done and presented them with the piece of the German flag they had cut off as souvenirs of their deed.

Apostolos' father could not believe what his son was relating. "They will kill you, they will kill us all, do you understand? They will kill us all." Apostolos watched as his father paced the floor, a mixture of pride in what his son had done and fear of the danger to his entire family.

"They won't find us, Father. No one saw us. We did it for Greece. We did it to show those Nazis bastards that they cannot claim the Parthenon. They cannot own Greece. They need to know what they are up against here."

Apostolos' father looked at his son. His emotions were confused. He feared for his son's life and for the lives of his whole family, but he knew in his heart he had enormous pride in the daring, the courage, and the patriotism his son had shown. "This piece you gave me, Apostolos, this piece of the flag, I know what it means to you, but we cannot keep it. If it is found, we will be killed." He took the piece of cloth that still displayed parts of the Nazi swastika, placed it in a bowl, placed newspapers over it, and lit a match as both father and son sat silently and watched the cloth burn, turn black, and then disintegrate into ash.

Apostolos then conveyed to Manolis what his father had done, and Manolis' mother, seeing the wisdom in what Apostolos' father had done, repeated the process in her home as Manolis watched the evidence of his actions disappear.

When word of the Nazi humiliation reached Hitler in the morning after the flag had been removed, he was in the middle of one of his self-amusements. He was engaged in one of his harmless but almost childish games. This particular one he called the "dressing game." It began when his valet put out the clothes he would wear on that day. The valet would leave the room and then cry out, "Starting!" The valet would time him to see how fast the Führer could dress himself, and when Hitler had finished the valet would check to see if he had broken his previous dressing speed record.

Moments after Hitler emerged from his room and headed for the dining area where he would have breakfast, he received a call from Joseph Goebbels, his propaganda minister. "*Mein Führer*," Goebbels began, "we have had an incident in Athens, nothing catastrophic, but hugely embarrassing. Some person or persons, we don't know yet, climbed up to the Parthenon and took down our flag, which has now disappeared. We have sent troops throughout the city to get some answers and find whoever did this, but so far we have not been successful."

Hitler, who had been seated at the breakfast table, stood, said nothing, and then smashed his fist on the table. "And we had how many guards there?" he shouted on the phone.

"About twenty," Goebbels sheepishly replied.

"Twenty! Twenty!" again shouted Hitler. "So our twenty guards could not see, hear, find, or kill one, two, or how ever many Greeks whom no one noticed climbing the Acropolis to the Parthenon and in front of all of Athens took down our flag! And this is the same army that is winning victories in country after country? This is the army that is conquering Europe?"

Hitler held the phone to his ear, but there was no response from his caller. The Führer, now bringing his rage down to a quiet and calm voice, simply said to Goebbels, "Mr. Minister, find out who did this, kill them, and control the spread of this news. And finally, and I order that this be done immediately, the twenty Germans who have embarrassed the nation and me personally must pay a price. Have them all executed." Hitler then hung up the phone.

Goebbels held the receiver that now had become silent and then called the commander in Athens. The following day the twenty German soldiers were executed, and their deaths were widely reported not only for Greek consumption but, even more so, for soldiers of the Reich who might have any doubt about what the consequences might be if they did not do their duty and honor their country. But after weeks of investigations and searches, the commander of the Athens occupation reported to Goebbels that those who had committed that brazen act against the German flag could not be found.

Klaus Schreiber sat in the comfortable chair in the living room of the home the Nazis had taken from a Greek family to house their occupying force. It was the common practice of the Germans to take a Greek house and force the rightful owners to leave everything and find some other accommodations for themselves and their families. Some moved in with other families, others returned to their brothers, sisters, cousins, aunts, and uncles who lived in small villages in rural Greece. Still others, with nowhere to go, lived as homeless people, each night seeking food and shelter somewhere in Athens.

Schreiber was reading the newspaper story that reported the execution of the German guards who had failed to protect the honor of the German flag and nation on the Acropolis. How stupid they were, he thought, they made us a laughing stock in Greece, they disgraced us, and they got what they deserved. His colleagues had noticed a change in Klaus over the past months, he had become even more serious than usual, seldom joked, and spent his private hours reading Hitler's speeches as well as the Führer's book, *Mein Kampf*, which by German law had become required reading in Germany though few, even Goebbels and Goering, had ever actually read it. But the sections Klaus did read struck a responsive chord in him. He followed and accepted Hitler's argument that the German people were a superior race whose destiny was to be a world ruler. He also accepted that Germany needed "living space," and that would eventually mean the control of Europe and even Russia. And Klaus was particularly receptive to Hitler's discussion of the Jews. In *Mein Kampf* Hitler had described an organized Jewish attempt to corrupt and destroy everything that was civilized in Western culture. The Jews, he wrote, raped German women in order to put Jewish blood into the pure German strain. Klaus read the material, thought about it, read it once again, and then internalized it. Hitler, believed Klaus, had pinpointed the problem as no one else had done. It all made sense to him now. Germany would lead the way. Who could stop us? he thought. All who have tried have failed. Klaus felt an enormous sense of pride. He was part of the greatest military machine the world had ever seen. What Napoleon did or even Alexander the Great had accomplished would pale before what the Third Reich would accomplish. Klaus felt good, he felt proud, as he put his copy of Hitler's book down and smiled.

He was part of something big, something great, he thought, and he felt content as he read the document ordering him to his next post, Thessaloniki. The word among the troops was that they were being ordered there to deal with what was described as "the problem." The "problem" was never defined or specified for Klaus or his colleagues, but for most there was little mystery about the order. The "problem," they all assumed, was the Jews.

In the weeks following the Nazi occupation of Greece, the country was theoretically divided into zones: the Germans held the key cities of Athens and Salonika; the Italians received an ill-defined joint control of Athens, but mostly the more rural parts of Greece; and the Bulgarians were given territory that was adjacent to their own border. The Germans, seeing the seeds of even greater potential trouble among the Greeks, allowed the Greek flag to fly on the Acropolis but only between the German swastika and the Italian flag. The Greeks characterized the German concession as like "Christ being between two thieves." The Germans were also aware of how fierce the potential for Greek resistance could be because of their experience in Crete, which they eventually succeeded in capturing but at an enormous cost. Hitler had lost more lives in one day in Crete, more than 4,000 men, than in any single day in the previous fifteen months in eleven countries.

While the Germans would give lip service to sharing the control of Greece with the Italians, it became clear from the first entrance of Nazi troops into Athens that it would be the Germans, not the Italians, deciding the fate of Greece. Even within Italy there was little confusion as to who was in charge. Mussolini seemed to be escaping widespread public condemnation for his Greek adventure, but his foreign minister Galeazzo Ciano did not, as the Italian public and press continuously referred to the Italian catastrophe in Greece as a situation that had resulted from Ciano's blunder.

Now civilians again after the Greek surrender to the Germans, Nicholaos Gantos and his brother Vasili remained in Athens doing odd jobs to simply pay for the fast rising prices of food for themselves and their uncle and aunt in whose home they lived. When they could, they sent money, or more often, food supplies to their parents and to their sister and Sarah ben Nathan who was living with them claiming to be a Greek with an assumed name to hide her Jewish ancestry.

Increasingly, just obtaining food for a day was becoming more and more difficult. The Germans were continuing the practice, which they were doing in every country they occupied, of draining all the country's economic resources for their own use. In Greece their two main economic interests were food and ores, which they used for munitions. The German troops lived in Greek homes and often looted them. Greek products such as olive oil, raisins, and figs were taken to feed their troops in Greece or sent for the troops in North Africa. The total cost of supporting the occupation forces was placed on Greece, which was gradually destroying the financial structure of the country. By 1942 the costs of the German occupation were reaching 90 percent of the Greek national income. And as more and more money was printed and circulated, inflation reached unsustainable levels. In addition, Great Britain had instituted a blockade that prevented needed food and supplies from entering the country. Now all of Greece, but particularly Athens, was in a severe crisis, and actual famine was gripping the country.

Nikos had just finished shaving one of his uncle's neighbors. The man offered to pay Nikos for the shave, but he refused the money. He knew the man's family had little food. In fact, Athens was in the midst of a genuine famine. Nikos sat at the table as his brother, who had been out hauling garbage, came into the house. Vasili had lost some weight, his hair was disheveled, and he brought into the house the odor of the garbage he had been lifting from the homes where German soldiers were quartered as well as from the hotels where the more high-ranking officers were living.

"Niko," began Vasili, "it's really bad out there. People are literally starving. I have seen dead bodies just abandoned in the street. It's unbelievable. Little children are walking around with their bones sticking out from their emaciated chests."

"They're raping the country," said Nikos. "They're simply raping the country."

"You know," said Vasili, " I actually saw some German soldiers offering some bread and cheese to some children, but then their commanding officer saw them, ordered them to stop, and told them that if it happened again they would be reported to Field Marshall Wilhelm Kepler. Apparently, he is the one who is giving the order to drain Greece of everything of value. I hear he is a cold-hearted, arrogant pig."

"Kepler?" questioned Nikos, "I hear he calls our friend Petros who works in the barber shop in the hotel for haircuts and for a shave. I wonder if it's the same one?"

"Niko, we've got to do something. I can't just sit by while I see those kids on the street begging for crumbs and stepping over famished dead bodies." Nikos slowly shook his head in agreement but not clear about what they could or should do.

In Berlin, Hitler was growing increasingly concerned about the reports of famine in Athens. He knew it could lead to trouble. He wanted the food and ore from Greece but did not want to be held responsible in the eyes of the world for the growing food crisis in Athens. "Blame it on the Italians," he told Goebbels. "After all, they technically also control the city, not just us."

In Rome Mussolini was receiving reports that the Italians were being identified as the ones causing the famine. Meeting once more with Ciano, he displayed his anger again, "I am thoroughly disgusted with the Germans since they signed the armistice with Greece without our knowledge. And now, the Germans have taken even the shoelaces from the Greeks, and they attempt to lay the blame for the economic situation on our backs. Galeazzo, go to Berlin, talk to Hitler, or Goebbels, or Goering and tell them we must solve this growing famine problem in Athens." Ciano left for Berlin, hoping to speak with Hitler directly, but the Führer told Goering he was disgusted with Ciano whom he blamed for dragging Germany into Greece and ordered Goering to meet with him.

Arriving in Berlin, Ciano was escorted into Goering's office and was seated in the chair situated directly in front of the Nazi minister's desk. Minutes later Goering walked in, holding a cup in his hand. "Coffee, Mr. Minister? Tea? Water? Can I get you anything?"

"Nothing, thank you," responded Ciano. "Field Marshall, Il Duce is concerned about the food situation in Greece. People are literally starving. We could all face real problems unless we get some basic foods to the people."

Goering rose from his chair, his large corpulent body showing no evidence of having ever experienced a reduction of food. "Minister Ciano," started Goering, "perhaps you have lost sight of what war is about. Let me show you a communication I have sent to our military commanders, including those in Greece." Goering handed the document to Ciano who carefully read the short paragraph:

> You have been sent to the occupied territories not to work for the welfare of the peoples entrusted to you, but to get hold as much as you can so that the German people can live… I could not care less when you say that people under your administration are dying of hunger. Let them perish so long as no German starves.

Ciano slowly handed the paper back to Goering and prepared to comment, but Goering continued, "We cannot worry unduly about the hunger of the Greeks. It is a misfortune that will strike many other peoples besides them. In the camps for Russian prisoners they have begun to eat each other. This year between twenty and thirty million persons will die of hunger in Russia. Perhaps it is well that it should be so, for certain nations must be decimated. But even if it were not, nothing can be done about it. It is obvious that if humanity is condemned to die of hunger, the last to die will be our two peoples."

Ciano felt as if he should say something but seemed unable to give any kind of response. He was not one to show sympathy for any of Italy's enemies, and especially for Greece, but he was struck by the unemotional, technical, almost clinical lack of any empathy displayed by Goering. He rose from his chair, shook the hand of the field marshall, and said, "Thank you for your time, Marshall Goering. I will report our meeting to Il Duce."

Goering smiled and patted Ciano on the back. "Tell Il Duce not to worry about Greece. Nothing will happen there. Our commander in Athens, Kepler, is one of our best. He knows his orders: Greeks come second, Germans and Italians first. He's tough, he won't let things get out of control."

Goering's assessment of Kepler was proving every day to be correct. The German pillaging of Greek food, supplies, and virtually anything and everything they could touch continued. The streets were literally filled with emaciated living beings and enormous numbers of corpses. Nikos, Vasili, Apostolos, and Manolis did what they could to ease the situation. When it was safe to do so, they stole food from German trucks and distributed it to families. They sabotaged trucks on rural roads leaving Athens for Salonika, increasingly with the help of a growing number of men and women who would strike at night and then disappear into the mountains. The response of Commander Kepler was to issue orders of "shoot to kill" anyone even approaching a German convoy truck and to intensify the invasion of Greek homes to take anything that might be considered of value.

For Nikos, there was only one way to stop, or at least disrupt, the horror he was seeing on the streets of Athens. Nikos lit his cigarette, ran his fingers through his hair, and sat with Vasili and his friend Petros Panolakis, one of the barbers in the shop located in the Grand Bretagne Hotel.

"This man Kepler," asked Nikos, "he lives at the hotel headquarters, doesn't he?"

"Yes," Petros said, "and so do the other senior officers. I see them almost every day. Most come into the shop for haircuts every three or four weeks."

"And what about Kepler himself, does he come in?"

Petros thought for a moment and then answered Nikos, "He's a little strange, doesn't talk or socialize much, at least with us. He wants his haircut done in his room, so one of us goes up there. He talks a little but not much. He's a pretty good tipper, though, I give him credit for that."

"Does he ever ask for a shave?" asked Nikos.

"Sure, not every day though. He's pretty fair and doesn't have much of a beard. I'd say every two or sometimes even three days he calls down and asks someone to come and give him a shave, the warm towels, the whole thing."

"Do you ever shave him, Petros?" asked Vasili.

"Many times," answered Petros, "but not always. It depends on how busy I am at the shop in the lobby. Kepler really doesn't care though. He's not that fussy about who it is, as long as they know what they're doing."

"Petros," said Nikos, "I want to meet Kepler, talk to him if I can, see what he's all about. The next time he calls for a shave, call me. I'll go up and do it. You know, Petros, that I know what I'm doing. I won't embarrass you."

"But, Niko," responded Petros, with a quizzical look on his face, "he's never seen you and he probably knows you don't work at the shop."

"I'll tell him I was just hired. That I was working in Piraeus, but business was slow there."

Petros hesitated, "I don't know, Niko, these people are mean bastards. I can't jeopardize the whole shop."

"Petros, don't worry. You know I wouldn't do anything to hurt you, your family, or the people you work with. I just want to get a sense of who this guy is. What makes him tick? How committed to Hitler and Nazi ideology is he?"

"Niko, promise me you won't do anything stupid, promise me! These people are vicious, believe me, they are vicious."

"Petros, you have my word, nothing stupid."

Within three days Petros called Nikos to tell him that Commander Kepler had called the shop to request someone come to his room and give him a shave and a face massage. Petros responded that someone would be up as soon as a barber was available. Nikos and Vasili quickly drove to the hotel. Nikos had not shaved for a week and his now dark beard covered his face. He also wore glasses although the lenses were simply plain glass. Speaking in German, which he had learned because of his university studies, he informed the guard standing outside the hotel that he worked for the barber shop and that he was reporting for his first day of work. At the same time, Vasili had gone to the back entrance to the hotel where the deliveries were made and the garbage was collected. He, too, disguised his appearance with a cap, dark glasses, and his own version of facial hair, a mustache he had grown over the past month.

Entering the hotel, Nikos proceeded up to Commander Kepler's suite, knocked on the door, and, when the German opened it, introduced himself in German as Takis Kutopodis, the barber, and was allowed in by the commander.

"Good morning, Commander," greeted Nikos in his near perfect German.

Kepler was surprised that the barber spoke German but seemed pleased. "Good morning, Mr., eh,

Mr., please, what was your name again?"

"Just call me Takis, sir. I studied German at the university, but these recent events have forced me to abandon my studies to care for my family. Hopefully, when all this is over, I can go back. I love the German language and German history and culture."

Kepler smiled. He seemed pleased that this Greek, at least, appreciated Germany, and he felt comfortable with one who could converse in his language. "Are you new to the shop, Takis? I have not seen you before."

"Yes, Commander, I fill in here when they need me. I have my own shop in Piraeus, but things are rather slow now, so I am here today and this whole week. I'm sure you will be pleased with my service, sir. I have been in this business since I was fifteen years old, and my customers always are satisfied."

"Then let's get started, Takis, and don't forget those hot towels. They relax me."

"Absolutely, sir, have no worries, just relax your head back, and I'll do the rest."

Nikos placed the warm towels on the commander's face to soften the beard, used the shaving brush to quickly lather the German's face, and then began his shaving routine.

"You handle the razor well, Takis, I can see why your customers return."

"Thank you, sir, " replied Nikos and as he finished

his shave suddenly took the wet towel, shoved it violently into the mouth of Kepler with his left hand, and with the razor in the other hand quickly plunged the shaving instrument into the neck and veins of the German. Blood gushed out into the towel, as Nikos continued to use the razor to slice into Kepler's neck. Within seconds, Kepler was dead.

Nikos carefully cleaned the blood from the floor, went to the window, signaled Vasili to come up with the large garbage bin, and waited. In minutes Vasili came in with the garbage bin. The brothers loaded Kepler's body into the bin, covered it with the garbage already in the receptacle, left through the back elevator, and placed the body in the small garbage truck. Driving it to one of the local cemeteries located behind a church, they quickly and quietly dug into the ground, placed the body in the hole, covered the grave with dirt and sod, and placed a gravestone written in Greek at the head of the grave.

Vasili looked at his brother, smiled, and said, "Let's shave off all the hair, Niko. You and I are in big trouble now."

In the days that followed the disappearance of Kepler remained a mystery to the Nazi high command. No one had seen him leave the hotel headquarters, and when Petros and the other barbers at the hotel were questioned, they all said the commander had not called them for services and if he had, one of them would have gone to the room as they had done so many times before. And besides, they said, they had not hired any new barber and had no intention of doing so. Nikos and Vasili deliberately made no contact with Petros, remained sequestered in their uncle's home for three days, and finally discussed their options.

Only one seemed safe: they would both go to the mountains, join the Greek resistance fighters there, those named the *andartes*, and do what they could to continue to disrupt the Nazi occupation of their country.

Another person was also leaving at approximately the same time. Klaus Schreiber, along with hundreds of others, boarded troop trucks and headed toward Thessaloniki with only the vague rumor that they were going there to address a problem.

CHAPTER EIGHT

MORDECAI BEN NATHAN SAT quietly in the old chair in the living room of the small house in which he was raised and now still lived with his parents. His father, Samuel, sat on the sofa reading the newspaper, when his mother, Rachel, entered the room.

"Is this a funeral or what?" she asked as she smiled. "Why is no one talking?"

"Do you talk while you read the paper, Rachel?" her husband asked as he placed the paper on the table.

"And Mortis? You are reading nothing, just sitting?" his mother asked as she bent over to gently kiss his forehead.

"Just thinking, Mother, just thinking," Mortis replied.

"Thinking? What is so important that makes you so deep in thought?" asked Rachel as she sat next to her husband.

Mortis looked at his parents and with a look of concern on his face said, "There is something very important we need to discuss. It is serious and could be dangerous for all of us."

Samuel, who was now fifty-three years old, seemed puzzled. Rachel, now fifty, said nothing, but her expression betrayed a look of concern.

"What is it, my son?" asked his mother. "is something wrong? Are you in some trouble?"

Mordecai arose from his chair and walked over to a briefcase that he used as an all-purpose accessory to carry his university papers, snacks, keys, and newspapers. He returned to his chair and looked again at his parents. "When you asked what's wrong, Mother, and what I'm thinking about, it comes down to one simple fact: we are Jews. And I have told you before that there has been much trouble with the Jews in Germany and now the Germans are here, here in Thessaloniki."

"But they have been here for months, Mortis, and nothing bad has happened to us or to our friends or to those in our synagogue," responded his father.

Mortis reached for the paper he had taken from his briefcase, "But, Mama, Papa, listen to the words of Hitler," and he proceeded to summarize what he was reading. "Hitler says the Jews are intending to destroy the Aryan race, which he claims is what the Germans are, and that the Jews want to 'plunder all nations and subjugate them as slaves of their international guild of criminals,' to quote him directly."

"That's nonsense," said Samuel, "that's crazy, the man must be crazy."

"And listen," Mortis went on, "he says he is successfully destroying the Jews in Germany and, listen carefully, the same, he says, needs to be done in other nations until the world is cleaned of Jews."

"Do you think he really means that, Mortis," asked his mother, "or is it just political talk?"

"Mother," Mortis replied, "he not only means it, it is happening. We need to leave Thessaloniki as soon as we can."

"Leave?" his mother asked with a tone of shock and surprise. "Leave? Where would we go? This is our home, and it has been the home of our family for hundreds of years."

Samuel did not immediately respond to his son's plea. In fact, he had seen growing evidence, small as it was, of the negative comments and literature that had appeared in Thessaloniki since the German occupation. Jewish publications had been suspended by the Nazis in the spring of 1941, and soon anti-Semitic publications had appeared. But the thought of leaving the city, abandoning all that he and the generations before had worked for, and running to hide in some remote place was too much for him to contemplate. He buried his face in the palms of his hands, said nothing, as his son watched his father attempting to not allow his wife and son see the tears coming down his face.

The Jews of Thessaloniki could look back on a long and successful history. In 1492 the Spanish monarchs, Ferdinand and Isabella, put forth the Alhambra Decree that called for the expulsion of Sephardic Jews. Some went to Italy and Portugal, but large numbers eventually went to Thessaloniki. Later other Ashkenazic Jews came to the city from Austria and Hungary. In 1519 Jews were more than 54 percent of the city's population. In subsequent decades Thessaloniki became the largest Jewish city in the world. At the beginning of the twentieth century the city had a population of 130,000, and 60,000 of those inhabitants were Sephardic Jews. The Jewish population considered Greece as their home. In the recent war against Mussolini's army, more than 13,000 Jews had served in the Greek army. In Thessaloniki itself there were thirty synagogues. In other parts of Greece, Jews also resided, their origins going back to antiquity. And now this Jewish son of Jewish parents was telling his mother and father to leave, abandon their home, their livelihood, and their history.

But Samuel ben Nathan knew he could not ignore his son's words. The Nazis had already occupied some Jewish homes and community buildings, and he had seen signs banning Jews from entering some cafes. Other fellow Jews he knew had been forced to turn their radios over to the Germans. Mortis told his parents that if they did not leave Greece itself they must at least go to some rural Greek village, as they had sent his sister Sarah to Nikos' family in Kalavryta, or they must go to the Italian-controlled sectors of occupied Greece.

"Are the Italians any better?" asked Rachel. "How do we know we would be safe there?"

"They're not the same as the Germans, Mother. They have even spoken out against German anti-Semitic propaganda, and there is no evidence that even Mussolini has spoken publicly and so negatively about Jews. It's something we need to seriously think about, and we don't have much time."

Mortis' assessment of the Italians was, however, only partially correct. He was right in telling his parents that the Italians, overall, showed no real signs of any planned and organized anti-Semitic activity. What he did not know was that in Italy, too, an anti-Semitic campaign was also active, although not as visible as that of the Nazis. A group of ten respected Italian professors had developed a paper claiming that the majority of Italians were of Aryan origin. It stated clearly that Jews did not belong to the Italian race because they were of non-European racial elements that were different than those of Italians. The result was that laws were passed that prohibited Jews from marrying "Aryans" or teaching in schools and universities, limited the amount of land they could own, and banned them from serving in the army and being members of the fascist party, even though many Jews supported Mussolini and his fascist ideology.

In Italy about 50,000 Jews were assimilated into the country, and Mussolini had publicly denied that the Jews of Italy presented any kind of problem. But Il Duce did nothing to stop the large numbers of racist publications that openly mocked the physical features of Jews and blacks and reinforced racial stereotypes such as the infantile nature of blacks and the moral depravity of the Jews. For most Italians these racist attacks were the work of others, not Mussolini, who carefully maintained his public image of a family man of good character. But in private ways, Mussolini revealed his true feelings about the Jews. Hearing that a restaurant owner in Rome had given an extra helping of meat to a Jewish customer and that a business in Milan had bought a gold watch for a Jewish employee when he lost his job, Mussolini gave his orders: "Close the restaurant down," he told the party leader in charge of economic issues. And his response to those who had presented the watch to their Jewish colleague was equally as direct: "The directors of that company, whoever they are, must receive a strong message. Expel them all from the party."

In his private time with Claretta, however, Mussolini expressed his real feelings about the Jews even more forcefully. His mistress, wearing a blue dress with her hair and makeup fully in place, had just returned from her stylist. Il Duce was standing by the window looking at the sunset when she walked in the room. Hearing her, he turned, smiled, and opened his arms in a welcoming gesture. "I like your hair," he said as he kissed her, took her hand, and led them both to the gold embroidered sofa placed at the corner of the room. "What did you do with it?"

Claretta seemed pleased with Il Duce's compliment. "I had it cut a little bit shorter," she replied, "and I had him sweep it a bit away from my face. I'm glad you approve. Now maybe you won't be looking at other women, my love."

"One new hair style is not enough to change a man, Claretta, but you know wherever I look, my eyes have only true love for you. By the way, is that hair person of yours a Jew?"

"I'm not sure, Benito, I pay no attention to those things. All I know is that he is very good at working with hair."

"Well, I hope he isn't one of them. These disgusting Jews, they should all be destroyed," he suddenly, without warning, blurted out.

"Benito, why do you say such a thing?"

Mussolini did not bother to answer her directly. "I will massacre the Jews as the Turks did. I have isolated 50,000 Arabs in Italy's North African colonies, and I can easily contain 50,000 Jews. I will build a little island and put them all on there."

Claretta tried but could not resist once again bringing up part of Mussolini's past. "But, Benito, my love, you know I know all about one of your former lovers, Margherita Sarfatti, and she was a Jew."

"You forget nothing, do you, Claretta. Yes, she was a Jew, but so what? I wasn't thinking about her background when I was with her, I was thinking of other things," he said as he forced a smile. "And besides, she meant nothing to me, absolutely nothing."

Claretta knew when to raise a subject and when to leave it, so she now changed her approach. "But, Benito," she said, "I think you ought to keep those views of the Jews to yourself. If you don't, the public will think you are just following Hitler and the Nazis, don't you think?"

"I don't know how people can believe that I am merely imitating Hitler," he snapped. "He wasn't even born at the time I first talked about these things. I must give the Italians a sense of race, so that they don't produce any mongrels, so that they don't ruin what is beautiful in us." Mussolini turned, placed his arm around Claretta, and simply said, "Claretta, you should not worry about such things. I'll leave your hairdresser alone, I promise. We will deal with the Jews in our way and let the Germans deal with them some other way."

In Thessaloniki the Germans now accelerated their campaign against the Greek Jews. Klaus Schreiber's unit had been ordered to retrieve Jewish scrolls and documents and take over the Jewish library. Klaus and his comrades went throughout the city enforcing their orders that Jewish-owned businesses were to be publicly identified with signs signifying that they were Jewish-owned. Returning from a day's deployment during which he posted those signs, Klaus removed his shoes and rested on the high back chair in the house where he and five other soldiers were quartered. The house had been taken over by the Germans as soon as the surrender of Greece had occurred, along with many other homes that had been confiscated to serve as residences for the occupying army.

"At least this house was not lived in by Jews," Klaus remarked to Heinrich, one of the young soldiers with whom he lived.

"I guess not," replied Heinrich. "There are Christian icons all over. Jesus, Mary, Archangel Michael, St. Paul, there must be one or two in every room."

"There are plenty of those," responded Klaus. "I wonder where those Greeks who lived here went? I think about that once in a while."

"Klaus!" exclaimed Heinrich. "Do I see a more compassionate side of you?"

"Well, the Greeks are Christians, just like the Germans. I wouldn't think about it for a second if this house had been occupied by Jews."

Heinrich paused, looked at Klaus, and finally asked, "Did you always think like that, Klaus? Or only since the war started?"

"I've read a lot about the Jews. Not only the Führer's views, but others' too. And I've thought about the role of the Jews in Europe over the centuries. They are different, Heinrich. They just are. I don't know if I believe all the stuff about them wanting to take over Western Civilization, but I know they control the wealth and there's something not only different, but something bad about them—how they look, how they talk, how they even smell. Hell, even the Catholic Church has been anti-Semitic for centuries."

"Well," said Heinrich, "I know you're right about the Catholics and especially the one who's Pope now. I'm Catholic, and I haven't heard from him any condemnation of the anti-Jewish policies and actions of what we're doing. If it's all right with him, I guess it's all right with me. So I guess we're both ready to carry out Krenzski's latest orders."

Nazi General Kurt von Krenzski had issued an order to mobilize Thessaloniki's male Jewish population for what was called "civilian labor." For many of Thessaloniki's Jews it had been clear for months that the low-key anti-Semitic activities were coming to a close. In the last six months some Jews had been arrested and others executed as "Communists." There had also been increasing numbers of anti-Jewish pieces in the local press.

For the ben Nathan family, Mordecai's urgent pleas to leave the city had come too late, and his parents had waited too long. On a hot Saturday in July 1942, German soldiers came to their home and ordered Mortis and his father to report to the area of the city known as Eleftheria (Freedom) Square to register for the labor detail. Mortis' mother was left behind since the decree had specified that only males between the ages of eighteen and fifty-five were to gather at the square. On that same day Klaus Schreiber's unit was ordered to monitor the activities of the Jews who had been gathered.

Early in the morning the Jewish men gathered at the square expecting to register for some labor detail. Some 10,000 men had been ordered from their homes to appear, and they gathered on what was developing into an extremely hot day. Every man had been forced to wear a yellow star upon which written, in both German and Greek, *Jude* and *Evari-*

os, respectively in German and Greek the word for "Jew." It soon became clear that this was to be no registration project, but hours of public humiliation for the Jews. Because it was the Jewish Sabbath, Mortis, his father, and the other men covered their heads with hats. Klaus and the other soldiers were ordered to walk through the lines of men and, with their rifles, knock off the hats of those who wore them. This was not only an insult to Jewish custom but created a situation in which, as the day wore on and the intense heat increased, many were impacted by heat exhaustion and fell to the ground. The Nazis in charge forced the men to engage in hours of physical drills. Those men who could not keep up with the drills were kicked and beaten. Others had water thrown on them and were ordered to continue the drills. As the hours passed and the heat became even more intense, larger numbers of men collapsed on the street. Local citizens watched this public humiliation from the windows in their homes, and a troop of German actors who had been brought to the city to entertain the troops broke into applause at what they were witnessing.

Mordecai was sweating profusely as he complied with the exercise drill commands of the Nazi officer in charge. Next to him his father gasped for breath, attempted to go on, but finally fell to the ground. A soldier rushed over, poured water on his head, and forcefully brought Samuel to his feet, commanding him to continue.

"Get up, Jew man," the soldier said in German.

"Leave him alone!" shouted Mortis, "He's my father, and he can't do any more."

The soldier slowly approached Mortis, then raised his rifle, and struck him sharply on the leg. "Then maybe you can do twice as much!" the soldier shouted. At that moment another soldier approached. It was Klaus.

Mortis looked at Klaus with a strange mixture of shock and hope. Was that really Klaus, he thought? Should he say something? What could he say? Klaus' face also betrayed recognition. Yes, it was Mortis, he was sure of it. Should he say something? He seemed frozen, not sure what his reaction should be. He looked Mortis directly in the eye, said nothing, and began to walk away.

"Klaus! Klaus!" yelled Mortis, "Klaus, it's me, Mortis, look at me, Klaus!"

The soldier standing with Mortis and his father stopped, looked at Klaus, and said, "Who is this man, Klaus? How does he know your name?"

Klaus stopped, turned to his soldier comrade, and said, "I don't know who he is, he must have heard someone calling my name. Maybe the sun and the heat have gone to his head." Klaus turned and again walked away.

By the end of the hours that the Jews had been subjected to ridicule, heat, and exhaustion, many were unable to walk. They were asked to line up again to be given orders to report for work on roads and airfields the Germans were building in Macedonia. Klaus was among those handing specific orders to the men as the lines passed by. Mortis and his father were, by chance, in the long line that was to pass by Klaus to receive their work order. He stood with the other soldiers, the paper orders in his hand. As Mortis approached, Klaus turned to his colleague and said, "This man gets no order, he's not a Jew."

The soldier with Klaus at first did not know how to respond. "What do you mean he's not a Jew? Do you know him? If he's not a Jew, why would he report for work orders and spend hours doing the drills?"

Klaus responded quickly and with authority. "I've seen him before. I think he's a Bulgarian or something, and he's not well up here," he said pointing his finger at his temple signifying that Mortis was not mentally stable. "He thinks he's a Jew, but I know he's not. Give him no papers or orders."

Mortis was then led by the other soldiers out of the line and asked to stand to the side. As his father approached Klaus, Mortis screamed out, "Klaus, Klaus, that's my father, please, Klaus, don't give him any papers! Please!"

The other soldiers looked to Klaus for some sign

or direction as to what to do. Klaus looked at his comrades, said nothing, and nodded a "yes" signaling that the man Mortis claimed was his father should be given work orders. Mortis became hysterical. "Klaus! Klaus! Please! Don't do this!" Klaus motioned two other soldiers assigned to this location to remove Mortis from the area and let him return to his home.

Exhausted, Mortis made his way back to his home and related to his mother what had happened to him and to his father, as she listened to her son's news with tears streaming down her face. "Mother, we need to go now, I hear that if we get to the Italian controlled part of Greece, there is no targeting of Jews. We need to go immediately."

"But what of your father, Mortis?" Rachel sobbed. "When can we be together and see him again?"

"I don't know, Mother. The Nazis will make him work on one of their projects. Perhaps they will then let him go. When this war is over, then we will all be together again."

Mortis convinced his mother that they both had to leave immediately. Packing only a few things, they left Thessaloniki, bound for either some rural village in an Italian-controlled zone or possibly Athens where his friend Nikos could give them help or guidance. What Mortis and his mother did not know was that his father would only be at a work site for a very short time. Within one month Samuel ben Nathan was placed on a crowded bus that headed north, its destination Auschwitz where, within two days of his arrival, he along with other Greek Jews were sent to gas chambers and killed.

The information Mortis had received about the Italians was correct. Contrary to Mussolini's boasts to Claretta, he had issued no direct orders to annihilate the Jews, and the Italian military in Greece refused to cooperate with the Nazis' "final solution" to the Jewish problem. Jews in Greece fled the country when they could, but most attempted to seek protection in the Italian zones of Greece.

The Italian commanders in Greece were strongly opposed to the German actions against the Jews. The Italians were shocked by what the Nazis were doing as the Germans continued to loot Jewish homes and businesses and destroy Jewish synagogues or use the few that remained as stables for horses. The Nazis desecrated Jewish cemeteries and took the tombstones of graves to use as raw material for a variety of building projects. The Nazis assessed the Italian reluctance to persecute the Jews as the result of being bought off by Jewish money, yet they had no evidence of that charge. The Italians were simply not infused with fanatic anti-Semitism and were more humane than the Nazi extremists. And it was this attitude that allowed Mortis and his mother to move with no difficulty from Thessaloniki to Athens, where Mortis immediately sought out his friend Nikolaos Gantos.

But Athens was not solely under Italian control, and increasingly the Germans took on a more prominent role in the city. Nikos himself, while not a Jew, had come to see firsthand the brutality of the Nazi hatred of the Jews. Prior to Mortis' arrival in Athens, Nikos had been brought to Nazi headquarters from a Jewish restaurant that he frequented once or twice each month. On this particular day he was eating with two friends when German SS officers entered the restaurant, walked over to a number of tables, including the one at which Nikos and his friends were sitting, and ordered twelve individuals from the restaurant to come with them immediately. The restaurant patrons were taken to the offices of the Nazi commander in charge of overseeing this particular district. Nikos and the eleven others were herded into to a large room that had little furniture, only a long table and four chairs. The detainees were lined up and told to be silent unless spoken to. An officer who identified himself as Major Radinski entered the room and stood before the men, who had been lined up, one standing next to another. Speaking German, the officer motioned the interpreter to be prepared to translate his message into Greek.

"I want, first of all, for each of you to identify yourselves," Radinski ordered, "your name, address, age, and religious affiliation." Each man, in turn, did as he was told. The ages varied, but nine of the twelve were between nineteen and twenty-five years of age. One person identified himself as a Catholic, seven as Greek Orthodox, and four as Jews.

Radinski then said, "I want the Jew named Nehamas to step forward."

Slowly, a medium-sized man, aged twenty-three, stepped forward from the others. Radinski nodded to the Nazi soldier standing on the side, and the soldier proceeded to lash the man with a whip until the man fell to the floor and was then removed from the room by another guard. Radinski removed a small sheet of paper from his pocket, gave it to the interpreter, and then spoke. "I am ordering that the man named Levy step forward." Nikos and the others stood silently, expecting that they were to witness a repeat of the same scene they had just seen. Slowly, a tall, thin man, with the beginning growth of a beard took two steps forward from the others. The interpreter, reading from the paper that he had been handed, proceeded to read aloud, "Major Radinski will personally execute before you the person named Levy for escaping, one week ago, from the building where he was being held under arrest. Beware! The same fate awaits you should you not adhere to the orders of one who speaks for the Third Reich of the German people."

Fear and panic filled the room as Radinski took his pistol, moved next to the man he had addressed, and shot the man Levy in the head, who fell to the floor in a pool of blood. As the man lay on the floor, Radinski stepped forward over the prostrate body and fired one more time. Putting the gun back in his holster, he motioned to one of the Nazi guards and said as he pointed to the dead man's shoes, "Remove them. They look new, and I like them."

CHAPTER NINE

WHEN THE IDENTIFICATION of the eight Greeks who claimed to be Christians was verified, they were released. Nikos and the others left the room to return to their homes, wondering what had happened to the three Jews who were not allowed to leave. Weeks later when Mortis and his mother came to Athens and arrived at the Gantos house, Nikos was fully aware of what danger his friend faced as well as the potential danger to his own family. It had been made clear to Athenians that any families who attempted to hide or aid any Jew being sought by the Nazis would themselves be punished and possibly killed.

Nikos and his uncle and aunt welcomed Mortis and his mother into their home and offered to help them however they could. As they sat in the small living room, Nikos' Aunt Penelope brought coffee and a tray of Greek sweets. "I know firsthand what you are facing," said Nikos as he conveyed to them the story of his encounter with the Nazis and the four Jews. "I don't know if they're all like that," Nikos continued, "but this Radinski was a sadistic, sick individual. So, as my uncle has said, you and your mother are welcome to stay here until something changes."

Mortis finished sipping his coffee and placed the cup on the adjacent table. Looking at Nikos' uncle and aunt he said, "You are very kind to allow us in your home, but we know we can't stay here. It will be too dangerous for all of you if they come looking to round up Jews as they did in Thessaloniki, and you do not cooperate or attempt to hide us. My mother and I deeply appreciate your offer, but I cannot put all of you in danger."

"But where will you go?" asked Nikos. "You can't keep running. Maybe you should go with your sister to my parents' home in Kalavryta. My mother tells me things have been quiet there, and there have been few signs of any Germans and your sister has fit in well as a relative of my parents and no one suspects she is a Jew."

Mortis thought for a moment, looked at his mother, and then said, "Niko, if your mother and father will have her, I will take my mother to them, but I cannot go. I cannot spend my days in hiding when I see what is happening. I don't know what has happened to my father, I may never see him again. I want my mother and sister to be safe. But for myself, I intend to stay and fight. I hear there is a guerrilla movement forming in the mountains to fight this occupation. I want to join them. And when I see what those Nazis do, even what a person like Klaus has become, I feel an anger and even a hatred I have never experienced before."

Mortis had told Nikos earlier of his experience with Klaus Schreiber in Thessaloniki. Nikos believed Mortis but still found it difficult to fully visualize that the person they both had considered as almost a brother had somehow turned into the individual Mortis described. Nikos looked at Mortis' mother and said, "Mrs. ben Nathan, we will get you to my parent's home where you will be with your daughter, and you will both be safe. And Mortis, I will join you to fight these barbarians in the mountains, but you must stay here, in this house, for a short time. I know someone who can connect us with the key people organizing the resistance. You may have forgotten, but I once told you that my mother, as a young girl in the village of Dorvitsa, was in love with a boy who left the village and became a priest. Well, that young man has gone much further than that. Today he is the archbishop of Athens, Archbishop Damaskinos.

Archbishop Damaskinos' baptized name was Dimetrios Papandreou. He had served in the Greek army during the Balkan Wars and afterward became a Greek Orthodox priest. He served as Bishop of Corinth and as an ambassador of the Ecumenical Patriarch in the United States. In 1938 he was elected Archbishop of Athens and took the name Damaskinos. A tall man, he was an imposing figure as he moved throughout Athens in his flowing black garment and full white beard. The German action against the Greek Jews was deeply troubling to him. The Jews had lived in Greece since ancient times, and while they practiced their own religion and customs, they had, in every other way, become fully assimilated into Greek society. They were full citizens and participated in the Greek military in defense of their homeland, which they considered to be Greece. When Nikos had called the archbishop's office and identified himself as the son of Melina, who Damaskinos had known as a young man from the village in which he lived, the religious leader immediately invited him to meet at his residence.

Nikos arrived at the residence at the appointed hour of 10:00 a.m. He was led into a large study with huge bookcases, each filled to capacity with various topics relating to religion, history, and biography. The walls were covered with icons of not only Jesus and the Virgin Mary but also of various saints of the Greek Orthodox Church. Nikos was directed to sit in a large chair that was next to a rectangular coffee table. Two other chairs encircled the table. The archbishop entered the room, and Nikos immediately stood, bowed his head, and kissed the religious man's hand.

"Good morning, Niko, it's good to meet you. And how is your good mother?" said Damaskinos as he seated himself in the chair opposite his visitor.

"Good morning to you, Your Eminence. It's good to finally meet you as well, and my mother is fine, still doing the usual village things," responded Nikos. "Thank you for seeing me. I need your advice and help. My former roommate in college, Mordecai ben Nathan, is a Jew. The Germans took his father someplace, we don't know where, away from home in Thessaloniki. Mordecai's sister is in Kalavryta living under an assumed name with my parents, and Mortis, that's what we call him, and his mother are at my uncle's house here in Athens. But I don't think it's safe for them to be with us, for their sake as well as for the well-being of my uncle and aunt."

Damaskinos sat up in his chair, stroked his beard with his hand, and thought for a moment before he spoke. "Niko," he started, "these Nazis are bad people. They are dangerous, and your friend, his mother, and your aunt and uncle, and you as well, could be in great danger. You must not keep your Jewish guests in the home any longer. Our Church, and I personally, cannot stand idly by while these murderers kidnap people, make them disappear into forced labor,

167

and then take them to other locations where we believe they are killed. I have already instructed all the parish priests under my jurisdiction to give sermons denouncing the German action against our Jewish friends and neighbors. The German commander, Wisliceny is his name, I think, has ordered Chief Rabbi Elias Barzilai to bring to him the numbers regarding the size of the Jewish population in Athens. He also told the rabbi that he wanted him to head up a new council that would create a Jewish police force to carry out Nazi demands on the Jews and issue and monitor new identity cards for all Athens Jews."

"Is the rabbi cooperating?" asked Nikos.

"No, he is not. He told the Germans he needed more time to collect all the information, and then he destroyed all the Jewish records and took my advice."

"Which was what?" asked Nikos.

"I told him to tell the entire Jewish community to leave Athens any way they could and as quickly as possible."

"Are they listening?" Nikos asked again.

"The rabbi has fled to the mountains to join the resistance, and the Jews in Athens are slowly, too slowly, I think, leaving. Some are going to rural Greek villages, some to Palestine, and others to various other places they believe to be safe."

"And what about my friend and his mother and sister? I'm not sure they would leave Greece or even know where to go and how to get there," said Nikos with a sense of despair and futility in his voice.

"There is not much time, Niko. I am about to issue a formal public statement against the German action against the Jews, which is certain to catch their attention. The time they need to receive my document and plan any reaction may give you and your friends a very short window of opportunity to find safety for them. Here is what I can do for you. I will issue an official baptismal certificate as a Greek Orthodox Christian for the sister you said is living with your parents. That way, even if the Germans do get to your village, she will be safe. Right now I think the best thing to do with your friend's mother is to have her go to the convent. We will dress her as a nun, and I'm sure the Germans will not even bother to go there. As far as your friend Mordecai, bring him here to me. I will give him clothes as a priest would wear, and anyone who asks will be told that he is my assistant who has just completed his seminary work and has been ordained. And when this terrible war is over, the family can then be reunited."

Nikos listened carefully to the plans put forth by the archbishop. "Your Eminence," he said, "what you have proposed for my friend and his family is most kind. I cannot thank you enough. I will have Mortis and his mother come immediately so that the things you suggested can be put in place." Nikos rose from his seat, once again went to kiss the archbishop's hand, but the archbishop put his arm around Nikos and, as he would if he were his own son, kissed him on both cheeks.

"God bless you, Niko, now go and bring your friends to me. I must prepare our official statement of protest to the Germans."

In the next three days Archbishop Damaskinos moved quickly and forcefully. He instructed all the priests under his jurisdiction to publicly condemn the Nazi actions against the Jews to their congregations. He then began working with the mayor of Athens to create false birth certificates indicating Greek Orthodox birth that he then ordered be distributed to hundreds of Jews in Athens. Meeting with renowned poet Angelos Sikelianos, he and the poet jointly drafted a statement that was to serve as a direct appeal to the German authorities to stop the Jewish persecutions. Damaskinos told his poet co-author that the statement must be clear and forceful, and both men, working through the night, finished the document by dawn. They then sent it as an official letter to the man the Nazis had assigned to deal with the Jewish "problem." He was SS officer, General Jurgen Stroop, the same man who had led the effort to destroy the Jewish Ghetto in Warsaw, Poland.

Stroop had developed a precise strategy to eliminate the Jews of Athens. Knowing that Jews would congregate on important holidays, he ordered the roundup of Jews on the evening of Yom Kippur. All Jews were ordered to appear at local community offices to register their names and identify their residences. Stroop was angered when only 200 Jews registered. At other times Stroop announced that the occupying forces were scheduling the delivery of a special flour to Athens for Jews to use to prepare matzoh for Passover, but to receive the flour the recipients had to register with the Nazi authorities. Few Jews responded to this aspect of Stroop's strategy either.

Sitting at his desk, in full military uniform, General Jurgen Stroop was reviewing documents and correspondence from Berlin, sipping coffee, and eating from a plate of Greek sweets that he particularly liked. A young soldier knocked on the door, entered, and stood at attention after offering the proper salute to the general.

"A letter for you, sir," said the young soldier, "delivered here in person from the office of the head of the Greek Church here in Athens."

Stroop placed his coffee cup down, thanked the soldier, and began to read. As he read the words on the paper, he became increasingly angry. It read:

The Greek Orthodox Church and the academic world of Greek people protest against the Persecution... The Greek people were deeply grieved to learn that the German occupation authorities have already started to put into effect a program of gradual deportation of the Greek Jewish community... and that the first group of deportees are already on their way to Poland...

According to the terms of the armistice, all Greek citizens, without distinction of race or religion, were to be treated equally by the Occupation authorities. In our national consciousness, all the children of Mother Greece are an inseparable unity—they are equal members of the national body irrespective of religion.... Our holy religion does not recognize superior or inferior qualities based on race or religion, as is stated in the Holy Bible, 'There is neither Jew or Greek' and thus condemns any attempt to discriminate or create racial or religious differences.

Today we are deeply concerned with the fate of 60,000 of our fellow citizens who are Jews. We have lived together in both slavery and freedom, and we have come to appreciate their feelings, their brotherly attitude, their economic activity, and their indefectible patriotism.

Stroop finished reading and with a flip of his hand threw the letter to the side of his desk. He then called for his two lieutenants who were waiting in the outer office. The two men came in and saluted the general. Stroop motioned them to be seated. The two officers could sense from the expression on Stroop's face that he was angry, but, if so, it was a controlled anger.

"Gentlemen," he started, "who is this Greek priest Damaskinos, and who does he think he is? He wrote me this letter saying that his church and Greeks generally 'protest' against the persecution of the Jews and that they are 'deeply concerned' about the fate of the Greek Jews."

"General," the tall lieutenant responded, "he is the archbishop of Athens and a very formidable and influential person here. He is widely respected by the Greeks."

"I really don't care how respected he is by Greeks. He needs to understand who controls his country now, and, contrary to his assertion of Greeks viewing all as equals, he needs to learn that we do not adhere to such a view. The nerve of this fool! No other country we have so far dominated has ever dared such a public protest against our policies. And these Greeks think they can force us down? If they're all equal, maybe we should eliminate all of them!"

"With due respect, Sir," said the other officer, "I'm not sure that would be wise or worth our time and effort. I believe the Führer has larger and more important plans for the Reich."

Stroop replied calmly, "Of course, you are correct, Lieutenant, but the gall of the man has gotten to me. And is he the one who is telling the Greek priests to condemn our Jewish policies and to discourage the Jews from registering?"

"I'm not sure, General, but rumor has it that such directives are coming from his office."

"Gentlemen," said Stroop, "go bring him here so that I can personally let him know how much I do not appreciate this ridiculous letter or what he has been telling his priests. And when you go to him, search his home. I wouldn't be surprised if he is hiding some Jews there, too."

The two officers accepted their general's directive as a personal order to them. Taking a small contingent of four soldiers with them, they drove to the residence and office of Archbishop Damaskinos. Days before Nikos had brought Mortis and his mother to the home of Damaskinos where he had arranged for Rachel ben Nathan to be taken to a nearby convent where she was to stay dressed and disguised as a Greek Orthodox nun. Mortis had remained with Damaskinos who had attired him with the clothing of a Greek parish priest and told him he was to tell anyone who inquired that he was serving as an administrative assistant to the archbishop.

When the Germans arrived at the door of the archbishop's residence, they knocked on the door, and a young priest, wearing a long black vestment, opened the door. With a somewhat quizzical look on his face when he saw the two officers and the four accompanying soldiers, he said, "Good morning, gentlemen, can I help you. I am Father Michael." Mortis was playing his part well. As "Father Michael," he escorted the officers into the study of the archbishop whereupon the religious leader was told that, on orders from General Shroop, the four soldiers would be moving throughout the residence.

"Please do," interjected Father Michael. "Our home and our faith are open to all. I can give you a tour if you would like."

"Thank you, Father, but that won't be necessary. My men can make their way around, and we won't be long," said one of the officers.

"As you wish, Lieutenant," said Mortis, as the soldiers began walking through the home, while the officers remained in the study with the archbishop.

The Nazi officers, not knowing how to officially address a Greek archbishop, simply said, "Father, we are here on orders of General Jurgen Stroop. He has ordered us to immediately escort you to his office where he desires to meet with you on an important matter."

Damaskinos now rose from his chair, approached the two officers, and moved to shake their hands. "And what are your names, gentlemen?" he calmly asked. After shaking each man's hand and receiving their names, he went on, "And what is the nature of this 'important matter' of which you speak?"

"It is in regard to your letter," responded the one officer.

"Oh, I see," said the archbishop. "So let's not keep the general waiting. Let us go immediately."

The archbishop and the German party immediately departed to meet with the general. The officers had conferred with the soldiers who had searched the house, and they reported that no other individual, other than his assistant, Father Michael, appeared to be living or hiding there. As they all walked out of Damaskinos' residence, the archbishop turned, smiled at Father Michael, and said, "Father, please adjust my schedule for today so that I can have the honor and opportunity to meet with General Shroop."

The drive from the archbishop's home to the Nazi headquarters took only twenty minutes, and when they arrived Damaskinos was brought to Shroop's office. The general made no attempt to rise from behind the desk to greet the religious leader but, with a motion of his hand, directed the archbishop to sit in the chair in front of the desk.

"I have received your letter, Mr. Archbishop, and I am not pleased," Stroop began. "Who do you think you are? You understand, I hope, that you, or any other Greek, do not control this country. We do. Is that understood?"

"Oh, I think that is very clear, General. You may control our country temporarily, but you do not control our history, our values, our religious beliefs, our humanity. Do you think you can do that as well? If so, you are badly mistaken." Damaskinos calmly touched the large crucifix that hung around his neck and then asked, "Are you a Christian, General?"

Stroop was now visibly upset and ignored the archbishop's question. "Listen, Bishop, or Archbishop, or whatever the hell your title is, we don't care what your history or feelings about Jews may be, we happen to think differently. The rumors I hear about what you are telling your priests to say and do is unacceptable and I am ordering you to cease immediately. Is that clear?"

Damaskinos leaned forward from his chair and, looking the general directly in the eye, responded, "General, it's not only the Greek people and the Church that condemn what you are doing, the God who made you and me and all Germans and Greeks and Jews condemns it as well. And you give me too much credit, General. I don't control the minds and conscience of our Greek parish priests. They are simply following the orders of an authority higher than you, me, Hitler, or anyone else. Their orders come from God."

"You are an arrogant man, Bishop. I thought you were supposed to show some humility and respect, I might add. You apparently have little regard for the potential harm we could bring to all of you Greeks if we so wished."

"Well, General, out of courtesy and respect I have sent you the letter for you alone to consider and await your response. I sense that this meeting is your response. Tomorrow, however, the letter will be published in the Greek press, so you will have to deal with a larger audience than just me."

Stroop's face was now red with outrage. "You had better not have that letter published," he yelled, "and if I see it in the morning newspapers, I warn you, you personally will suffer the consequences. I will give the order to execute you by firing squad!"

Damaskinos sat quietly, rose from his chair, and prepared to leave the room. Looking for a final time at Stroop, he quietly said, "According to the traditions of the Greek Orthodox Church, our prelates are hanged, not shot. Please respect our traditions."

RESISTANCE
AND RETALIATION
1943-1944

CHAPTER TEN

I N THE DAYS FOLLOWING DAM-askinos' meeting with General Stroop, decisions were being made in various locations.

Stroop, after calming down from the defiance the archbishop had shown, was counseled by an aide to not do anything to harm the religious leader. The aide told him that Damaskinos' final remark about requesting not to be shot, but rather hanged, was a historic reference to the time in the nineteenth century when the Greek archbishop was hanged by the Turks, an act that inspired the Greeks to even greater strength and determination to resist the Turks. The aide told Stroop that a similar thing could happen now if the archbishop were to be killed by any manner, whether by firing squad or by hanging.

"Let him go, General," said the aide, "he's not worth the problems we will have if we kill him. We can instill fear in the people simply by continuing to hunt down the Jews and punishing those who aid or hide them."

Stroop's instincts were to go after Damaskinos, but he also knew he did not need some large-scale uprising in Athens, so the general took the aide's advice, but he felt he could not sit by and take no action. Sitting at his desk, he wrote an order that directed the occupying Nazi troops to find and round up all parish priests who were giving pro-Jewish sermons or in any way aiding Jews and warn them that they were to immediately cease such activities or suffer the consequences of their actions. And he made clear that the consequence would be arrest and possible execution.

Miles away in London another decision was being made. Winston Churchill was contemplating how Great Britain could stop, or at least weaken, the Nazi war machine. He knew it was impractical to take the war directly to the Führer with British troops, so after the Battle of Britain, in which the German air force was unable, in spite of constant bombing raids, to bring Britain to her knees, he ordered the creation of a force of highly trained troops that he called the "hunter class." These men were to bring, "a reign of terror" to the Nazis. Churchill said they were to engage in sabotage actions that would leave, "a trail of German corpses behind." This group, named the Special Operations Executive (SOE), would use tactics such as labor unrest, propaganda, strikes, industrial and military sabotage, terror against traitors, boycotts, riots, and any other means to harm the Nazi effort and the German leaders.

After meeting with his appointed head of the SOE, Hugh Dalton, Churchill said good night and told Dalton, "And now, set Europe ablaze." The SOE followed Churchill's orders by inserting more than 500 agents, including sixty women, into Nazi-occupied countries in Europe, including Greece, to spy and to kill those whose elimination would disrupt the Nazi war effort.

From the beginning of the occupation the Greeks had shown their defiance of the enemy troops with public actions that signaled to the Italians and Germans that they would not be able to control a compliant population without substantial and sustained effort. The lowering of the Nazi flag from the Acropolis should have been an early warning that the Greeks were prepared to be bold and daring in their resistance. Greeks in the thousands regularly marched through the streets of Athens, defying the occupying forces to stop them as they sang the national anthem and shouted, "Long live Greece. Long live Freedom." The crowds openly carried banners calling for death to any fellow Greek who collaborated with the enemy. When British prisoners of war were marched through Constitution Square, citizens spontaneously broke into applause, not for the Germans guarding them but for the British.

In more secretive ways the Greek resistance by the *andartes*, or guerrillas, began soon after the German occupation. Guerrilla warfare was not new to Greeks or to their history. Their fight for independence against the Ottoman Turks in 1821 had essentially been waged by bands of *andartes* who slowly eroded the hold of the occupying Turks. Now, against the Germans or Italians, these contemporary guerrilla bands hid in the mountains and moved from there to launch their various tactics of assassination and disruption of the enemy war effort. They were supplied with the day-to-day necessities for survival by Greeks who lived in the villages. Their tactics against the enemy were varied. They sabotaged telephone systems, which cut the Nazis off from communications; they hid bombs in cans of olive oil and set them off in areas occupied by some Italian but mostly German troops. These bands of guerrillas engaged in assassination, targeting German officers or even low-ranking Nazi soldiers. Against the wishes of their parents, who feared negative comments by fellow Greeks, girls and women joined the resistance forces making speeches in villages and in churches, organizing food supplies, and fighting in combat actions as well.

For Nikos Gantos and Mortis ben Nathan, the decision as to what they would do next came swiftly.

They knew they could not sit idly by as persecution and famine gripped their country. Both men decided to go to the mountains to join the growing resistance movement being formed in these difficult to access locations. Nikos and Mortis had chosen to go with a Republican resistance group, the National Republican Greek League (EDES) under the leadership of Napoleon Zervas. Nikos' brother Vasili made the decision to go with Aris Velouchiotis' group, the National Liberation Army, which also had a political wing, the National Liberation Front (EAM).

Prior to leaving, Nikos had a spirited discussion with Vasili. Both brothers now had grown long, full beards, as had most of the men who had fled to the mountains to plan and execute actions against the German and Italian occupying forces. Nikos and his brother met at the edge of a soccer field where both men had played as young boys. Nikos lit his cigarette and offered one to his brother. Vasili accepted the offer, took the cigarette, lit it, and joined Nikos in inhaling and exhaling clouds of smoke that seemed to hang in the air.

"Vasili," began Nikos, "I don't understand why you are going with the Velouchiotis group. You know, everyone says they are Communists."

Vasili inhaled on his cigarette slowly and slowly exhaled. "Some are Communists, some are not," he responded. "But even if they all are Communists, what does that matter? Right now that group is giving the Nazis something to worry about and are working to drive them out of our country. Isn't that what every Greek wants?"

"But it's more than that, Vasili. They want to get rid of our king and run Greece as a Communist country," answered Nikos.

"And would that be so bad, Niko? Our king, first of all, he's not even a Greek, and, more importantly, where is he? He's left the country, hiding safely in London or someplace. He ought to be leading the fight against these invaders. And why do we need a king? I thought we were the inventors of democracy. The group you're with, Niko, wants the king to return and do what he did before for the Greek people—nothing!"

"I'm not in Zervas' group because they want the king back. Frankly, I think he's a waste of time and money for us. But I am for a real Greek democracy. You're right, Vasili, we did invent the democratic idea, so now you think a Communist Greece would be better?"

"Better than what we've had under a king," Vasili responded. "At least these Communists promise some kind of equal distribution of the country's wealth so that we can live decently."

Nikos seemed surprised at his brother's remarks. "Yes, that's what they promise, but it's just words, just promises. Where have the Communists ever done it? In Russia? Hardly. Even an idiot like Hitler is smart enough to see the danger in their ideas. There's not one example where those promises were kept or realized. And your leader, this man Velouchiotis, I hear he's crazy, that he kills as many Greeks as he does Nazis or Italians."

Vasili paused, collected his thoughts, and said, "He is different, a bit strange, yes. But no one hates the Germans more or is more a Greek patriot than he is. Yes, he has killed Greeks, but only those who are traitors, those who collaborate with the enemy. And I don't blame him, those traitors should all be shot." Nikos and his brother continued talking and disagreeing for another half-hour. Then finally both men had said what was on their mind, rose from the bench, gave one another a strong embrace, and left for their specific guerrilla groups, known in Greece as the *andartiko*.

The guerrilla band that Nikos and Mortis had joined was, indeed, different from that which Nikos' brother, Vasili, had joined. Napolean Zervas, the leader of Nikos' band, EDES, was suspicious of the group with which Vasili was affiliated. Zervas saw them as dangerous Communists whose ultimate plan was to bring Soviet-style Communism to Greece once the war was over. He was a staunch supporter of Republican government but said he would support a Greek constitutional monarchy when the war was over. He welcomed British help in Greece against the Axis powers, and consequently it was Zervas' group of *andartes* favored by Churchill, who also feared a postwar Communist Greece and was a strong supporter of the Greek king. Churchill's feelings about the EAM/ELAS band, led by Velouchiotis, were negative, but that sentiment was not always held by British troops who were actually in Greece. Many Brits in Greece had urged Churchill to support Velouchiotis' group because they told the prime minister that they were not all Communists, and, more importantly, they were the only really effective resistance group operating. They informed Churchill that among the Greek people support for the king was very weak, but Churchill ignored their advice and gave the EAM/ELAS guerrillas no support, hoping that ultimately they would not succeed. And Churchill was particularly concerned about reports he was receiving about the guerrilla leader, Aris Velouchiotis.

Aris Velouchiotis was not his real name. He was baptized Athanasios Klaras when he was born in Lamia, Greece. Early in his life he was attracted to Communist ideology and was arrested numerous times prior to the outbreak of war for his Communist ideas and actions. Jailed in a Corfu prison in 1939, he signed a "statement of renunciation" that, in effect, meant he had renounced his Communist ideas, but few who knew him believed that was the case. At the outbreak of WWII he was drafted but showed undisciplined behavior and was sent to a special squad filled with soldiers who had demonstrated "disciplinary" problems. In 1942 he went to the mountains and began organizing resistance groups. It was then that he assumed the name of Aris Velouchiotis, a combination of the Greek word for Ares, the god of war, and Velouchi, which was the name of the local mountain. His initial group of guerrillas was only fifteen men, but the group quickly grew as more and more Greeks sought ways to resist those who had invaded the country. Soon his group numbered more than 50,000 men and women.

Velouchiotis led a small group of his *andartes* into a local Greek village early on a cold and damp morning. Vasili had been selected to be a part of the group, and they followed their leader into the small village. Velouchiotis led his men holding a Greek flag while he and his band of followers sang the national anthem as they marched. After assuring the local villagers that they would not be harmed, he went to the village center to speak to the assembled crowd. A small man, he had an exceptionally full and long dark beard, and he openly carried a weapon and wore a belt of bullets strapped diagonally across his chest. As the villagers stood silently waiting for him to begin, Velouchiotis slowly and deliberately began to speak.

"Fellow Greeks," he began, "we come to let you know that you are not alone. With your help we will rid our beloved Greece of those who think they can subdue us. We seek a society of equals, not slaves to some outside barbarians. We ask you to help us by giving us food and clothes, opening your homes to us, joining us. Together we will prevail, have no doubt about that. Tell us about the Italian and German locations, where they are, what they are doing, and we will strike, we will be free, join us, join us in saving our Fatherland!"

Vasili watched Velouchiotis' speech from the sidelines, marveling at how, in a soft voice and manner, he could hold the attention of everyone and make his intelligent and carefully reasoned case to those assembled. He was a charismatic leader, thought Vasili, and he had not witnessed anything in Velouchiotis that others had characterized as a brutal or sadistic streak. After the leader had finished speaking to the villagers, the guerrillas stayed in the village that evening, welcomed into the homes of the local people.

The following morning Vasili was awakened by a loud voice coming from outside the home where he had spent the night. Dressing quickly and securing his weapon, he went out to see what was happening and whether he was needed in any way. One of the guerrillas, a man named Stavros, was being aggressively questioned by Velouchiotis. An older woman had complained that Stavros, who had spent the night in her home, had gone into the bedroom of her nineteen-year-old daughter and attempted to sexually assault the young woman. Velouchiotis moved close to Stavros, only a matter of inches separating the two men's faces.

"Did you enter the girl's room?" Velouchiotis asked in a quiet manner.

"I did, Aris, but it was a mistake. It was late, I was tired, and I made a mistake and opened the door to her room," answered Stavros.

"A mistake?" asked Velouchiotis in a tone of disbelief. "And did the girl make a mistake when she screamed and her mother came into the room to find you in there?"

"I-I did nothing," stammered Stavros, "I did not touch the girl."

"But your intention was to more than 'touch' her, wasn't it, Stavros?" Velouchiotis said, with increasing anger in his voice.

"Yes, it was his intention!" yelled out the young girl who had been the object of Stavros' attention. "He came to my bed and attempted to undress me!"

Velouchiotis had heard enough. He was not one to delay action. Pulling out his pistol, he approached the man and said, "I have told everyone that I cannot tolerate inappropriate behavior of my men with any woman. You have heard me preach this rule many times, yet you chose to disregard it. You are not worthy of being called a man." Finishing his last sentence Velouchiotis pulled the trigger on his pistol that had been aimed at the man's heart. As the assembled crew watched in horror, Stavros fell to the ground dead. "Let this be a lesson to every man," Velouchiotis said, "our rules are our rules, they are not to be violated." Vasili watched the episode, shocked by what he had seen. He now saw another side of Aris, just as his brother had reported.

Velouchiotis had indeed told his guerrilla troops that they were not to engage in any sexual behavior among themselves or with local village women. He told his *andartes* that their sole focus was to attack and disable the Nazis. Others in his group saw it differently. They felt it was an unnatural demand on his men and women to banish sex from their minds, and some had heard that while he was in prison in Corfu years before, Velouchiotis had been brutally tortured, including torture to his genitals, that now made him incapable of sexual activity. Others in the group dismissed those stories and were convinced that he was, in fact, a homosexual, who had no immediate outlet for his desires and so forbade sexual activity for everyone.

In the following weeks Vasili continued to see the violent nature of his leader. Velouchiotis spoke passionately about prohibiting the Greek king from returning to Greece and suggested that if he did return, the price that he must pay for abandoning the country would be his assassination. On two other occasions Vasili had witnessed his leader's plan for those Greeks who sympathized or actually helped or collaborated with the Germans. In the city of Astros, he had witnessed Velouchiotis personally killing a Greek merchant who was voluntarily giving food supplies to Nazi soldiers. In another instance, this time high in their mountain headquarters, Velouchiotis had overheard one of his men saying he disagreed with the periodic assassination of German soldiers. "They are not all bad persons," he had said, "they are just young soldiers following orders, just like we do from Aris." Velouchiotis ordered two of his closest confidantes to take the man farther up in the mountain, knock him unconscious, and then throw him over the edge. Rather than being silent about the incident, Velouchiotis gathered his men and women and told them exactly what he had done. "Fellow comrades," he began as he addressed the large crowd, "if you are not with us, you are against us, and if you are against us, we cannot let you live. My methods may be judged as harsh, but they are nothing compared to what will happen to all of us if the Nazis continue to control our nation."

Velouchiotis also had plans to overcome or eliminate all other Greek resistance groups. Hopefully, he thought, they would join him, but if not, he was prepared to take more direct action. He was particularly negative toward Napoleon Zervas, who he believed was an ambitious man who would seek special office or favors if the king returned to power in Greece. Velouchiotis, who hated the monarchy, believed Zervas was a monarchist by convenience, not someone who really wanted a king, but rather his goal was what he might receive from that monarch. He was a hypocrite, thought Aris, and if there was something he could not tolerate, it was hypocrisy. When the right time came, Aris thought, he would kill Zervas.

But rather than distancing himself from Zervas, or even planning to kill him, a unique and daring plan brought both Velouchiotis' group and Zervas' men together to work jointly on a bold guerrilla initiative. It was Churchill's Special Operation Executive, the SOE, that planned a major act of sabotage against occupying Nazi forces. The long-range goal was not only to attack German forces in Greece but also to obstruct Nazi forces in North Africa under the command of Field Marshall Erwin Rommel. This could be done by destroying a viaduct rail bridge that connected Thessaloniki to the Greek port of Piraeus. The bridge was one of the key links to supplying Rommel's troops. There were as many as forty to fifty trains carrying these supplies each day. If the route could be disrupted, Churchill believed, the Germans would have to reinforce their efforts in North Africa, which would force them to abandon, or at least delay, the Nazi planned invasion of Russia.

The specific target decided upon by the SOE was the Gorgopotamos Bridge, and the action was given the code name, Operation Harling. The plan was complicated since the British operatives would have to parachute into enemy territory and would then be met by the two factions of the Greek resistance, the guerrilla forces of both Zervas and Velouchiotis. Both of these resistance leaders were suspicious of each other's allegiance and loyalty to the Greek cause of liberation. The plan called for the two factions to work together to sabotage the bridge, although they had never before cooperated on anything. The plan was to divide the saboteurs into seven groups, with the Zervas and Velouchiotis groups scheduled to attack the Italian garrison positions at the two ends of the bridge, while other groups destroyed rail tracks, cut telephone lines, and prevented enemy reinforcements from coming to rescue the enemy positions that had been attacked. A special group, made up of demolition experts from SOE, had the job of actually demolishing the bridge.

At first the plan had problems. The only native Greek who was a part of the parachute drop group was Themistocles Marinos, whose orders were to meet up with Aris Velouchiotis. Marinos, meeting with the guerrilla leader, faced a suspicious man.

"Who are you and who sent you?" asked Velouchiotis.

Marinos, who had been recruited by the British SOE for the operation, seemed shocked by the question. "I am a Greek like you, and I am part of the SOE plan to destroy the bridge," he answered.

Velouchiotis was not convinced. "How do I know you are not a spy, a spy of the king or a collaborator with the Germans?"

Marinos was now angry. He and his group had risked their lives by parachuting into enemy territory, and now this self-appointed guerrilla leader was questioning his motives and loyalty. "Listen, my friend," said Marinos, "why don't you read what the plan is and follow orders. I don't have time to waste talking to people whose egos are more important than this mission."

Velouchiotis looked intently at Marinos, slowly walked away toward one of his lieutenants, and said softly, "Be prepared to execute this man, he is not one of us."

The person Velouchiotis was speaking to quickly responded, "Aris, you are mistaken, these men are part of the SOE contingent. I know this man, he is from my home village."

Velouchiotis said nothing, realizing that at times, too many times in fact, he reacted impulsively, not bothering to know the facts of the situation. Acknowledging his error, he walked back to Marinos and said, "If we must work together on this, so be it."

Within two days the plan was ready to be executed. Under the dark of night, at 11:00 p.m., the various groups moved into their assigned positions, and the attack began. The two guerrilla groups began their attack at each end of the bridge, distracting the enemy forces whose assignment was to guard the bridge. The third group, the demolition team, now moved into place. The leader of the team blew a whistle, indicating that he was about to set off the explosion. The Greek guerrilla forces fighting near the bridge now retreated out of harm's way, and the explosions were triggered. After a thunderous noise and a flash of flames that lit up the night sky, the bridge fell. As the British and Greek saboteurs watched from a distance, smiles broke out, cheers were heard, and the men turned to each other and shook hands. The attack was a major blow to the Nazi war plan. It showed Churchill that his faith in the SOE was justified and that successful joint operations could be planned and executed with local resistance forces.

Hitler's reaction was quite different. Receiving the news of the successful operation by British and Greek forces, he paced the floor, and then called for an immediate emergency meeting with his trusted advisors.

"This bridge must be repaired with all deliberate speed," Hitler said. "Unless we can supply our troops in North Africa immediately, we will lose valuable time in wrapping up that operation so that we can concentrate our efforts on the Soviet invasion. We have already lost valuable time because of what these Greeks have done." The bridge could not be repaired quickly, and six weeks passed before it was capable of being used again.

Aris Velouchiotis was pleased with the results of the operation but vowed to no longer cooperate with the Greek guerrillas under Zervas' leadership or with the British as well. A passionate anti-monarchist, he continued to distrust the pro-monarchist Zervas group and the British, who, under Churchill, would not abandon their support of the Greek king. If his plans for Greece's Communist future were to be realized, his opponents had to be eliminated, and Aris made plans in his mind to assassinate Napoleon Zervas. Velouchiotis' violent nature, and impulsive behavior, began to trouble Vasili. He was sympathetic to the views of Velouchiotis, which were clearly Communist-inspired, but it was his leader's tactics that troubled him. What Vasili began to see in Greece's future was a potential civil war, which he believed would be a disaster for the country.

Velouchiotis justified his harsh tactics by telling his followers that unless they dealt strongly with the occupying forces, and dealt just as harshly with any Greek who supported and collaborated with the Italians and Germans, they would all meet an even stronger and more violent fate from the enemies who were allowed to continue to control the country.

"Our goals," he told the assembled men and women in the camp high in the mountains of the Arcadia region of Greece, "are straightforward. We want four basic things. First, a social democratic government. Second, a denunciation of King George for treason. Third, a purge of all anti-democratic elements in the government, and fourth, free elections by Greeks to establish their government. But first, of course, we must liberate our country and do whatever is necessary to defeat these fascist Germans and Italians, these barbarians."

Velouchiotis was not a flamboyant leader. He gave his speeches in a monotone yet was able to hold the attention of his village audiences by the force of his message. He instinctively knew that when villagers heard that some German scholars were claiming that the contemporary inhabitants of Greece were not true Greeks descended from the glory generations of past ancient Greek history but rather were now of Slavic stock, he would inevitably receive a positive response of people willing and able to join his ranks.

"The only so-called Greek who is not a Greek," Aris said to his audiences, "is the current king of Greece.

He is a German and has abandoned his adopted country as a running coward." Aris now held his audience in rapt attention. "They say we are murderers. Yes, we slaughter, and we are ready to slaughter any Greek who helps or sympathizes with those who have ravaged our country. Who did the British come to for help when we sabotaged the bridge? They came to us. Others say we are Communists. Is that charge a matter of shame? The march toward Communism is the future for all of us. Capitalism, not Communism, breaks up the family and annihilates national frontiers in quest of profits. We will not ever give up our arms until we have national liberation and popular rule."

But Vasili was aware that the "Communism" of Velouchiotis was hardly the brand espoused by Lenin and Marx. Velouchiotis spoke of wanting to stop the exploitation of the people by rich plutocrats but continued to speak of the value of private property, and he gave no hints of being anti-religion. Moving from village to village, his guerrillas first sought out the local priest to secure his blessing, and afterward many of the priests joined in various resistance parades.

Vasili, writing to his brother Nikos, tried to explain his attraction to the Velouchiotis *andartes*. "If there are some Communists among us," he wrote, "they are a strange kind. We all pray together, go to

tis and his warriors' exploits against the enemy were now talked about throughout Greece. But gradually the other, darker side of the Velouchiotis campaigns also became known throughout the nation.

Nikos, serving as part of the guerrilla forces of Napoleon Zervas, continued to be troubled by his brother's association with Velouchiotis. Stories reached Zervas, who then conveyed them to his followers, which worried Nikos. He wrote to his brother and asked to meet with him at a time when both guerrilla groups were in close proximity to one another. Weeks later the opportunity came, and the brothers met near a monastery located between the two camps.

Meeting after dark, the brothers approached one another, shook hands, and then proceeded to hug one another. Vasili had maintained his long, thick, beard, very much like that of his leader, Aris Velouchiotis. Nikos had a thick mustache, but the remainder of his face was now clean shaven.

"You have lost some weight," said Nikos to his brother, "you need to eat more."

"I'm fine," replied Vasili. "I needed to lose a few pounds anyway, and I feel better. You look good. How are things going for you and the Zervas camp?"

"I feel good," replied Nikos. "I could use a little more sleep, but other than that, we're doing OK. We are doing some real damage to the Germans and Italians."

"We are, too," said Vasili, "so much so that the Germans don't know how to figure us out or where to find us."

Nikos placed his rifle on the ground, hesitated for a moment before he spoke, and then said what had been bothering him. "You know, Vasili, it's not only the Germans who don't know how to figure all of you out. It's also Zervas, it's me, and it's many of our countrymen. We don't understand Velouchiotis' murderous rampage. If it's the Nazis or the Italians, fine. But why all the Greeks that are being killed either personally by him or by others under orders from him? We get reports that he executes Greek villagers who he determines are cattle thieves, that he tortures prisoners, especially other Greeks, and that he personally executed a man for supposedly stealing a chicken for his starving family to eat."

"He is a very passionate man, Niko," said Vasili. "He is a Greek patriot, and he has empowered villagers, set up democratic councils they never had so that these common peasants can govern themselves and not follow the thieving Greek collaborator government the Nazis have established or continue to listen to the richest Greeks who care nothing for us. He has a vision for a new Greece that can emerge after the war is over."

"A new Greece?" questioned Nikos. "You mean a Communist Greece that will never, ever take hold or last in our country. Greeks are individualists, Vasili, not collectivists. And will this 'new Greece' follow the tactics that have been reported about your leader? That when he kills those Greeks he thinks are enemy collaborators, he then mutilates their corpses? Is that what the 'new Greece' will be about, Vasili?"

"Niko, I don't know where you hear those things. All I can tell you is what I wrote to you, that I personally have only witnessed a few instances where Velouchiotis did these kinds of things. That he has no sympathy for any Greek who works with or for the Germans or Italians is certainly true, and I know he has killed some of them, but I have to tell you, when it comes to dealing with Greek traitors, I feel the same way he does. What should we do with these traitors, Niko, just let them sell out our country and then forgive them when it's all over? What would you do?"

Nikos had no immediate answer. He looked down to the ground as if he was thinking about what he would say. Finally he spoke, "I'm not sure. Maybe when the war is over, they should be tried by our country and sent to jail. Maybe they should be forced to leave the country. I guess I don't know except that it bothers me that we are killing each other and that we are creating divisions between your group and mine that are poisoning us and can only lead to catastrophe."

The brothers knew that at least for now there would be no agreement between them, but both were determined that these events should not and could not destroy their blood bond as brothers. Once again, before returning to their respective camps, they shook hands, once again hugged one another, and promised to keep in touch.

In Athens, reports of the *andartes'* terror tactics and assassinations were coming to the German and Italian command centers. Since the most numerous incidents were happening against the Nazis, the Italians did not seem overly alarmed at what was developing high in the mountains and small villages of Greece. The Nazi headquarters, however, was becoming increasingly concerned, but as yet no specific orders had come from Berlin as to what the German strategic response to these resistance tactics should be.

Meanwhile, still stationed in Athens, Klaus Schreiber was continuing his daily patrols, basically on the lookout for any possible organized resistance activities in the city. In some ways, Klaus enjoyed being in Athens. As he walked the streets he was surrounded by reminders of those things he had been studying at the university in Thessaloniki. He walked by the ancient Agora where citizens came not only to engage in commerce but also to serve as citizen legislators and where many of the philosophers he had been studying spoke and taught their followers. He saw where

Socrates had been tried and where he had taken the hemlock that ended his life but not his influence. He walked around the Acropolis and the ruins of the Parthenon and marveled at the accomplishments of these ancient Greeks.

At times he wished he could be here under different circumstances, not in uniform and holding a rifle but as a civilian, a student, perhaps someday a professor, studying these places. He had hoped that someday Greece would be the subject of his teaching and scholarship. He had read about some of the actions of the Greek mountain guerrilla forces and had heard that their numbers were increasing every week. He wondered what Hitler's response would be once he had been fully apprised of the Greek attacks on German positions and convoys and other sabotage incidents including the assassination of German officers and soldiers. In some way he hoped that he might be ordered to pursue these guerrillas. Patroling Athens day after day was certainly safe, but he was increasingly bored. The days were long and repetitious, and at least pursuing these guerrillas would be challenging, more dangerous to be sure, but more important for a German victory.

When word came about the destruction of the Gorgopotamos Bridge, he felt that something was about to happen in terms of a German response. Certainly Hitler could not let such a setback go unchallenged. Certainly he would not let a band of peasant guerrillas stop his plans and jeopardize the thus far successful German war machine.

Schreiber did not know that his instincts were correct. In Berlin Hitler called for a meeting with three men. Among the four of them, they would determine a strategy that would send a clear, harsh message to these Greeks and to anyone else in Europe who dared defy the Third Reich and challenge its leader, Adolf Hitler.

CHAPTER ELEVEN

THE FÜHRER WAS IN HIS STUDY, slowly and carefully petting his dog, Blondi. The dog had been given to him by a top aide, Martin Borman, and soon became a favorite of Hitler. He attempted to teach the dog tricks, and the animal always slept in Hitler's bedroom. So important had Blondi become that an army sergeant's full-time assignment was to attend to the animal. Even in the middle of important meetings, Hitler would call for a break in the discussion and personally walk Blondi. A knock was now heard on the study door. Hitler asked the person to enter, and the young soldier announced that the three men their leader had summoned had arrived. The soldier took charge of Blondi, left the room, and told the three officers who were waiting that the Führer was prepared to meet with them. The three men entered the study, greeted their leader, and then sat at a long conference table situated in the middle of room. The conference table was surrounded by large wooden bookcases filled with various genres of books. If the three men had had time to inspect the books, they would have seen a variety of titles. There were works by Guido von List who wrote on the theme of racial purity but believed such a policy could be achieved by political means. The men would also have noticed a book dealing with a subject dear to Hitler's heart: mass psychology, written by Gustave Le Bon who had argued that in large groups individuals lose their ability to think and are persuaded by the endless repetition of certain ideas. They might also have noticed a book entitled *The Protocols of the Elders of Zion*, which made the case that there was a secret Jewish plan for taking over the world. Hitler's visitors may have been surprised by seeing novels dealing with cowboys and Indians, written by Karl May, a fellow German who had never been to the United States. What would not surprise anyone would be the dozen or more copies of the Führer's autobiography, *Mein Kampf* or *My Struggle,* which by law had become required reading in Germany after Hitler became chancellor in 1933. Through the book's royalties Hitler had become a multimillionaire. But the three men, Herman Goering, Heinrich Himmler, and Joseph Goebbels had not been summoned by the leader to discuss books or literature. Sitting at the conference table, with Hitler seated at the head, the three Nazi officers were curious about why they had been summoned.

Hitler opened the meeting and addressed the problem. "Gentlemen," he began, "the situation in Greece is getting out of control. We are facing an organized resistance against our troops consisting of open defiance, sabotage, and assassination. We all know the damage they inflicted with the destruction of the Gorgopotamos Bridge. They have thrown a roadblock to our plans, but they now have gone far beyond that. Just days ago, in the middle of Athens, in broad daylight with German troops patroling the streets, three of our soldiers were assassinated by sniper fire coming somewhere from a high-rise apartment location. We could not identify or capture the assassins. And in the rural areas these bands of guerrillas are living off the land, firing up local villagers and recruiting people to their resistance movement. Their numbers have grown, by our estimates, to more than thirty or forty thousand people. We cannot allow this to continue. We cannot allow chaos to overcome Greece, not only for our own plans but also for the image and message it sends throughout Europe. How do each of you see the situation?"

Goering was the first to respond to Hitler. He was the leader of the Luftwaffe, the German Air Force. He had acquired fame as a WWI flying ace hero and was a person of huge appetites of all kinds. He was fat and eating constantly; he was was known to have eaten ten lobsters at a single meal. He wore flamboyant uniforms and clothes and would often greet guests at his home dressed in various costumes. He had begun painting his fingernails and applying rouge to his face, but for this meeting he had wisely refrained from using such makeup for his audience with his leader.

But this eccentric behavior often masked a more violent, vicious side, absent any moral code or conscience. Together with Himmler, he had organized the concentration camps and was an early advocate of eliminating the Jews by mass murder. When he had once been asked if arranging for the murder of individuals, Jews, and non-Jews had bothered his conscience, he had answered, "I have no conscience. My conscience is Adolf Hitler."

"We should have never been in Greece," Goering said. "These bungling Italians forced us to go there, and we are wasting men, money, and valuable time trying to hold that country in our grip for no good reason. If it hadn't been for that idiot Mussolini and his stupid son-in-law Ciano, Greece would have stayed neutral or probably even been with us. Have we forgotten that their king is a German? I think we should get out as quickly as possible, move everyone and everything to the Eastern border to prepare for our invasion of Russia. That's where we will win this war not in little, unimportant Greece."

Hitler did not respond. Moving the lock of hair that fell over his forehead, he knew Goering was probably correct but that an immediate withdrawal from Greece was not feasible. He now looked to Himmler. "And what is your position, Heinrich?"

Heinrich Himmler's appearance did not seem to fit his position in the Third Reich. He looked and acted like a college professor, an academic who wrote scholarly works for learned journals. He was, in fact, the head of the SS (*Schutzstaffel*, a paramilitary group for the Nazi Party) and the Gestapo (*Geheime Staatspolizei*, the Nazi secret police). His SS had become a huge and dreaded force, its numbers exceeding 250,000 persons. He had amassed huge power and could personally designate virtually anyone as an enemy of the Reich and order his or her execution. His colleagues viewed him as a cold, passionless individual, and he seldom raised his voice or lost his temper. He was a believer in the occult and was careful to plan for his own protection. Himmler's job was to protect Hitler from any direct connection with the mass murders, and he protected himself from Hitler by secretly keeping a file of information against the Führer that could be used against him, if the leader ever decided to eliminate Himmler himself.

"We cannot just leave Greece," he began. "You

must understand, *Mein Führer*, that these bands of guerrillas are not just Greek patriots; the most effective ones and the ones doing the most damage against us are Communists. Their goal is not just to liberate their country from us and the Italians. Their goal, whether they admit it or not, is a Communist Greece. For that reason alone, we must immediately stop this insurgency, and we must do it with the harshest means available. These Greeks will not understand reason and half measures. They are tough. You saw what they did to the Italians with half the resources and the battle they gave us even though we vastly outnumbered them. They will pick us off, one by one, unless we show them that they will pay an enormous price for what they are doing. For every German they kill or attack, we should, *Mein Führer*, kill ten, twenty, or fifty of them." Himmler stopped speaking, wiped a bead of sweat from the thin mustache over his upper lip, and turned to look at Goebbels.

"What you say is true," Hitler said. "We cannot leave them just yet, we cannot, and, yes, they are tough. I actually admire these Greeks, you all know that, but this assault on us cannot continue. So what are your thoughts, Joseph?"

A small man who walked with a limp, Joseph Goebbels' official title was Minister of Propaganda and Enlightenment. Goebbels was a master of propaganda, ritual, theatre, and manipulation of the masses through mass spectacles and mass media. Jealous of others whom he perceived as being closer to Hitler than himself, he constantly praised the Führer and was quick to agree with virtually any position his leader articulated. He, like Hitler, was a Jew hater who encouraged Hitler's views on the topic. A married man and the father of six children, Goebbels also had the reputation as a compulsive womanizer.

"*Mein Führer,*" Goebbels began, "I too do not think we can leave Greece yet. Marshall Goering is, of course, correct; we should have never been in Greece except for the inept egomaniac Mussolini, but we are there. And we do know of your admiration for the culture and history of Greece. Many of our troops either feel the same way or at least know of your past statements. I believe if we are to stop this resistance movement, we must change those attitudes."

Hitler seemed somewhat perplexed, and his face betrayed a lack of understanding of what Goebbels had said. "Explain that, Herr Goebbels, I'm not sure where you are headed in your thinking."

Goebbels thought for a moment, waiting to state his case as precisely as possible. "*Mein Führer,*" he started, "even many of our troops in Greece seem enamored with the country. They try to visit the historic sites when they can—the Acropolis, the Agora,

Delphi, the Mycenae remains, the theatre at Epid-
aurus. They in effect become tourists. If they are to
act with force against the Greek resistance, we must
prepare them mentally first. Recently there has been
some scholarship that claims that the Greeks of today are not the direct descendants of the ancients.
These works claim that the original Greek blood has
been changed by Slavic invasions and the Semitic invasions of the Phoenicians."

"And how valid are such claims?" interrupted
Himmler.

"Some say they are legitimate, some claim they
are bogus. I don't know where the truth is, and,
frankly, it doesn't matter," answered Goebbels. "The
truth should never obstruct our goals. We need to
tell our troops that these claims are true—that Slavic and Semitic blood has poisoned that of the glorious ancients, that these Greeks we see in the streets
are clearly not descendants of those who built those
sites our soldiers visit. And also because of this our
men should never engage in sexual relations with
Greek women because the offspring of such unions
will be individuals not of pure German Aryan blood
but rather of creatures who have polluted our blood.
An approach like this, *Mein Führer*, will leave little
doubt in our soldiers' minds that to kill these Greeks
who dare kill us is not a great loss but a positive act."

Hitler did not immediately respond. He stood up

from his chair and paced the room. The other three men in the room also said nothing, knowing that to speak would interrupt Hitler's train of thought. The leader returned to his seat and finally spoke, "I'm not sure I believe any of those things you report about Greek history, Herr Goebbels, but I do agree with you that whether they are true or not makes no difference. If that is what it takes to harden the resolve of our troops, so be it. Begin the process, Joseph. Frankly, the real reason I believe we must act with extreme force is that, as Heinrich has said, the real threat in Greece is these Communist guerrillas. We cannot launch an invasion of Stalin's Communist Soviet Union and leave Greece in the hands of these Communist bandits. Gentlemen, let us spend the next minutes drawing the order to our commanders in Greece."

During the next hours Hitler and his key leaders discussed the wording of orders and the extent of the punishment that would be inflicted on those who attacked German troops. Their first communication was to the Nazi officers in Greece:

If the German conduct of war is not to suffer grievous damage through such methods, it must be made clear to the adversary that all sabotage troops will be exterminated, without exception, to the last man.

This means that the chances of saving their lives is nil.

Recognizing the lack of German troop experience in dealing with the terror tactics of guerrilla warfare, the communication went on to say that all civilians were to be regarded as potential enemies. Germans in Greece were warned to view any Greek friendly to Germans with suspicion because the Greek character was devious and cunning. The friendly Greek, the communication went on to say, would always want something in return. "Better to shoot once too often," the document concluded, "than once too seldom."

In the official order from Hitler the tone and extent of the Nazi response to the Greek resistance was clear. It read:

> The enemy has thrown into bandit warfare fanatic, Communist-trained fighters who will not stop at any act of violence. The troops are thereby authorized and ordered in the struggle to take any measures without restriction even against women and children if these are necessary for success. Humanitarian considerations of any kind are a crime against the Germans.

As the orders reached Greece, steps were immediately begun to indoctrinate the troops with the anti-Greek propaganda Goebbels had recommended.

The Greek resisters were described to the German soldiers as Communists, criminals, and racially inferior people. The soldiers were told that it was the duty of every German soldier to use brutal force of arms to break the resistance forces and that any soldier who refused would be brought before a military court and punished. Along with his fellow soldiers, Klaus Schreiber listened silently to the orders of the commanding officer.

In the days that immediately followed, even more specific orders were given to the troops. They were informed that any man found having intimate or sexual relations with a Greek woman would be executed. All armed Greek men were to be shot on the spot, and those villages from which any shots had been fired against Germans were to be totally destroyed. Every attack on Germans was to result in punishment of Greeks. If the actual shooter could not be identified, the key leaders of the village—the mayor, the priest, the doctor, and village elders—were to be executed in public. And, the orders specified, for every German soldier shot, one hundred Greeks were to be killed. Listening to the orders from his commanding officer, Klaus Schreiber looked straight ahead, and only one thought ran through his mind: Is this war? What have we become?

In their respective mountain retreats, Napoleon Zervas and Aris Velouchiotis received the news of the Nazi orders as soon as couriers from the villages could bring them. Zervas was troubled by what he now saw as an impossible situation. To stop the raids on the Germans would mean that there would be no hope for eventual liberation. But to continue those raids would mean the mass murder of innocent countrymen. He felt helpless. For the moment, he thought, he would halt his group's activities, perhaps then make a strike, wait for the German response to see if they would actually act on what they threatened, and then make some final decision.

In the other remote mountain encampment, Aris Velouchiotis was not troubled by indecision or what he perceived to be a dilemma. Gathering his key leaders, he sat on a large rock around a campfire. It was a clear, quiet evening, and the stars in the sky seemed particularly bright. In his quiet, controlled voice, sometimes hardly more than a whisper, he felt he had to inform his resistance fighters what the Nazi orders would mean. "Our enemy has spoken," he began, "but they are just words. They cannot make us tremble, they cannot bring us to our knees. We are Greeks; they apparently have forgotten that. In our veins flows the blood of those who pushed back the Persian Empire and of those who broke the chains of 400 years of Turkish oppression. Fellow combatants, we will not, we cannot, stop. We will fight until every German Hun is driven from our land. The time for speeches is over. We must plan our next assault." Aris stopped speaking. Those listening to him did not react. There was no applause, no verbal shouts of support. Each man and woman knew the gravity of the situation. They knew they had to continue, but they also knew what the consequences would probably be for many of their fellow Greeks. Slowly, silently they left the campfire site and moved into their tents.

The days ahead would be the testing time. German troops moved from village to village seeking information about the location and plans of the *andartes*. Klaus Schreiber was particularly useful to the Nazi command because he spoke and understood the Greek language. He was assigned to question local people for information but seldom received any useful insights. He had been especially frustrated by the lack of information provided by the residents of a small village on the outskirts of Corinth. Weeks before another Nazi unit had come to the village to seek information, and one of the soldiers had completely disappeared; when the unit prepared to leave the village, the soldier was missing. Klaus' interrogation of the villagers about the incident revealed nothing. One old man told him that the soldier may have deserted or perhaps had suffered some deadly natural accident. What Klaus did not know and never discovered was that the soldier had encountered a unique and deadly resistance strategy.

For young German soldiers away from their homeland, the order from on high that they were to not have contact of any kind with Greek women was an order certain to be ignored if possible. For many soldiers the lure of young Greek village girls was a temptation difficult to resist. And for some young Greek girls, their gender was a resistance tool they possessed that they were eager to use. The story that no one would reveal to Klaus was that when this previous Nazi unit entered the village two sisters, young attractive Greek girls, had smiled flirtatiously at the German soldiers walking through their village. That evening the Nazis established camp about one half mile outside the village, and one young soldier, Kurt Braden, decided to take his chances, leave the campsite, and walk back to the village to find the young girls who he believed had smiled at him in such a tempting manner.

Arriving at the village at 11:00 in the evening, the soldier found that the village was quiet; people had left the town square, the few shops were closed, and the only movement on the streets was that of four stray cats, seeking food that had fallen from the tables of the local village restaurant. The girls' father, a large mustached man of forty-two, had told his daughters of his intense hatred of the Germans and how, if he did not have so many family obligations, he too would go to the mountains to join the resistance. He yearned for the opportunity to do his part, and when the soldier came to the door of his modest home and demanded to see the man's daughters, he instantly knew his chance had come.

Calling his older daughter, he told her in Greek, which the soldier obviously did not understand, what he had in mind. He instructed her to walk with the soldier through the olive trees that were part of the family's parcel of land. He also conveyed to his daughter that he would be out of sight but close by. Contrary to his normal behavior and contrary to the norms of any Greek village, the father pointed to the small clock on the wall and communicated to the soldier that his daughter must return in exactly one hour. Somehow, though they spoke different languages, the young soldier nodded his understanding of the father's conditions, and the two young people, the Nazi soldier and the older Greek village girl, walked away from the house toward the olive trees.

Within ten minutes the girl's father had left the house, retrieved an object from the small shed where he kept tools, and followed a different path to the olive trees where he knew the soldier would be with his daughter. As the two young people sat on two large rocks that served as chairs and tried with difficulty to communicate, the father slowly advanced from behind and with one swift blow of an ax came down on the soldier's head. His daughter screamed and quickly moved away from the severed, blood-soaked body that fell to the ground. The father ordered his daughter to return to their home and then proceeded to dismember the dead German into pieces and bury those pieces in three different locations. Smiling as he finished his task, he returned to his home. He felt proud; he had at last done something to rid his country of these invaders.

Klaus and his colleagues continued to be instructed to place all Greeks in the category of potential enemies, not worthy of humane considerations. They were told, day after day, that the guerillas were inhuman criminals who were racially inferior. The soldiers were told that the Greeks were "crafty" and that the soldiers would have to be even more crafty than the enemy and should not hesitate to be ruthless against them. They were told to memorize and repeat the admonition, "Better shoot once too often rather than once too seldom." The only solution to the guerrilla tactics they were asked to believe was to meet terror from them with even more terror.

Klaus' unit attempted to send two men to the guerrillas posing as deserters who wanted to join the resistance forces, but Velouchiotis, after intense interrogation, walked away, motioned Vasili Gantos to follow him, and simply said to him, "Kill the bastards, they are lying." Vasili took the two soldiers, sat them on two chairs, and then proceeded to fire two shots into each of their heads. Later that evening, the two bodies were placed on the road where they were found by Nazi patrols.

The increase in incidents such as these made the Germans determined to stop the Greek assault by extreme methods of terror. The village of Komeno gave them an excuse they were seeking. Vasili and five other men were sent to the village by Velouchiotis to secure food and supplies. While in the village a two-man German reconnaissance team came into the village, saw the guerrillas who were carrying weapons, quickly turned around, and drove back to their headquarters where they reported their sighting of armed guerrillas. The Nazi commander, Colonel Joseph Salminger, who had been unsuccessful thus far in eliminating the *andartes*, now saw his opportunity. Bringing his men together, he lied to them and told them that German soldiers had been killed and that the Greek terrorists could not be allowed to continue these assaults. Salminger told his troops, "If we cannot yet hit directly at these guerrillas, we will destroy their mothers, fathers, sisters, brothers, wives, husbands, and children." Klaus and the other soldiers sat silently as Salminger went on for another fifteen minutes about how the men must not hold back from killing women and children. "They are not women and children," emphasized the Colonel, "you must view them and remember they are sharpshooters, and they want to shoot at you." Then Salminger gave his explicit order, "You are to go into the village of Komeno and leave nothing standing, I repeat, nothing standing."

At 5:00 a.m. on the following morning Klaus, along with the others, began the attack. Houses were stormed, and as frightened villagers began to run seeking safety they were shot. Bodies, men, women, children, were falling to the ground throughout the village. Some villagers jumped into the river and were lucky enough to swim to the other side to safety, but others were left helpless as German soldiers fired at every person they could see and then set fire to village homes. Screams of people running for cover or coming upon the sight of corpses of their loved ones could be heard everywhere. Klaus opened the door of a home, saw an old man sitting alone, and fired one shot to the man's chest as the man fell to the floor. Klaus then lit matches and set the house aflame. Outside in the village streets, some residents were on the ground wounded as German soldiers slowly walked the streets giving "mercy shots" to their heads to end their suffering. A village priest ran out begging for the carnage to stop and was met by the end of a German rifle to his head, while another soldier emptied three bullets into the priest's head and chest. Those villagers who did not leave their houses were burnt alive, as Nazi troops systematically set fire to each village structure. When it was over, more than 300 villagers had been killed and the village transformed into a flaming bed of ashes. Colonel Salminger was pleased. Not one German soldier had died, and a lesson had ben sent to the guerrillas. "This," Salminger announced, "is just a beginning of what we will do. Stop your actions or hundreds more of your countrymen and families will die."

CHAPTER TWELVE

THE SLAUGHTER OF INNOCENT people at Komeno was cause for concern in both the guerrilla and Nazi camps. Nikos approached Napoleon Zervas who was sitting in a chair looking forward at no particular object. "Napoleon," asked Nikos in a soft voice that conveyed concern, "are you all right? Is anything wrong?"

Zervas looked up and was slow to respond. "Niko," he finally said, "I think our hands are tied. We cannot continue to resist if the price we pay is what happened at Komeno. I am told that more than three hundred people were killed, the village torched, and nothing remains but ashes, dead bodies, and some ragged children wandering around looking for food and their mothers and fathers. These Germans are not soldiers, they are barbarians in the truest sense of that word. For every one of them we kill, they kill fifty or a hundred Greeks." Zervas seemed unable to continue to speak and shook his head as if not believing what he had just reported.

Nikos understood the truth of what Zervas had just said. He could not respond with some workable solution. He thought of his own family living in Kalavryta. Finally, he spoke, "Maybe, Napoleon, we need to stop our activities for a while, let things cool down, let the Germans believe they have succeeded in intimidating us. Maybe they will let their guard down, and then we can strike in some different way, maybe not directly against the soldiers but rather only hit their truck convoys, disrupt their communication options. I don't know, but maybe their response won't be as forceful or so vicious." Zervas listened carefully to Nikos' ideas, knowing immediately that they made sense. There was no guarantee of a German letup, but it was worth a try.

"You make sense, Niko, it's worth a try," responded Zervas, who rose from the chair, shook Nikos' hand, and walked outside into the cool, fresh air. But as he walked, other thoughts surfaced in his head. If they couldn't strike the Germans effectively right now, why not just focus on the Italians? Continuing to walk briskly, Zervas began mentally constructing a plan.

What happened in Komeno had an impact in the German camp as well. Klaus was unusually quiet, not responding to his fellow soldiers. He seemed depressed. Various thoughts were running through his head about what he had done. What kind of war is this anyway? We see no enemy army, we shoot at no enemy forces wearing uniforms. Instead we fire at any Greek we see; we kill old men, women, children. What have we become? Klaus thoughts were interrupted by a tap on his shoulder from another soldier, Herman Schultz.

"Klaus," Schultz said, "are you all right? You seem to be dazed or something."

Klaus looked at his comrade. "Herman, what did you feel, did you feel anything when you sprayed bullets at those people in Komeno? Did what we did bother you?"

Schultz sat next to Klaus and took no time to respond. "Klaus, I did what I was ordered to do. Do you think I like killing people? I can tell you I do not, but I know if I do not follow orders, either the Greeks or my commanding officer will kill me. It's not pretty, my friend, but the logic is simple."

"But there has to be a better way, Herman. I did what you did, too. I know I killed at least five women, three old people, and, I think, two or three children. Frankly, it makes me sick. It's just not right. Is this the only way we can crush this Greek resistance? There's got to be a better way. The world is watching us, Herman, they are watching. I want to be proud of Germany, not ashamed of my country."

"Klaus, the best advice I can give you is twofold. First, don't let anyone here even catch a hint that you are not proud of Germany. And second, even if it hurts, follow orders, just follow orders. If you don't, you will not survive this war alive, believe me."

High in the mountains of the Arcadia region of Greece one other group was responding to the news of the Komeno massacre. Aris Velouchiotis brought his key leaders together, among them Vasili Gantos. Standing erect before his men, Aris began, "They must pay for this butchery comrades, they must and will pay! These people are animals not humans, and they must be hunted down and killed like we would any wild animals. There is no place for sympathy, no place for honor, no place for compromise. We must kill as many of these Nazi vermin as we can."

Vasili was the first to respond. Standing with his rifle at his side, be began, "Aris, no one here, least of all me, disagrees with what you say about these Germans, but I do think we need to consider the consequences of what we are doing. Yes, we sabotage trucks, cut lines of communication, and kill a German soldier once in a while. But are these actions good for our country, our fellow countrymen? The three hundred that were murdered in Komeno were our fellow Greeks, not some people in some far off land. And if tomorrow or even today we kill two or three more Nazis, what will we have gained if they respond by demolishing more villages and killing three hundred more Greeks? I just think we need to pause, think this through, and not be driven by emotion."

Velouchiotis liked and respected Vasili, but in this instance he was not sympathetic to his logic or argument. "The answer, Vasili, is No! I hope I am making that clear. No is the answer to the implied question of whether we should stop our attacks on the Germans. Do we think these barbarians are rational men? They are all brainwashed fascists who believe the speeches and racist teachings of that pervert they call a leader, Hitler. We cannot stop. If we stop, they win. If we stop, we lose our Fatherland. If we stop, we are cowards. If some Greeks must die in this process of liberating our country, that is a price that must be paid. The only response we must have is to be as brutal, or even more brutal, to them as they are willing to be toward us. I hope everything is clear. In three days we will strike again."

Velouchiotis then revealed his plan. Villagers from Kalavryta had sent word to him that a convoy of German soldiers would be passing on the outskirts of the village in a few days. Aris instructed his men to intercept the Nazi convoy, kill the soldiers, and dispose of their bodies so that no trace of them could be found. Since Vasili was from Kalavryta, he knew the region well and was assigned to lead the attack.

Hiding between the high rocks that surrounded the road, the Greek *andartes* struck the convoy as it rolled past in the dark of night. The Greeks shot the tires of the trucks, swooped on the Nazis with grenades, and threw cans of gasoline at the trucks followed by burning flares. As the soldiers attempted to leave the trucks in panic, the guerrillas utilized the machine guns they had stolen from the Italians to kill the fleeing Germans. The attack was a success. Eighty German soldiers were killed, twenty others captured. Velouchiotis was pleased with the mission and praised Vasili for his leadership in the operation.

In German headquarters there was a flurry of activity as word reached them that more than one hundred of their men were missing, probably killed or captured by the Greek resistance forces. When it was finally verified that the convoy had been ambushed and scores killed, the news was met with increased determination to use the harshest measures against the Greeks. The commander of the German division, General Karl von Le Suire called in his subordinates, Major Ebersberger, and his lieutenant, Hauptmann Dohnert. "Major," started Le Suire, "precisely what do we know about the guerrillas who led the attack on our troops?"

Ebersberger stood at attention as he addressed his commanding officer. "General, we are almost sure it was the Velouchiotis band. The Zervas group has actually slowed down their actions in response to our reprisals, but this Velouchiotis man, the man is apparently a lunatic."

"Perhaps," responded Le Suire, "but he's the kind of lunatic I wish was on our side. I almost respect his recklessness. But let me be clear, what I am about to say is not a recommendation, it is an order. Understood?"

Ebersberger nodded. Dohnert knew his place was to say nothing. Whatever the order Le Suire was about to give would be his responsibility to actually carry out.

Le Suire assumed a more relaxed posture. "Sit, Gentlemen," he said, and both Ebersberger and Dohnert moved to sit in the chairs placed before Le Suire's desk. The general began speaking again. "I am hereby ordering the mission I will call Operation Kalavryta. The essence of this mission is the following: every village, from our headquarters to Kalavryta, is to be destroyed. Greeks who flee when they see us must all be shot. We will report that we had come peacefully, we were attacked, and when the Greeks attempted to run, we shot them. When we finally enter Kalavryta, this is what I am also ordering." Le Suire stopped, then seemed to divert from his line of thought. "Gentlemen, do either of you know anything about the history of the village of Kalavryta?"

Ebersberger and Dohnert both simultaneously

shook their heads. "I know nothing special, General," said Ebersberger.

"Nor do I, Sir," added Dohnert.

"Well," started Le Suire, "let me give you a quick, condensed version in Greek history. It was in Kalavryta, in 1821, that the Greek Revolution against the Turks started and the revolutionary flag first raised. It was in Kalavryta that the Greeks first made the call of 'freedom or death' to their Ottoman oppressors. This village is important to all Greeks, and for that reason alone we will inflict destruction they will never forget. Kalavryta is a place that is the modern birthplace of the Greek spirit of freedom and independence. Gentlemen, Germany will eradicate that spirit."

Ebersberger and Dohnert sensed that there was something different in the way Le Suire was relating the history of Kalavryta. Both wondered what he would say next. Was some special, unique approach being contemplated in his mind to kill off every vestige of the total Greek resistance? Answers to their questions came quickly.

Le Suire stood from his chair and came around to the front of the desk. Pulling up another chair, he sat directly in front of his two subordinates, a gesture that seemed to the two officers to be somewhat strange. The general leaned forward and began to detail his plan. "Gentlemen, this is how this operation will be different. This is how, when we are finished, it will send chills, panic, and terror into the center of the resistance movement. After Kalavryta, I believe there will not be a resistance movement." Le Suire then detailed his orders to Ebersberger. The major and Dohnert returned to their troops to convey the order and plan the assault.

Sitting with the large group of fellow soldiers, Klaus was troubled by what he was hearing. He had not, as yet, recovered from his experience in Komeno. The random, indiscriminate killing of men, women, and children could not leave his mind. He had slept little since that day in Komeno. He still could not comprehend why he and the others were in Greece. What kind of threat was Greece? None, he concluded. What kind of prize to the Reich was Greece? Once again, he concluded that Greece was no prize at all. So why all the slaughter? He knew the Greeks pretty well, he thought. His best friends had been Greeks. He could understand why the Germans and Italians would be resented. If he were a Greek, Klaus thought, he probably would feel the same way. But Klaus was particularly troubled by the order to move on Kalavryta. Almost five years before he had visited the village with his friend and roommate, Nikos Gantos. He had met Nikos' mother and young sister, Eleni, and his younger brother, Vasili. Nikos' father had been away that weekend, so he was the only family member Klaus had not met. They had all welcomed him, treated him as a member of the family. They were good and decent people, and now he was being ordered to go into that village and repeat what he had done in Komeno. After hearing the briefing from his commanding officer, Klaus returned to his bed. Lying on his back, his eyes wide open, he simply starred at the ceiling above him. He could not erase from his mind what had been told to the troops about the unique aspect of the mission labeled, *Unternehmen Kalavryta*, Operation Kalavryta.

General Le Suire had planned the operation so that its completion would send a clear and powerful message to those in the mountains who, the general thought, foolishly believed they could intimidate or defeat the army of the Third Reich. This operation would be different. There would be no wholesale, indiscriminate killing of everyone within the aim of a German rifle. Here, the goal would be to leave scores of grieving widows and children.

As German trucks and motorcycles approached the outskirts of Kalavryta, the village elders ordered the younger people to go house to house to inform the people to not do anything unusual. They were ordered not to retreat and hide in their homes or to take any measures that might provoke retaliation or violence by the Nazis. Women were told to continue their household chores or their work in the fields. The old men were told to remain at the coffee house and follow their normal daily routines. Children at play outside were not to be disturbed or frightened. This village had done nothing to provoke or anger the Germans, and there was no reason to believe that the village was a target for any conflict or reprisal.

Entering the village, German troops disembarked from the trucks and took positions throughout the village. Klaus took his position in front of the building that served as the village schoolhouse. Major Ebersberger had delegated the implementation of the plan to Hauptmann Dohnert. Knowing that Klaus was fluent in Greek, Dohnert summoned him to his side and told him to translate his message to the assembled villagers. After Dohnert spoke, Klaus immediately translated his words. "All males," the order read, "aged twelve and above of the village of Kalavryta are to leave their present location and gather at that small hill on the east side of the village." As Klaus read, he pointed toward the location where the males were to gather. "In addition," Klaus continued, "all women and children are to report to the village school and wait there until receiving further orders."

Confusion now permeated the village residents. No one had any idea of what was happening. Could the Germans be trying to recruit Greek men to their side? Why were women and children being separated from the men? Some women began crying, others bluntly asked questions that the Germans did not understand and did not bother to attempt to respond to. Slowly, Klaus and his fellow soldiers moved from house to house making sure that all the designated males were moving to the appointed location and that women and children were going to the schoolhouse. Klaus felt nervous as he approached the one house in the village he clearly recognized. He had slept there. He had been welcomed there during family dinners. It was the family home of Nikos Gantos. Turning to the soldier next to him, Klaus tapped him on the shoulder and simply said, "Soldier, you take that house, I'll do the two next door."

As the soldier ordered Nikos' family out of the house, Klaus looked back, seeing an older man walk out. That must be Nikos' father, he guessed, and then a woman he clearly recognized: Nikos' mother. Two other women also left the house. One was about his age, and the second was a pretty young girl of about fifteen. Klaus did not know that the slightly older woman, the one about his age, was Mortis' sister, but the younger girl looked familiar, yet somehow different. He stared at her and she stared back toward him, and for both it was a moment of recognition. She had only been about ten or eleven, Klaus remembered, a child when he last saw her. Now some five years later she had become a young woman, maybe fifteen or sixteen. The girl was Nikos' sister, Eleni, and suddenly everything was clear in his mind. Klaus quickly turned away, not wanting her to perhaps recognize his face. But it was too late. As a girl of eleven she had met and liked Nikos' friend Klaus Schreiber, who she also thought was very handsome. Seeing that face again now she was convinced it was that same Klaus. There was no doubt about it, she thought, but what should she do? Should she say something? Call his name? She decided to do nothing. Perhaps calling his name would make things worse for them and for him. But she was comforted to know that it was Klaus. He knew the family, certainly he would not be part of anything that would harm them or the others.

Slowly, without looking back, the women of the Gantos household were gathered with the other village women and children and led to the schoolhouse where they were ordered to just wait until further notice. Closing the door to the school, everyone not only heard the sound of the door being shut but also the sounds of locks that secured the doors from anyone seeking to leave. And along with the other young boys and men of the village, Nikos' father walked toward the hill outside the village. Five hundred males from Kalavryta finally assembled at the designated location. Klaus and the other troops were also ordered to gather at the hill location.

Nazi commander Dohnert then gave the order, simply saying, "Fire." Immediately German soldiers raised their machine guns and sprays of lethal bullets filled the air, hitting men and boys alike who had been standing close together. Screams and curses filled the air as the continuous shooting slaughtered row after row of helpless male villagers. Bodies fell over bodies, as the ground became a sea of dark red blood. In a matter of minutes, it was over. More than five hundred males had been massacred. In the schoolhouse women could only hear the continuous gunfire; some screamed, some simply buried their heads in their hands and sobbed continuously. The small children were crying, but few women made any attempt to comfort them, intuitively knowing what had happened to their men.

The Germans made no attempt to bury the dead. Returning to the village center, another unauthorized order was given by Dohnert to ensure that all of Greece would tremble at the might of the German war machine. The order was to set fire to the schoolhouse, and soldiers moved to set matches to the all-wooden structure and then prepared to leave the village as the schoolhouse fire grew in intensity. As the heat and smoke intensified, the screams of panic and pleas for help could be heard. Klaus seemed frozen. He seemed unable to move. "Klaus!" yelled one of his colleagues, "Come on, we're leaving. You'll miss the truck! Come on!"

Klaus had little time to think. He blurted out, "I'll be there, I need to go back, I lost something important my mother gave me! I'll catch up! I'll be right there!" Klaus ran back toward the schoolhouse, raised his rifle, and shot off the locks that had secured the door shut. Quickly running toward the moving troop truck, he shouted out in Greek, "The door is open! The door is open! Get out! Get out!" Reaching the truck he boarded with the help of soldiers who lifted him in. As the truck sped away, he saw people leaving the burning schoolhouse. Klaus sat in the truck, saying nothing. His mind was racing with thoughts of what he had done. If his superiors knew exactly what he had done just moments before, he was a dead man. And if they knew what he had done on that hill where the men had been massacred, he would also die. As the Greek males from the village had stood there helplessly being mowed down, he had purposely directed his shots into the ground, refusing to aim at anyone. He had deliberately made it a point to kill no one. This was not war any longer, he thought, this was madness. He felt as though he were living a terrible nightmare. He didn't know if he could take it any longer. But what could he do? He began to cry and hid his tear-soaked face in his hands, hoping none of his fellow soldiers would see what had happened to him.

When word of the massacre at Kalavryta reached both the Zervas and Velouchiotis camps, there was shock and anger. Nikos and Mortis told Zervas they had to immediately go to the village. Vasili told Ve-louchiotis that he had to go to his home village as well. Meeting in what had been the village square of Kalavryta, Nikos, Vasili, and Mortis seemed unable to speak as they looked around the village. The death toll from the surrounding villages and Kalavryta was nearly seven hundred people. The villages were de-stroyed, most burned to the ground. More than one thousand homes were looted and two thousand live-stock stolen by the German troops. And in Kalavry-ta, five hundred corpses were lying on the ground. For days Nikos, Vasili, Mortis, and other men who had survived from surrounding villages buried the dead, as women and small children wept at the sight of their bullet-ridden fathers, husbands, brothers, and sons.

Nikos, Vasili, and Mortis finished their tasks. Nikos' father was dead. By some miracle, some un-known Nazi soldier had opened the schoolhouse door, which had allowed his mother, sister, and the other women to survive. But survive to what? The women had no husbands, brothers, sons, or grand-sons. They had no homes, no church, no village. Nikos was particularly enraged by what his sister, Eleni, told him.

"Niko, one of the men who were here to kill our father and the others was Klaus. I saw him, it was Klaus."

Nikos seemed stunned at first, unable to respond to his sister. Finally, he said, "Eleni, are you sure? Are you absolutely sure? You have seen him only one time, and you were very young. Maybe it was just someone who resembled Klaus."

"No, Niko!" insisted Eleni, "no! It was Klaus, I'm sure of it. He was one of the murderers, I know what I saw, and I will never, ever, forget it!"

Nikos did not pursue it any further. Klaus, Klaus Schreiber, he kept repeating the name in his mind. He kept thinking about this person he had called his "brother," this person he had invited into his own home, this same person who now had been part of a killing team that had killed his father. It was something he could never forget or ever forgive.

Nikos gathered the survivors and knew there was little he could say, but he tried. "For many of us, it seems as though our lives are over. We have lost everything we loved and everything we owned. There is little I can say to comfort you, or my mother, or sister, or me. But somehow, somehow, we must go on. These murders cannot go unchallenged. We are not cowards like those who slaughter unarmed, innocent people. We are Greeks. They were savages when we were writing philosophy and inventing theatre, and they have remained savages. They can kill our bodies, but they cannot kill our heritage, our history, our determination, or our spirit. These savages will pay a heavy price for their deeds. And we will prevail!"

There was no applause, only silence. At least, for the moment, the Germans had accomplished their goal: they had broken the hearts of these Greeks who now experienced more sorrow than seemed humanly possible. Perhaps, many in the village thought, they would be better off if they too had died, for what was there to live for?

Far from this sorrowful scene in Kalavryta, events in Italy were moving quickly, events that would change the course of the war and the future of Greece itself. Italy was also on the mind of Napoleon Zervas. Returning to their campsite and meeting with their leader, Nikos and Mortis now were informed of what Zervas had been contemplating as a response to the German atrocities. Strange at it seemed to them at first, Zervas told Nikos and Mortis that a way to strike at Germany was to strike at Italy. And the way to do that was to assassinate Benito Mussolini.

TOWARD FREEDOM
1943-1944

CHAPTER THIRTEEN

When Nikos and Mortis heard Zervas' words, their first reaction was to question whether they had actually heard him correctly. Did he say that someone would assassinate Mussolini? Or had they really heard what they thought he had said—that he wanted them to kill the Italian leader? Nikos first spoke for clarification. "Napoleon, if you are saying what I think you said, I don't know what such an action will do to help us with the German ravaging of our people and villages."

Mortis seemed surprised by Zervas' statement as well. "Like Nikos, I don't see how that helps us with the Nazis, and, besides, it seems like you are asking us to go on a suicide mission. Mussolini goes nowhere without security made up of the best soldiers he has. I doubt we could ever even get close to him."

Zervas, who had his rifle strapped across his chest, took the weapon off his shoulder, placed it upright against the wall, and motioned Nikos and Mortis to move closer to him. Looking at both men, he said, "Listen to me. Eliminating Mussolini will change everything. When he goes, there is no real leader to succeed him. His fascist movement in Italy will fall apart, the Italian troops in Greece will leave. Most of them, you both know, have no desire to be here anyway, and there never has been strong support in Italy for their Greek invasion, particularly since it has led to their worldwide humiliation. I continually get reports that his son-in-law, Ciano, is intensely disliked for many reasons but especially for his major role in pushing Mussolini to attack our country. Frankly, if you could kill them both, you probably would be doing both Greece and Italy a great service. With Mussolini out of the picture, his movement then in chaos, and the Italian troops called home, the Germans then will have to spread themselves so thin if they hope to control the entire country that they will not be able to do it effectively. That means our resistance can operate more effectively and with less fear of their reprisals. And I can guarantee that Hitler has too many other worries about survival from both the East and the West to send thousands more troops to Greece."

"But why us, Napoleon?" questioned Nikos, "and what about Mortis' point about Mussolini's security?"

"Because you are the only two who have a chance of success," answered Zervas. "Niko, your reputation as a sniper has become almost a legend in Greece. Our men are still talking in amazement about what you did to kill those Nazi soldiers in broad daylight in the middle of the day in Athens. And Mortis, your ability to speak, read, and understand Italian makes you the perfect person to navigate through Italy."

"And what am I supposed to do?" asked Nikos smiling. "Walk around pretending I'm a deaf mute?" Mortis could not help finding Nikos' comment amusing.

"Actually," Zervas said, "that's not a bad idea. I was trying to think of a way so that you would not stand out. In fact, that's a very good idea, Niko. When you cross the border into Italy, you say nothing except to Mortis and you act as though you hear nothing. And Mortis, your afflicted companion you should identify as your 'cousin' who is with you because he cannot operate on his own."

"OK," said Nikos, "I hear or say nothing. That still does not get us close to Mussolini and his security detail."

"Niko, with your ability with a rifle, you don't have to get 'close.' Every year on the date of Mussolini's ascension to power, there is a huge parade in Rome. He travels in an open car, stands up the entire way waving to the crowd as if he were an ancient

Roman emperor. Along the route there are a number of tall buildings. In two or three of those buildings are the Rome offices of Greek shipping companies. The Italians, because they rely on these companies to ship their products throughout the Mediterranean and beyond, have never attempted to interfere with the businesses. We will arrange for you to use one of those sites for your kill. You can do this, Niko, I know you can. And after you have accomplished your mission, you and Mortis should stay in Italy for a week or two and then come home."

"You make it sound so easy, Napoleon," said Mortis, "but it will not be that simple."

"No, it won't." echoed Nikos. "A million things could go wrong in that environment, and if they do, we are all dead men. But, Mortis, we will do it, we must do it for Greece. Practice your Italian, Mortis. Unfortunately, I won't be able to hear how well you speak." Nikos smiled again.

Within a week Nikos and Mortis prepared for their mission. They determined that the best way for them to enter Italy was on one of the Greek merchant ships that routinely went from Greece to Italy to load Italian goods destined for export. Zervas made the arrangements with the Greek shipping companies, and Nikos and Mortis arrived in Naples, disguised as part of the crew whose task was to load crates of olive oil for transport to other market destinations. Their actual task: to eliminate Il Duce.

Although Benito Mussolini knew nothing of the Greek plot against him, things were not going well for the Italian leader. Italian troops were suffering huge casualties on the North Africa front. More than half of the Axis battalions were Italian, and they had lost more than 17,000 men. The Italian population was open to Mussolini's grand designs as long as the casualties to their sons, husbands, and brothers were relatively low. But the debacle in Greece and particularly the huge losses in North Africa were altering the public's perception of their leader.

Even Il Duce's own son-in-law was increasingly feeling that the war was going badly and that Mussolini leadership was weak and controlled primarily by Nazi Germany. Galeazzo Ciano was disturbed by rumors that the Germans were blaming the negative progress of the war effort on the Italians. He was also concerned by other intelligence indicating that the Allies were planning to hit the Axis powers from the south, possibly through Greece, or perhaps Sicily. Ciano sensed that the war effort of the Axis was destined to fail if the Allied invasion was launched through Sicily and then moved through the whole of Italy. Allied bombing of parts of Italy had already begun, and Ciano saw further escalation of bombing as not only destroying the country but his own future as well. Increasingly, Ciano wanted to explore ways for Italy to seek an armistice and leave the war. But Ciano knew that Mussolini would never agree to what he would see as defeat.

"You must swear to me that what I say is confidential," Ciano said to his friend, Dino Grandi. "Even my wife cannot know of this." Ciano seemed nervous as he spoke and then quickly reached for his pack of cigarettes, took one from the package, and lit it. "The time has come. We cannot deny it any longer. We must end this war, and the only way that can happen is if we have new leadership. Il Duce must step down."

Grandi slowly nodded his head in agreement. "Unfortunately, Galeazzo, I think you are right. If we continue as we are, Italy is headed for disaster. Already there are food shortages and the number of worker strikes grow daily. But what about your family, your wife? How can you deal with that? As well as with Il Duce? Are you sure you want to be out front and visible if we replace Il Duce?"

Ciano now paced the floor as he exhaled a cloud of white smoke. "No doubt," he said, "it's difficult. I wish it could be another way, but it cannot. I will have to talk to my wife and explain to her that this is probably best for her father as well. I really don't know how she will react."

"Don't you think you should talk to Mussolini and personally tell him of your concerns for him and for the country?"

"No, that would not be a good idea. I know my father-in-law. He will never agree to step down. Somehow he still thinks that with Hitler's support of Italy, we will win. I don't think he allows himself to face the facts."

"Then what should we do next?" asked Grandi.

"Although we haven't met for years, we need to convene the Grand Council and invite Il Duce to speak to us and make his report on the conduct and future of the war. After he speaks, we all must decide, did he make a case to remain as our leader or not? And then we all need to vote."

Besides the negative aspects of the war effort, Mussolini faced other troubles as well. To placate the growing public call for Ciano to resign, Mussolini made him ambassador to the Vatican, a position in which he was sure to cause little trouble to the war effort or to Mussolini himself. Il Duce's health also continued to be an issue. The stomach pains continued, and his doctor now said that a case of dysentery had triggered ulcer problems that confined him to bed for weeks at a time. Even when he was not restricted to bed rest, Mussolini no longer made the trips to Italian cities and towns so that he could read the pulse of the people and they could see their leader in person. For Nikos and Mortis, now safely based in Italy, this became a problem. No longer was Mussolini as visible as he had always been. No longer were there frequent press reports of where Il Duce was or where he was going. Their prospective target was increasingly hard to locate.

If illness, bad war news, and public unrest were not enough to aggravate Mussolini's ulcer, his wife Rachel no longer seemed willing to ignore what she knew were her husband's infidelities, particularly his liaison with Claretta Petacci. What specifically had inflamed Rachel was that her husband had moved Claretta to Villa Fiordaliso, a residence close to where she and Mussolini lived. Her anger now reached a point of no return. Rachel phoned her husband and told him that she was going to see and confront Claretta about the affair. Il Duce listened to his wife's shrill voice and, seemingly too exhausted to do anything, simply replied, "Do as you wish." Mussolini then phoned Claretta to warn her about what was about to happen.

"She is coming to you," he warned his mistress. Lying to Claretta, he went on, "I tried to dissuade her, but it was not possible. Don't let her in. She is out of control, and I fear she may be armed."

A strong rain would not subside as Rachel came to Claretta's residence and was allowed in by the security guard who had been assigned there. "You wanted to see me?" said Claretta as she nervously led her unwelcomed guest into the sitting room.

Rachel seemed eager to confront Claretta. "Yes," she replied, as her voice rose, "I wanted to see you, to tell you something, that you must go away, that there is no need of you. No one wants you! Go away and leave my husband in peace!"

Claretta at first seemed composed. "You are mistaken if you believe you can give me orders."

The mistress' calm tone angered Rachel. "He doesn't love you at all!" she shouted. "He told me yesterday that he doesn't love you and that if you would go away it would give him pleasure. He loves only me, do you understand?"

"You are wrong, Signora, very wrong, let me show you," Claretta said as she quickly opened a drawer and held a handful of letters. "These are from him, letters that are proof of his love for me!"

Rachel ignored the letters. Coldly she responded, "They don't interest me." But then Rachel moved toward Claretta, grabbed her by her arm, and began insulting her. "Do you take pride in being a whore? A kept whore!"

Rachel's hold on Claretta was broken by the ringing of the phone. It was Mussolini. Speaking first to Claretta and then to Rachel, he pleaded with the women to calm down and asked his wife to return to their home. The call seemed to calm Rachel. Stepping back from her threatening position, her voice now in measured tones, she said to Claretta, "I did not come here to threaten you. I have not even come here out of jealousy. Il Duce needs peace, and it is necessary to put an end to this scandal you have created by your presence here. If you really love him, you must give up seeing him."

Claretta now lost control of her emotions and buried her head in her hands as tears streamed down her face. Recovering, she burst out, "Il Duce cannot live without me. You may not want to hear that, but it is true, it is true!"

"It isn't true!" yelled back Rachel. "Let me get my husband on the phone again so that you can hear the truth from him directly." Picking up the phone, Rachel called her husband and pushed Claretta to the receiver where she heard Mussolini's voice.

"My wife is right, Claretta. It's time to end it." Mussolini's voice was clear and firm as he lied one more time to Claretta and to Rachel.

Claretta burst into tears again as Rachel turned to exit the villa. Turning around, she faced Claretta one more time and spoke loudly as she left through the door, "You'll get what you deserve, Signora!" Returning to her home, she went to the bathroom, locked the door, took a bottle of bleach from the cabinet, and poured a portion down her throat. A maid forced open the door, made Rachel vomit, and called a doctor. Hours after the doctor had treated her , she began to return to normal.

Mussolini was told what had happened and attempted to phone Rachel over and over to determine her condition. Finally he sent a note asking if Rachel wanted to see him. She responded that she did want him; her husband went to ask for forgiveness and stayed with her throughout the night. But as he sat by her side he could not erase his desire to once again be with Claretta.

In their small apartment in Rome Nikos and Mortis were growing restless and frustrated. How could they ever get their chance at Mussolini? No one seemed to know where he was; for weeks he had not been seen publicly, and news coverage of the Italian leader had been absent or exceptionally vague. Mortis spent the days walking the streets talking to average Italians, trying to gain a sense of where the Italian public was in regard to the war. The message he managed to send back to Greece via the merchant ships was that for Italians the war was perceived as going from bad to worse.

By mid-1943 Allied parachutists had landed in Sicily. The Allied attack from the south was beginning, not through Greece, as many had assumed, but through Sicily and would inevitably move into Italy itself. The mood of the Italians was very clear, Mortis reported: sue for an armistice. End the war. But their leader, Mussolini, thought otherwise. He would look again to his friend Hitler for help. He was confident the Führer would not fail him, and he excitedly responded to Hitler's call for the two men to meet.

When they met at an eighteenth-century castle near Feltre in Italy, Mussolini's reception by Hitler was not what he had expected. The German leader opened with a lengthy monologue, which concluded with his dissatisfaction with the conduct of the Italian army. Il Duce sat silently listening as Hitler complained that, "the organization of your army is manifestly bad. This war cannot go on indefinitely, and we can only win with additional manpower and will. Is the will and manpower there in Italy, Il Duce? I hope so, but it is not now evident." The Führer's statement was interrupted by a messenger who stepped into the room and handed the Italian leader a note.

"*Mein Führer*, I have been informed that the enemy has begun bombing Rome and various points on our railways." Mussolini put the note down and waited for Hitler's response.

Hitler ignored the message regarding the Allied bombing and immediately continued his criticism of the Italian inadequacy in waging the war. Finally he finished, shook Mussolini's hand as if he had not taken almost an hour criticizing the Italian, and left to return to Berlin.

After the Germans had departed, General Ambrosio, who had accompanied Mussolini to the meeting, urged him to speak up to Hitler. "You have to speak clearly to the Germans," he urged. "They want to use Italy as a rampart, and they don't give a damn if it ruins her. You are Hitler's friend. Make him understand our thinking. We ought to break loose and think of our own problems. Il Duce, we must face the facts, We must be out of this war within two weeks."

Mussolini at first seemed unsure of what to say. He saw that the potential for total collapse was near, yet the desire to maintain power consumed him. Finally, looking directly at Ambrosia, he said, almost defiantly, "Are we ready to erase twenty years of power at one stroke?"

Ambrosia did not respond, but in his mind it now became clear that Mussolini either did not comprehend what was happening to Italy or, more likely, appeared to be more concerned about himself than the nation. General Ambrosia left the meeting with Mussolini, returned to Rome, and said to the Secretary of State for Foreign Affairs, Giuseppe Bastianini, "He no longer can lead. He must go."

To address the concerns of the fascist leaders who now had questions about Mussolini's leadership, Il Duce was asked to convene the most important body of fascist Italy, the Grand Council, a group that had not met for more than five years. The meeting opened with the party secretary, Carlo Scorza, leading the assembled group in a loud welcome of *"Saluto al Duce!"* Mussolini spoke for almost two hours, explaining and rationalizing Italian setbacks in the war yet proclaiming confidently that Italy would remain in the war, Hitler would never surrender, and that victory would ultimately be theirs. All the council members did not agree with Mussolini's assessment, and a spirited debate followed, lasting for another nine hours. Finally, a motion was made to remove Mussolini from his position. Il Duce could not believe what he had just heard. "What motion is this?" he yelled at the group. "We are at war, Gentlemen, we cannot abandon the vision for Italy. We cannot abandon our German friends. We cannot capitulate. I have led this nation to greatness! To greatness! Is this the reward of my nation? I demand a roll call." Mussolini's face was red, his voice seemed hoarse, and, as he spoke, he unconsciously put his hand to his abdomen as if such a move could relieve the pain he was experiencing in his stomach.

The party secretary, responding to Mussolini's order, began to call the roll. Only a few of the council members were casting their vote for Mussolini. Moving from council member to council member, the party secretary finally came to Galeazzo Ciano, Mussolini's son-in-law. "And, Mr. Ciano," the secretary asked, "how will you cast your vote?"

Ciano hesitated, looked quickly at Mussolini, and then looked directly at the secretary. "My vote is for removal," he said as his eyes dropped now to stare at the floor.

Mussolini seemed frozen. He looked directly at his daughter's husband and slowly shook his head. He rose from his chair and left the room.

By the time Mussolini reached his home, it was 4:00 in the morning. Sleeping only a few hours, he awoke and informed his wife of what had transpired at the council meeting hours before. He was depressed, and Rachel could see it in his face and eyes. "I hope you had them all arrested," she said, angered at what these men who had risen to power because of her husband were now doing by turning against him. "Who do they think they are?" she asked defiantly. Her voice was now increasing in volume and intensity. "They are nobodies, you made them all, and now they do this? Why do you hesitate? Arrest them right away!"

Mussolini was in no mood to argue. Quietly he looked at Rachel, raised his hand as if to say "stop," and then said, "Not yet. I'll do it tomorrow morning."

Rachel was not satisfied. "Don't you understand?" she said. "Tomorrow morning will be too late. Grandi, Ciano, and the others will have already disappeared."

Mussolini had not fully comprehended the significance of the vote, which essentially had been one of no-confidence, and he believed that with a few changes, the critics would be silenced and his position would be secure. Returning to his office, he called Claretta to inform her about what had happened at the council and told her he would personally see the king about the matter. Claretta warned Mussolini not to go to the king, fearing that for some reason she could not explain, it would make things worse. "I just have a very bad feeling about it, Benito," she told her lover.

Mussolini ignored her warning as some sort of foolish woman's intuition. Pale and mentally exhausted, he sat down at a table in his office and quickly ate a dinner of soup, boiled vegetables, and water that had been brought to him. He had mentally decided that unless he heard something directly from the king himself, he would assume that the council vote had no bearing on his continuing leadership. His train of thought was suddenly interrupted by a telephone call. The message to Mussolini was that he was to appear before the king the following day at 5:00 p.m., and he was ordered to arrive in civilian, not military, clothes. The request, particularly the specification about his apparel, was strange, he thought. It was, most likely a sign of trouble, but he would soon find out.

"What should I wear?" Mussolini asked his wife after he had hung up the phone.

Rachel looked at her husband in disbelief. Was this man who had led Italy for more than twenty years really this naïve? Was he so blind to what was happening? "No!" she responded loudly to his question. "No! You shouldn't go to the king if he told you to wear civilian clothes. Don't you understand? He's ordering you to come like that in order to arrest you without drawing attention. Listen to me! Last night I told you that the meeting of the Grand Council would be dangerous for you, and you didn't listen to me. I also told you to have everyone arrested last night. Do you remember?"

Mussolini said nothing but turned around and walked into his bedroom to the closet and selected a blue linen suit to wear for his meeting with the king. After showing the suit to Rachel, he turned to walk back into the room and said to his wife, "But, Rachel, don't you understand that it's impossible for the king to turn against me? I have the military behind me. To turn against me would mean suicide for him." Mussolini entered the room and slowly closed the door.

The evening was still exceptionally warm when Mussolini arrived to speak to King Victor Emmanuel III. The two men shook hands and immediately the king asked Mussolini to tell him his version of the Grand Council's vote of no-confidence. The king, immaculately dressed in a gray marshall's uniform and pants with red stripes at the seams, listened carefully, and when Il Duce finished, spoke. "This is a serious matter and things cannot go on like this. Italy is

265

falling to pieces, and our soldiers do not want to fight anymore. It is even rumored that the Alpine Brigade, supposedly one of our very best, is on the verge of mutiny. And it has been reported to me, Benito, that our troops are singing unflattering songs about you. If you are not yet, you are close to being the most hated man in Italy."

Mussolini remained standing as the king spoke, unsure of what was to come next.

"The Grand Council vote," the king continued, "does reflect the country's feelings about your leadership and must be respected."

Even with the strong language the king had used, Mussolini was sure his position was necessary for Italy, but he felt, out of protocol, he should offer his resignation although he was convinced the king would never accept his offer. "In that case," Il Duce said, "I should tender my resignation."

The king lost no time in giving his reply. "I have to tell you that I unconditionally accept it and am appointing Marshall Pietro Badoglio as premier."

Mussolini was stunned. Unable to collect his thoughts immediately, he said nothing and slumped into a chair that was immediately to his left. The king then told his now resigned former premier that he would be placed under the king's personal protection because of the potential danger he faced from angry Italians. "I may be the only friend you have, Benito," Victor Emmanuel said, "so this is for your own good." The meeting lasted less than thirty minutes. The king then escorted Mussolini to the door, and Il Duce looked for the automobile in which he had arrived. It was not there.

CHAPTER FOURTEEN

OOKING AT THE SCENE BEFORE him, Mussolini saw policemen and an ambulance. A police captain approached him and said in a calm, measured manner, "It appears you are in danger, Il Duce. I have been ordered to ensure your safety."

Mussolini's face conveyed confusion. "I don't think I'm in danger, but if you insist, please take a seat in my automobile. Do you know where the driver parked it?"

The police captain directed Mussolini's attention to an ambulance that was parked a few feet away. Pointing to the vehicle, he said, "You'll be safer here." Four policemen then came forward, surrounded Mussolini, and directed him to enter the ambulance. Benito Mussolini was now officially under arrest.

The news of Mussolini's fall from power spread quickly, first through the Italian news media and then throughout Europe. Sitting in a small café, Nikos slowly shook his head as Mortis translated the news from the Italian newspaper. Placing his small espresso cup on the table, he leaned closer to Mortis and, speaking Greek, said to his friend, "It looks like our mission is over, Mortis. Maybe we don't have to kill Mussolini. Maybe the Italians will do it for us or at least exile him to some remote place where he can't do any harm."

The news reports had been silent about where Mussolini was being held or what plans the government had for him. "You may be right, Niko," Mortis replied. "Maybe he's dead already, but he probably is in some remote place until the Italians decide what to do with him. Niko, I think you should return to Greece, there's nothing you can do here now."

"And what about you?" Nikos asked. "Aren't we going back together? There's nothing left for you to do here either."

"I think I'll stay just a while longer. Maybe I can hear things, gather information, talk to people about what Mussolini being out of the picture means for Greece. I can't believe the Germans are just going to let this happen. If the Americans and the British get control of Italy, they are that much closer to moving directly on Germany from the south. And if German troops come into Italy to save it or conquer it, they will be spreading themselves even thinner than they already are. Something's got to give. They can't be fighting on the western front, on the east against the Russians, and against the Americans and the British on the south and still try to keep Greece under their control. This might be a break for Greece, Niko. If after a few weeks I feel I'm not being useful here, I'll join you back home."

"All right," responded Nikos, "I'll go back but be careful. Don't stay too long."

Mortis nodded his head. Both men shook hands, embraced, and Nikos prepared to leave on the Greek merchant ship that was returning to the port at Piraeus in Greece.

The Italy that Mortis stayed to observe was collapsing. Remarkably, those who had sworn allegiance to Mussolini were nowhere to be seen. There were no protests or demonstrations in response to his ouster from power. The king and his new premier, Badoglio, publicly announced their allegiance to Germany and their commitment to continue the war, but behind the scenes, they were attempting to seek an armistice with the Allies. Street mobs tore down any symbols of fascism, and armed force had to be used against demonstrators who were demanding an end to the war. The economy was also collapsing, and, as Mortis had predicted, the Germans were not about to allow Italy to leave the war.

In Germany, Hitler responded to Mussolini's fall

from power. Once again he convened a meeting of his key advisors. The men who gathered to meet with the Führer were shocked by their leader's appearance. His left arm and leg were trembling, and he tried to mask the condition by pressing his leg against some nearby object and by holding his left hand awkwardly with his right hand. When he stood and when he walked, he was hunched over, and his complexion seemed almost gray. The men he had summoned all felt that he now looked old, that pressure and exhaustion had caused him to age very quickly.

Foreign Minister Joachim von Ribbentrop, Joseph Goebbels, Admiral Karl Doenitz, and General Erwin Rommel were directed by Hitler to be seated at the small table that he kept in his office for meetings with a few people. Hitler seemed shocked by Mussolini's fall. "I'm afraid Il Duce is not a true revolutionary as I am," he stated. "He is so bound to his own Italian people that he lacks the broad qualities of a worldwide revolutionary and insurrectionist." Hitler told his assembled officers that he feared treason in the newly established Italian government. "Look at the situation with their General Geloso. He had a Jewish mistress and was working with British intelligence. Together, Geloso and the British set up a call girl service in Geloso's villa to get information from the Italian officers, which was then passed on to Allied forces."

Rommel, Goebbels, and Doenitz looked at each other. This was information they had not known. "*Mein Führer*," said Goebbels, "I'm not surprised. These Italians are not loyal to us nor are they fighters. Their first priorities are women, wine, and the latest fashions."

Hitler held his left arm more tightly with his right hand and temporarily the trembling seemed to stop. Rommel and Doenitz noticed Hitler's movements but acted as though they had not. "You may be right Joseph," Hitler responded, "but Mussolini and his fascists are the only friends we have. If this new government seeks peace with the Allies, it will cause us much trouble. We must free Mussolini and restore the fascists to power. Gentlemen, we need to control Italy and capture all that riffraff that have interrupted our plans."

"What do you propose, *Mein Führer*?" asked Rommel.

"We must send troops to Rome and capture the king and the new government," Hitler said forcefully.

"But not into the Vatican, I hope," pleaded Doenitz.

Hitler now raised his voice even louder and stood up from where he had been seated. He had no religious affiliation. His view of Christianity was that it was a religion of hypocrisy that had outlived its usefulness. He had technically been a Catholic, but his only connection now was when he had told Goebbels years before that the elaborately staged Nuremberg rallies should be modeled on the Catholic Mass. "I'll go right into the Vatican," Hitler said, "do you think the Vatican embarrasses me? We'll take that over right away. It's all the same to me. That rabble diplomatic corps is in there. We'll get that bunch of swine out of there. Later we can make apologies." Hitler stopped; taking a deep breath, he once again sat in the chair.

Goebbels, who most often echoed Hitler's ideas, now spoke up. "I'm not sure that will achieve our purpose, *Mein Führer*. The Vatican is not our target, the king and his government are. We don't need any additional worldwide negatives by targeting the Vatican."

Hitler, recognizing the logic of Goebbels caution, did not respond to his minister's comments. "We must free Mussolini," he repeated.

Ribbentrop seemed skeptical, but Goebbels nodded his head in agreement with Hitler's comment on rescuing Mussolini. "Perhaps," Ribbentrop offered, "we are overly optimistic about the ability of Il Duce to lead a fascist comeback. Even his own army could not save him from arrest."

Hitler, confident in his own insight and judgment, virtually dismissed Ribbentrop's reservations. "These are matters that a soldier cannot comprehend," Hitler replied. "Only a man with political insight can see clearly."

Rommel, too, had reservations. He cautioned that there were not yet enough German troops in Italy and advised that such an action be delayed. Hitler argued that they could not wait and that they must locate where Mussolini was being held and rescue him. After giving the order to rescue Mussolini, Hitler dismissed his officers and, referring to Il Duce, said, "Gentlemen, I am happy to live at a time when, apart from myself, there is another statesman living who will stand out in history as a great and unique figure."

In Berlin SS Captain Otto Skorzeny was drinking beer in a hotel when he received orders to report to Hitler's headquarters. Hitler gave him top-secret orders for a mission code named Operation Eiche (Oak). The order was to find and rescue Mussolini. For days after his meeting with his leader Skorzeny seemed frustrated. It was difficult to locate where Mussolini had been taken and apparently hidden. Finally German intelligence received information that the Italian leader was being held in a central Italian ski resort, the Campo Imperatore Hotel, a location some 6,300 feet above sea level. In a daring raid made up of German gliders and Nazi paratroopers, the Germans swept into the location and found Mussolini. Skorzeny looked at him and said, "Il Duce, the Führer has sent me to free you."

Mussolini reached over, hugged the German officer, and said to Skorzeny, "I knew my friend Adolf Hitler would not leave me in the lurch." Mussolini was placed in a German glider plane that flew him to safety and to a meeting with Adolf Hitler. Without having to fire one shot, Il Duce was again a free man.

Hitler was ecstatic at what Skorzeny had done. He picked up the phone, called his captain, and said, "Today you have carried out a mission that will go down in history."

When Mussolini and Hitler were finally reunited, the Führer was troubled by the appearance and emotional state of his Italian ally. Mussolini seemed to have lost all of his old energy and enthusiasm. He somehow looked smaller, as if he had shrunken, and his ambition seemed to be missing. He seemed to want nothing more than to go to his home. Hitler was disturbed by the fact that Mussolini appeared to have no desire to seek revenge against those who had stripped him of his position and power. To Hitler this was another sign of Il Duce's weakness and limitations. The Führer addressed Mussolini directly, "I don't doubt that you will agree with me in believing that one of the first acts of the new government will have to be to sentence to death the traitors of the Grand Council. I judge Count Ciano four times a traitor—a traitor to his country, a traitor to fascism, a traitor to the alliance with Germany, and a traitor to his family. If I were in your place, perhaps nothing would have stopped me from rendering justice with my own hands. But I advise you that the death sentence be carried out in Italy."

Mussolini, his body tired, his voice weak, seemed shocked by Hitler's demand. Looking directly at the Führer, he said, "But you are talking about the husband of the daughter whom I adore, the father of my grandchildren."

Hitler seemed cold and unmoved by Mussolini's family ties. "All the more reason Ciano merits punishment in that not only has he failed in fidelity toward his country but in fidelity to his family."

Through his wife, Galeazzo Ciano attempted to offer some explanation to Mussolini for why he had voted to remove him from power. Mussolini seemed receptive to his daughter Edda's arguments, but her mother was not. "I will spit in his face if he comes near me!" Rachel burst out. Personally confronting her son-in-law, Rachel harshly said, "If you didn't like the post Il Duce had assigned you, you could have resigned." Ciano attempted to interrupt, but Rachel went on, "Il Duce is not a piece of furniture that you can put in the sunroom when someone's tired of it. You have erred, and it may be that someday you will have to pay for this."

Mussolini now felt defeated, unable to cope with the fact that his son-in-law had betrayed him. His daughter was begging for forgiveness for her husband, and his wife continued her angry and hateful words toward Ciano. Hitler's demand that Ciano be executed and that Mussolini now head up a counter state to oppose the Badoglio state in the south of Italy added to his increasing anxiety.

Mussolini felt he had to talk to Hitler to express his reservations about returning to power in what would be a German puppet state in northern Italy. Once again he traveled to Germany and was received by Hitler. "I am, my friend," Mussolini said to Hitler as he sat in a chair, his body bent over, his eyes swollen from exhaustion, worry, and indecision, "I am a sick man, Adolf. I believe I may have cancer. I don't know how much time I really have."

Hitler stood, paced the floor for a full two minutes, turned to Mussolini, and pointed his finger directly at him. "You must and will head this new Italian government," he said in a brutal, unsympathetic tone. "Northern Italy will have to meet the fate of Poland if you don't accept. And as far as Ciano, he will not be handed over to the Italians, he will be hanged here in Germany." Mussolini, unable to change Hitler's mind, was immediately established as the head of the new fascist state, the Italian Socialist Republic of Salo, the name taken from a small town on the banks of Lake Garda.

Galeazzo Ciano had attempted to come to Germany for protection after Hitler had rescued Mussolini. Hitler, who had wanted Ciano punished and hanged in Germany, changed his mind and decided that the punishment should be done by those he had betrayed and the death sentence carried out in Italy. Ciano was put on a German plane and flown to Verona, Italy, where he was scheduled to stand trial along with the other so-called "conspirators and traitors to fascism."

In Rome Mortis tried to make sense of the quick turn of events he was hearing reported on the Italian media. He conveyed to his British intelligence contacts that he believed that Mussolini's new role would not last long. The Italian people and the condition of the Italian economy would not, he reported, allow Il Duce to regain full power or to last long in whatever new position he now held. German troops, Mortis reported, were entering Italy in large numbers, and he said he believed the Nazis would now occupy more areas in Greece that had previously been controlled by the Italians. He felt that it was only a matter of time before Italy would either seek a peace or be defeated by Allied forces. Mortis said that he would try to send reports from wherever the Ciano trial was to be held. Within days Mortis learned that the trial was to be held in Verona.

From the day of his arrest Ciano understood what fate awaited him. In his mind he told himself that he would be aggressive toward those who now held him, tell the judges what he thought of them, and shout out that he believed the entire trial to be a fraud and a sham. One of his fellow prisoners, who had been charged along with him with conspiracy and treason, attempted to calm him down. "Do you really have it in your head to put us all in danger?" he pleaded.

Ciano would not budge. "You must understand," he replied, "that this trial is nothing but a tragic clown show. Our fate already has been decided elsewhere, and no one, I say no one of us, will succeed in saving himself. Is it possible that after so many years you haven't gotten to know that big coward Mussolini?"

During the trial Ciano's defiant tone seemed to become tempered as he tried to explain and rationalize his vote to oust Mussolini from power during the meeting of the Grand Council. Mortis had managed to join those who were spectators at the trial and observed Ciano unsuccessfully attempt to explain away what had been deemed the actions of a traitor. He was silently amused when, after Ciano had tried to give his side of the story, other spectators at the trial began screaming, "To death, Traitor! It's not the truth." At the trial's end Ciano's original prediction proved correct. The vote to find Ciano guilty was unanimous. Only one of the alleged conspirators was spared the penalty of death, and he was sentenced to thirty years in prison. Ciano responded with an outburst of anger to the judge's announcement that he was to be executed. The other condemned men sat silently as the judge announced their fate.

Ciano's death sentence placed Mussolini in a position he wished to avoid but could not. Il Duce's wife, Rachel, who had never liked Ciano, showed no sympathy for her son-in-law since she viewed him as one who had betrayed her husband. Hitler, who had always believed Ciano was anti-German and the main reason for the Italian involvement and embarrassment in invading Greece, also showed little sympathy for Mussolini's family dilemma. In Hitler's view Ciano was a traitor not only to Mussolini but also to fascism itself. The Italian leader was torn. To pardon Ciano and save him from the penalty of death would, in his mind, convey to Hitler weakness and an inability to deal appropriately with anyone who dared oppose him or attempted to undermine his fascist ideology. But to not spare Ciano would mean sending his own son-in-law, his daughter's husband, his grandchildren's father, to his death. Hitler, while making his position clear to Mussolini, attempted to remove himself from the situation, placing it squarely on Mussolini. "This matter is out of our hands," the Führer said to Joseph Goebbels. "It is a matter for Mussolini and the Italians."

Mussolini was unable to sleep, his stomach ulcers once again giving him trouble. His daughter Edda went to see her father to plead her case for her husband's life. Edda, while being the favorite of her father, had never been afraid of him or shy about defying his wishes. There was no smile on her face as she walked briskly into her father's office where he had been reviewing correspondence from Italian business people who were becoming increasingly concerned about the declining prospects of an Axis victory in the war.

"Father, we must talk," Edda said, as she moved to seat herself in the chair that was placed next to a large conference table where Il Duce had spread out the correspondence from a dozen or more of the businessmen. "What is all this about there being difficulties in getting Galeazzo out? With just several determined men, I myself could see to it that he escaped and with very little trouble." Her voice began to rise in pitch. "Father, do you hear me? Why can't you get him out?"

Mussolini seemed unable to provide an answer. He hesitated. Then attempting to calm his daughter down he said, "Edda, it is not as simple as you think. He is now also guarded by German SS troops. There are many people in our country who have followed me who view his actions as those of a traitor to our cause."

"Traitor?!" screamed Edda. "He is my husband, do you forget that? He is the father of my children, your grandchildren. What are you talking about? Are you blinded by your position? Are you some weakling afraid of your so-called friend, Hitler? This is your family, Father. Your family! Who will be the traitor if you allow him to be killed? You will have committed a greater treason, the one God Himself cannot forgive, you will have betrayed your own blood." Edda was now standing, nervously pacing back and forth in the room, slamming her hand on the table as she spoke.

"Edda," her father interrupted, "this has all gone too far. Galeazzo's words and actions are too public. It is no longer in my power to separate Galeazzo's fate from that of the other accused of the same charges as he has been."

Edda now lost any semblance of control and composure. Screaming at her father, she walked directly in front of him and pointed her finger in his face. "You are all mad! You are all mad! The war is lost, and it is useless to harbor illusions. The Germans will resist for a few more months but not longer. I wished they would win, but now there is nothing more to be done. Do you understand? Do you?" She began to cry, and tears came to her father's eyes as well.

Edda now realized she would get no help from her father. She now stood face to face with the man she believed was either so weak or so consumed with his own situation that he was willing to allow his daughter's husband to be killed. Screaming again as she prepared to leave the room, she now severed any ties of respect, love, or blood with her father. "Between us it is finished! Finished forever! And if you knelt before me dying of thirst and asked me for a glass of water, I would throw it on the ground before your eyes." Uncontrollably weeping, she ran out of the room. Her father slumped into his chair contemplating what he wanted to do but could not do. He had lost almost all his power, he was on the verge of losing the war, and now he had lost his beloved daughter. Yet, for some reason he himself could not fully comprehend, he could not change course. He picked up the phone, called the leader of the tribunal that was to carry out the death sentences of those who, along with Ciano, had been accused of treason, and said to him, "My wish is that the tribunal render justice without favor to anyone."

In prison, waiting for his sentence to be carried out, Ciano attempted to present a posture of defiance and arrogance to his fellow prisoners. "This trial is a sham," he repeated to the others. "This trial was nothing but a tragic clown show, "he continuously repeated. "Our fate was not decided here in Italy; it was decided in Germany. And that coward Mussolini will do nothing." There were five others besides Ciano who were determined to be traitors to Mussolini and to fascism and were sentenced to die: Emilio de Bono, Carlo Parachi, Tullio Cianetti, Luciano Gottardi, and Giovani Marinelli. All of them found it difficult to believe that Ciano's own father-in-law, Benito Mussolini, would not at the eleventh hour intervene to at least save him from death.

The six men, three of them puffing cigarettes some of which had burned down to tobacco stubs, sat on hard benches. "Galeazzo," said Tullio Cianetti, "I can't believe Il Duce will let this happen, especially to you. And, my friend, with your good words, hopefully we will all be out of here alive."

"Tullio," Ciano said as his hands gestured a motion conveying the message, don't you understand? "It won't happen. Mussolini is under the influence of that circle of whores and pimps that for some years has plagued Italian political life and brought the country to the brink of abyss. I personally accept calmly what is to be my infamous destiny. I suggest all of you do the same."

Within days the time came. A priest came to Ciano's cell to give him his final communion and offer prayers. Ciano looked at the priest, thanked him for coming, and said to him, "I believe they will shoot us in the back to signify that we are traitors."

The priest did not respond. Making the sign of the cross over Ciano's head, he began to leave the cell, saying as he departed, "May God save your soul, my son."

The next morning the six men were placed in a police van and driven to a location outside of Verona. Old folding chairs were placed on the ground, each next to the other. Twenty individuals were on hand to witness the event. Ciano asked to be able to face the firing squad, but his request was refused. The men were tied to their chairs, and all but Ciano were blindfolded. He had refused the blindfold. The charges against the men were read out loud, and before the order to fire was given, two of the accused yelled out, "Long live Duce, Long live Italy." As the riflemen began firing, Ciano attempted to turn his chair, so that he could face his executioners. Chairs toppled to the ground as bullets riddled the bodies of the six men. Ciano, in his chair, fell to the ground but appeared to not yet be dead. One of the executioners walked over to the strewn bodies to see if indeed they were dead. Seeing that Ciano appeared to still be alive, he fired a final bullet into his head. German SS troops were present to observe the executions and to report back to Hitler that the sentences had been carried out. Cameras filmed the execution so that the Italian public would also have no doubt that justice had been served.

The day of the execution Mussolini deliberately was absent from public view, so that no one could seek a last minute pardon for any of the six men. Public reports were that Il Duce was sick, that he had a fever and insomnia. When Mussolini finally received the report that the executions had taken place, he, at first in the presence of others, conveyed an attitude of indifference. Later, when everyone had left the room, he sat in a chair, dropped his head into his two hands, and burst into tears. When he later reported to Rachel, he told her, "From that morning, I have begun to die."

CHAPTER FIFTEEN

O N SEPTEMBER 8, 1943, GEN-eral Dwight D. Eisenhower was prepar-ing for an attack on the Italian mainland when he sent a message that changed the direction of the war. "The Italian government has surrendered its forces unconditionally," Eisenhower said. "Hostilities between the armed forces of the United Nations and those of Italy terminate at once."

While many, including the citizens of Italy, were pleased with the news, the exit of Italy from the war was met with mixed reactions in Greece. Greeks were happy that one of their attackers and occupiers was no longer to be on their streets and in their villages, but the Italians had not been a universally hated presence. They had killed some Greeks, to be sure, but they had not engaged in the brutal, indiscrimi-nate, wholesale butchery and citizen executions that had become common with the Nazis in Greece. And now that the Italians would be gone, it meant that the Germans would be occupying and controlling the entire country. For Mortis, the Italian surrender meant that his role in Italy was over. He knew that somewhere and somehow Hitler and the Germans were hiding and protecting Mussolini. Il Duce was no longer a key player, he now presented no threat to anyone, and Mortis believed that inevitably he would be captured or found dead somewhere. Mortis packed his meager belongings, boarded the Greek merchant ship, and headed back to Greece to once again join the resistance.

In Greece, the two major resistance groups headed by Aris Velouchiotis and Napoleon Zervas were taking different paths. Zervas continued to be supported by Churchill and the British who had two key goals: maintain British influence in Greece and the Mediterranean and get the Nazis and Communist sympathizers out of Greece. Zervas was becoming more cautious in his actions against the Germans, concerned that the brutal Nazi reprisals were doing more harm to Greece than the resistance actions were hurting the Germans. In his assessment of the war's events outside of Greece, Zervas saw a likely German defeat, which, unless something were done with British help, would most likely leave Greece in the hands of the Velouchiotis group whom he viewed as Communists.

For Napoleon Zervas the enemy increasingly became not so much the Nazis but his fellow Greeks who wanted to make the country a Communist state.

Velouchiotis saw a brighter future. With the Italians gone and the Allies closing in on all sides on the Germans, he, too, saw an ultimate Nazi defeat evolving. For Velouchiotis, the conflict increasingly became one of two separate fronts. He ordered his guerrilla fighters to not let up but increase their sabotage and assassination efforts against the Germans. However, he told them to not hesitate to use killing force against any fellow Greeks who stood in the way of his agenda, whether they be Nazi collaborators or Greeks who opposed his Communist visions. As Velouchiotis assessed conditions in the country, he was confident that a postwar Greece looked as if it could very well be a Communist Greece.

The surrender of Italy affected Nikos' bother, Vasili, and Nikos' former friend and classmate. Klaus Schreiber. Even though they were allied with the two opposing resistance groups, Nikos and Vasili made it a point to get together every five or six weeks to talk and ask about each other's well-being. They would often meet at their uncle's house in Athens, a small, but comfortable residence about twenty minutes by car from the center of the city.

The men's aunt, Penelope, had prepared a dinner of chicken cooked in a tomato sauce, salad, olives, bread, wine, and fruit for dessert. After she and her husband had joined the two brothers for dinner, they left the room so the brothers could speak privately. Nikos finished drinking his wine, took the napkin to wipe his mouth, and began speaking to Vasili.

"I'm disappointed in Zervas," Nikos began. "He seems too cautious, looking to the British all the time. Most of the things I've been able to do against the Germans I've really done on my own. I'm pretty sure he doesn't know anything about my actions."

"I hear he's not sure who the enemy really is, Niko," added Vasili, "if it's the Nazis or if it's my group."

"That's pretty much true," responded Nikos, "and I think he's leaning more toward the idea that your man Velouchiotis is more of a long-term threat."

"What about you, Niko, do you feel the same way?"

Nikos was in no mood to begin a long philosophical debate with his brother about his negative feelings about a potential Communist Greece. "You know what I think, Vasili, let's not go over that topic again. What I do know is that I'm going to continue the fight against the Germans whether with Zervas or not."

"You mean, go it alone?" asked Vasili.

"Well, I could. In some ways it's safer that way. No one to mess up plans, no witnesses to what I might do. But I hear there may be another option."

"Like what? With whom?" Vasili seemed curious.

"There's a special force of Greek-American volunteers who have been specially trained to help liberate Greece. They are scheduled to come here within two or three weeks. I'm going to volunteer to operate with them. I hear they are looking to get help from your group, so you could volunteer, too, and we would have a chance to be together in this fight, on the same side for a change."

Vasili thought about what Nikos had just said. He reached for a cigarette, lit one, and finally said, "That sounds interesting. I didn't know about such an American effort. You know, Niko, I just might join you. I've been thinking a lot lately, about what I'm doing and what that purpose is. My head is OK with the fact that we kill these German monsters, I can handle that easyily. But I do have trouble sleeping at night when I see the brutality some of my group are inflicting on fellow Greeks. And we are doing some good things for the country right now, but I do have doubts about working toward a Communist Greece."

The Velouchiotis *andartes* had established areas of the rural countryside that they labeled, "Free Greece." These areas had virtually no German presence. People's councils and courts were set up to create local citizen participation and governance. And attempts were being made to radically change the role of women in Greek society. Most village women were either poorly educated or not educated at all. Their assigned role was to present a dowry to a prospective husband, marry, have children, work in the fields, manage the home, and be as publicly invisible as possible. Velouchiotis' ELAS guerillas passed out pamphlets and other literature advocating a new role for these "modern" women who were already active partners in the resistance movement where they were serving as nurses and as key players in acquiring and distributing supplies, as well as fighting side by side with men, using the same weapons of war to kill the Nazis invaders. In addition to their program for a new role and status for women, the ELAS fighters were also attracting young people through their calls for increased education and larger opportunities for the young to use their talents through new economic opportunities. It was through a vision of a new Greek society that the Velouchiotis guerillas were gaining new converts and followers, while Zervas' group seemed only to advocate a return to monarchy with no agenda for social change.

Vasili embraced all these initiatives; they were needed, he believed, and they were good for Greece. But something bothered him about all this turning into a Communist Greece. It all sounded so good in theory, but he had doubts about its actually being able to work. He had come to the conclusion that his brother Nikos had been right when, at the beginning, he had warned him about joining with Velouchiotis. The Greeks have always been, and always will be, individualists, Nikos had said, and true Communism will never be accepted or work in Greece. And Vasili found it more difficult each day to witness the brutal nature of Velouchiotis as he attacked fellow Greeks. It was now even more pronounced since the Nazis had organized what they called "Security Battalions" made up of Greeks who followed Nazi orders and were especially hostile to fellow Greeks connected in any way to Communist theory, ideology, or actions. These Security Battalions also showed few restraints in regard to killing other Greeks who appeared to be Communists or Communist sympathizers. A climate was developing in which Greeks on one side or the other had no reservations about brutalizing or killing other Greeks. Unless something intervened to change things, Vasili thought, the country's long-range problem would probably not be the Nazis. It would be the Greeks themselves in a civil war. Such thoughts had troubled Vasili for months, so now when his brother offered the possibility of another avenue, by joining with this new unit of special Greek-American forces, he was receptive. "Niko," he said, "let me know when these Americans come. I want to join you."

While Nikos and Vasili were assessing their current situations and what they could do, Klaus Schreiber was dealing with his own troubling thoughts. For the most part, he had been a loyal soldier, obedient to the orders of his commanding officer. He had participated in the raids on villages, the burning of homes, and even the execution of Greeks who had been deemed collaborators with the guerrilla resistance forces. He had, of course, not always followed orders precisely, such as when he had fired his shots into the ground rather than at the men and boys at the mass execution in Kalavryta. But he had now reached a point where he could kill no more. He was a soldier. but not a murderer. He simply wanted to study and teach Greek language, history, and culture. He was not, in his mind, an enemy of these people; he was an admirer of them, and now he was caught in in what he concluded was a useless, losing enterprise. Klaus' earlier admiration for the views of Adolf Hitler were also diminishing in importance in his mind. Why should this war continue, he asked himself? Why should he kill or be killed? But what were his options? Refuse to follow orders? That was a certain death sentence. Desert to the guerrillas? That was another certain death sentence either from his own Germans or, most likely, from the guerrillas who would probably not believe his sudden change of allegiance. He now was hoping for a German defeat or peace treaty, which would bring him home as quickly as possible. It was probably unlikely, he thought, that he could go back to the university in Thessaloniki. He would have to start over, probably in Germany if anything was left after the Americans or Russians were finished bombing the country or invading it. And he also had a powerful desire to somehow connect with Nikos and Mortis, who had been friends, almost brothers. Where were they now, he asked himself? He felt that somehow, someway, he would try to seek them out before he left Greece. Perhaps they could, at least for a while, forget the horror of this war. He didn't know if he could ever find them, but he vowed to himself that he would try.

As they awaited the arrival of the Greek-American special forces unit, Nikos and Vasili gradually disengaged themselves from the two groups with whom they had been allied. Vasili sought to not be involved in shooting actions against the Germans but rather devoted his time to working with the village councils and the newly created village court systems in various parts "Free Greece." Nikos, with Zervas' knowledge, embarked on a number of solo missions. Neither seeking nor receiving approval from Zervas, Nikos moved from one location to another. Acting alone, he would disguise himself as a mechanic and disable German convoy trucks. At other times he would assume the identity of a gas station attendant and fill German cars and trucks with tainted gasoline, which would disable the vehicles after five or ten miles of driving. Working with bakers and butchers, he poisoned food delivered to Nazi troops so that severe cases of stomach cramps and diarrhea were certain outcomes. But most of all Nikos used his incredible skill as a sharpshooter to disable vehicles and assassinate German soldiers both in rural locations and again in the busy streets of Athens. Positioning himself at strategic locations, he seldom missed his targets, killing ten Nazi soldiers in a five- to seven-day period. So skillful was he with his rifle and with his precautions that no trace or clue was ever traced back to Nikos or to his family. In the Nazi headquarters in Athens this unidentified assassin was given the code name "the Rifle," and orders were given to track him down and execute him. But Nikos left no clues, and day after day continued with his deadly actions.

Zervas hoped somehow to stop the Nazi wholesale killings of innocent people and decided to explore ways to halt the carnage. His plan was simple, he told his men, "If we stop our attacks on the Germans, they will hopefully stop destroying our villages and killing our people. Time is on our side. If the war continues as it is going now, the Russians and Americans will soon close in on Germany. The Germans must then surrender, and their troops will leave our land. We need patience, not more killing of Greeks." Zervas spent the night composing a detailed document outlining his proposal and setting down rules by which all sides could operate. He asked Mortis to act as courier of the document to the Nazi regional commander who had established headquarters in the town of Tripoli in central Greece.

Giving the document to Mortis, Zervas instructed him to deliver it to the German officer and hopefully receive a reply that he could bring back to the Zervas camp. Mortis, having no other means of transportation, rode to Tripoli by horseback. The German headquarters was located in what had been the local municipal office; Mortis nervously approached the building and was stopped by the Nazi armed guard. Speaking in German, which Mortis barely understood, the guard said, "What business do you have here?"

Mortis held up the envelope with Zervas' document and attempted to convey his message in his limited and flawed knowledge of the German language. "I come here as a peaceful representative of Colonel Napoleon Zervas, the leader of the EDES organization. I have been instructed to present this document to your commanding officer."

The guard, only partially understanding what Mortis had said, motioned him to step forward. As Mortis came forward, the guard searched him for any weapons or explosives. "Wait here," the guard ordered as he motioned to his colleague guard to stand with Mortis as he entered the building to tell the commander of Mortis' arrival. Within minutes the guard returned from the building and motioned Mortis to enter.

Entering the office, he saw General Frederick Mueller sitting behind his desk. He handed the general the document and said, "General, I have been instructed to bring this communication from Napoleon Zervas, the leader of the EDES group, to you for your consideration and reply. With your permission, General, I will wait for your reply so that I might convey it back to Colonel Zervas."

Mueller accepted the envelope from Mortis and instructed him to be seated as he opened the envelope and began reading the contents. Reading the document slowly, he finished, put the paper on his desk and calmly said to Mortis, "Surely, this is some kind of joke, isn't it?"

Mortis did not know how to react at first but then said, "Sir, this is not a joke, Colonel Zervas is serious about his proposal so that the bloodshed and killing can stop."

"My answer Mr.? Mr.? what is your name?"

"Mortis, sir, Mortis."

"Mortis?" questioned Mueller again. "What kind of name is that? Are you a Greek?"

"Yes General, I am."

"Well, give me your full name, a name I can identify as Greek," said the general.

"My full name is Mordecai, General."

"Mordecai?" Mueller had a quizzical look on his face. "That's not very Greek. What is your full name?"

"Mordecai ben Nathan, General."

Mueller now immediately understood who the man before him was. "You are a Jew. Yes?"

"Yes, I am, General, a Greek Jew."

"I see," said Mueller calmly.

What Mortis did not know was that General Frederick Mueller had ordered numerous attacks on Greek villages, insisting on killing dozens of Greeks for any remote connection in deed or thought to any resistance group. He had ordered the torching of houses with gasoline in village after village whether or not any persons were in those houses. He had no reservations about killing women and children and had on numerous occasions taken particular satisfaction in identifying Jews and placing them on trucks that had the gas chambers as their destination.

Mueller tapped his pen on his desk as he completed his discussion with Mortis. "Mr. ben Nathan, I thank you for coming. If you will step outside for a moment, I will compose a reply to Colonel Zervas that you can return to him. As you leave, please ask the guard outside the door to please come in."

"Yes, General," said Mortis," I will be outside and await your reply. Thank you for seeing me."

"Thank you as well," said Mueller.

Leaving the room, Mortis motioned to the guard

that the general wished to see him. The guard entered the general's office, stood stiffly at attention, and saluted. The guard was a young man, just recently having celebrated his twentieth birthday.

'What is your name, soldier?" asked Mueller.

"Hohenberg, sir, Martin Hohenberg."

"Well, Mr. Hohenberg, I am giving you an order. You are to walk with the man who just left my office away from this building and execute him. He is one of the Jewish-Greek resistance fighters who will want to kill you and me unless we act first. Shoot him in the head, be sure he is dead. Pin a yellow star on his shirt with his name, which I will give you. Then dump his body in the main square in this city after dark. By morning the body will be found, and Mr. Zervas will have his answer to his proposal. You are dismissed, Mr. Hohenberg." The young soldier saluted again, left the office, and motioned Mortis to follow him.

The next morning the citizens of Tripoli awoke, and a large crowd gathered as Mortis' lifeless body lay in the middle of the town center, a yellow Star of David with his name written on it pinned to his bloodied shirt. Zervas had his answer, and not long after, through the informal communication channels that carried news from village to village, both Nikos and Vasili had received the news. Nikos was shocked and for hours he simply stared at whatever was placed before him. His best friend was gone in this senseless, barbaric thing called modern war. And he was also angry, convincing himself that the Germans would pay heavily for what they had done. He was eager to join the Greek-Americans who were coming now.

In 1942 the United States had created the Office of Strategic Services, the focus of which was clandestine operations. The agency had now formed a specialized American unit to operate against the Nazis in Greece. The unit consisted of about 200 enlisted men and officers who were all Americans of Greek descent and were familiar with the language and culture of the nation of their fathers and grandfathers. All the men were volunteers who had received special training in the mountains of Colorado so as to simulate as best as possible the environment in which they would have to operate in the rugged mountains of Greece. The mission was to aid guerrilla and British forces in liberating Greece from Nazi occupation. The commander of the American unit was Stan Peterson, whose baptized name was Stellios Petropoulos. It was with this American presence that Nikos and Vasili sought to connect.

Within days of the arrival of the Greek-Americans, Nikos and Vasili had made contact with Lieutenant Peterson and had set a time and place to meet. Peterson had made inquiries about both men and had received positive answers. The Americans were eager to have some native Greek connections of men who knew not only the geography of the nation but also where the enemy was located, what resistance actions had been taken against them, and what strategies had been employed in the past. The meeting was set for noon at a seaside cafe in the city of Nafplio.

Nikos and Vasili arrived in Nafplio, and approached the man in the American army uniform sitting alone at the designated cafe. Since Peterson, the Greek-American, could speak and understand Greek, they all spoke in the native language.

"Lieutenant," said Nikos, "just so you know, it's becoming harder and harder when you look at any Greek here to determine who they are and what side they are on. The Velouchiotis and Zervas guerrillas are spending as much time watching out for fellow Greeks as they are the Nazis. And these new Security Battalions that are made up of Greeks, which the Nazis have created as anti-Communist forces, are also killing fellow Greeks."

Peterson reached for some additional sugar for his coffee, then looked up at his new acquaintances. "I have been briefed about all the Greek on Greek conflicts and violence, Gentlemen. While I'm sure it's important, that's not why we are here. Our mission is to take out Nazi positions and personnel. Period. We cannot, and will not, get involved in issues that are internal to Greece."

"We understand, Lieutenant," said Vasili, "but we think for your own good and for the smooth operation of your mission you should at least be aware of these divisions and the growing conflict between them."

"And I appreciate that," responded Peterson, "so let's get on to how you both can work with us. I have heard about your skill with the rifle as a sniper, Niko, but what do you bring to our mission, Vasili?"

"I'm pretty good with explosives and various booby-traps, lieutenant. There are a number of decimated structures and dead Germans who would, if they could speak, vouch for my work. Niko shoots them down, I blow them up." Vasili smiled. It was a look of satisfaction and accomplishment.

"Well, good," said Peterson. "I think we can all work together very well. Maybe we old country and new country Greeks can really cooperate. Maybe we can start a new trend among Greeks everywhere."

Peterson decided that events outside of Greece would shape their approaches within the country. As American forces worked their way up the Italian geographic "boot," other Allied forces struck from the west on the beaches of Normandy on D-Day, and Russian forces in the east moved into the Balkans, Peterson believed the Germans would begin moving out of Greece so as not to be trapped there by the Soviets centered in the Balkans. And these Germans would seek to exit Greece by truck and rail; for Peterson and his fellow Americans and his newly found Greek native fighters these would be prime targets.

Peterson along with twenty others in his unit, including Nikos and Vasili, set out on their mission. Vasili's task was to strategically place bombs on the railroad tracks, and Nikos' assignment was to kill any Germans who either tried to neutralize the bombs or escape from the train once the explosives had been detonated. Besides the placed bombs, the Americans were armed with bazookas, automatic rifles, submachine guns, and hand grenades. As the trains slowed down to switch tracks, the signal was given, and the explosives were activated. Huge sounds filled the air as the explosions began and fire consumed the cars of the train. When they could, German soldiers from the train sought to escape the inferno, but when one was fortunate enough to leave the train, his luck ran out as Nikos and the other American sharpshooters dropped the Nazi soldiers to the ground with a barrage of bullets.

For Nikos and Vasili the cooperation with the unique unit of Greek-American soldiers filled the void both had experienced in their respective guerrilla camps. Nikos admired the planning, skill, and preparation of the Americans who could hit the Germans and not be concerned about German retaliation against Greek villages. And Vasili felt relaxed, knowing that he could focus on the Nazis and not fellow Greeks as Velouchiotis increasingly was doing. Both brothers continued to work with the Americans for the duration of their stay in Greece. The unit operated for the next four months and succeeded in carrying out numerous sabotage actions against German train and truck convoys. Only one American was killed during the operation, and seven were wounded. An unofficial report cited 675 Germans killed by the Greek-American unit in conjunction with their native Greek partners.

While efforts against the Germans were successful, the conflict in Greece was taking a turn that both Nikos and his brother had feared would happen. Gradually, who was defined as the enemy was changing. When the news had reached Athens earlier that Italy had surrendered, Athenians celebrated in the streets when Nazi soldiers were not present. They were even joined by Italian soldiers who were selling their guns and equipment to the Greek resistance fighters. Many of the Italian soldiers who had been stationed in the Greek mountains deserted to work with the Greek resistance against the Germans. The D-Day invasion and the Soviet advance into the Balkans signaled to most Greeks that it was now only a matter of months or even possibly weeks before the Germans would be defeated. The most potent enemy Greeks were beginning to see were other Greeks.

Open conflict was now occurring between the Velou-chiotis forces, who were assumed by virtually every-one to be anti-monarchist and pro-Communist, and the Zervas group, allied with the British who were pro-monarchist and strongly anti-Communist.

The prospect of a Communist Greece was a scenario Winston Churchill and the British felt they could not allow to happen since a Soviet control of Greece would mean a Soviet control of the entire eastern Mediterranean and control of the gateway to the Middle East.

Churchill decided to act. His plan was to personally go to Moscow, meet with Joseph Stalin, and see what could be done to divert the Soviet dictator's obvious desire to control the entire Balkans, including Greece. President Franklin Roosevelt, sitting in Washington, was not invited but was informed that the U.S. could have a representative at the meeting. Roosevelt, his political instincts now set on high alert, was worried about what kind of deal Churchill might make with Stalin.

Churchill and Stalin had met once before when the British leader had first visited Moscow two years earlier. At that time Stalin had been both personally charming and openly insulting toward Churchill, and both men had functioned under the influence of a steady consumption of food and even more liquor. For this second meeting Churchill's agenda was clear: a decision had to be made regarding who, among their two nations, would control what in a postwar era. Meeting in the Kremlin, Churchill took the initiative, saying, "Let us settle our affairs in the Balkans." Stalin, who, of course, knew that his troops had already penetrated deeply into the region, was not surprised.

"Absolutely," replied Stalin, "let's talk about it."

The discussion went on for hours as a steady supply of alcohol filled the glasses of the two men. The talks continued into the early hours of the following day. Finally, Churchill reached for a piece of paper, took a pen from his pocket, and began to write numbers on the paper. The numbers reflected what Churchill proposed should be the amount of influence the two nations should have in the liberated areas. Churchill wrote: Rumania, 90 percent for Russia, 10 percent for Britain; Greece, 90 percent for Britain, 10 percent for Russia; Bulgaria, 75 percent for Russia, 25 percent for Britain; Yugoslavia and Hungry, a 50-50 split for both countries. Churchill took the scrap of paper and slid it across the table to Stalin. The Russian picked the paper up, studied it, and reached for a blue pencil and made a large check mark on it signaling his approval, and slid the paper back across the table to Churchill. Churchill looked at the check mark on the paper, nodded approval, and then said, "Might it not be thought rather cynical if it seemed we had disposed of these issues, so fateful to millions of people, in such an offhand manner? Let us burn the paper."

Listening to Churchill, Stalin appeared unmoved by any concerns of what others might think about how two men had decided the fate of countries and people by passing a piece of scrap paper between them. At Stalingrad and now in the Balkans Soviet troops had prevailed, and Stalin was determined to have the spoils of war, no matter what the rest of the world might think. Responding to Churchill's suggestion that they burn the piece of paper, Stalin smiled and said, "No, you keep it." In matter of hours both men had secured what they wanted. Churchill succeeded in receiving a guarantee that Russia would not intervene or support the Greek Communists, and Stalin left with assurances that Great Britain would not seek to stop the Soviet domination of other Balkan nations.

The Churchill-Stalin plans for the post-war world were still only plans. There was still fighting and killing on numerous European fronts, and all of the factions of the exiled Greek government and the resistance groups knew nothing about the Soviet-British agreement. Hitler had suffered staggering losses in his plan to invade Russia. The Germans had lost more than 250,000 soldiers before the Nazis surrendered to the Soviet army in Stalingrad. The Allied invasion in Sicily and Italy, the massive action of the Allies on D-Day, and the steady movement of Soviet troops into Eastern Europe were placing Hitler in a desperate position.

His troubles continued to mount not only from his external enemies but also from those within Germany. He had barely and luckily escaped an attempt on his life, and he continuously received reports of other plots to assassinate him. Increasingly, he stayed in the Reich Chancellery, only occasionally venturing out to speak publicly or to review troops. The trembling in his hand and leg was becoming worse, and his efforts to try to hide the trembling no longer were working. The dinner parties that had been characterized by jovial conversation and the viewing and discussing of the latest movies now ceased. He deliberately refused to invite military men to dine with him, almost fearful that the only reports and news they would bring would be bad news. Hitler's dinner companions now were his secretaries, periodically his valet and chauffer, and his mistress Eva Braun.

The Führer found it increasingly difficult to sleep and began, for the first time in a serious way, to contemplate what he would do if Germany would have to surrender or if he himself was actually captured. He vowed to himself that he would never, in his lifetime, allow those things to happen. Once again he summoned Goebbels and Goering to assess the increasingly bleak situation. The call to Goering had caught him by surprise, and the urgency of the meeting with the Führer left him little time to dress in his full military attire. He came to the meeting in colorful plaid pants and a somewhat gaudy bright orange shirt. "I'm sorry, *Mein Führer*," he said as he entered Hitler's study. "I wanted to come as quickly as I could, given the important tone of the message I received, and thus had little time to dress more formally."

Goebbels who had arrived minutes earlier dressed in full military attire did his best to say nothing. He suppressed a smile as Goering entered the room.

Hitler seemed unfazed by Goering's apparel. He looked tired; obviously he had not slept well, thought Goering as he greeted his leader. Even Goebbels, who had more personal contact with the Führer, was shocked by Hitler's appearance. He seemed to have aged ten years in just the past months.

"How are you, *Mein Führer*," asked Goebbels, seeking to break the awkward silence of the moment.

"I am well," said Hitler with little enthusiasm or conviction in his voice. "There is little time for social conversation, Gentlemen. We have a serious situation at hand. We must take quick action, or I'm afraid all will be lost."

Goering responded, "Our air force is doing its best, but we have too many fronts now. I believe we must consolidate our strength to defend the Reich."

Goebbels slowly nodded his head. "Marshall Goering is right, *Mein Führer*, it makes no sense to continue to have troops in Italy. Italy is lost. We must face that. And it especially makes no sense to have more than 70,000 of our men in Greece, a country we don't want or need. Unless we can defend our home borders from the Americans on the west and the Russians from the east, all really will be lost."

Hitler, weeks before, had come to the same conclusion but had wanted to hear from his advisors, hoping that something dramatic would alter the situation. Nothing dramatic had happened. "I agree with you gentlemen. I will give the order. By October we must leave Athens and then all of Greece."

CHAPTER SIXTEEN

As Hitler's order became known by the Nazi troops stationed in Athens, there were mixed feelings. The resistance forces in Greece had not made for a safe and tranquil occupation, but at least the war was not a wholesale battle of one army against another army as their colleagues had faced at Stalingrad or at Normandy. They all understood that they would now most likely all be returning to Germany to attempt to fend off the powerful assaults of the Americans and the Russians. Their next assignment would be to defend the homeland that they all knew would be a vicious, bloody battle many of them would not survive.

Klaus thought constantly about what lay ahead. He was tired, very tired of the war, the killing, the brutality. He knew in his mind and heart that Germany's days in the war were numbered, and he instinctively felt that when he returned to Germany to fight the Allied forces his chances of survival were slim. Though he had developed reservations about the German cause during at least the past year, he had followed orders, done his duty, and was viewed by his commanding offices as a young man destined for better things, perhaps a career as an officer in the nation's army. But his commanding officers did not know his real inner thoughts about the war and even about some options that had crossed his mind. He knew the Greek language well, and he was familiar with the Greek way of life. Perhaps, he thought to himself, he could simply abandon his uniform, dress as a civilian, and disappear into Greek society where he could find work and perhaps return to his studies. But thoughts such as these did not linger long. He knew he would follow with his comrades, leave Athens, return to Germany, and pray that he could survive as the war would end. Time, however, was running out, and the lingering thought that he needed to find Nikos and Mortis before he left Greece would not leave him. Since he knew where Nikos' uncle lived in Athens, he decided to attempt to contact Nikos and Mortis through Nikos' relatives. In full uniform and armed with his rifle, he went to the home of the uncle and knocked on the door. An elderly man opened the door and momentarily starred at Klaus.

"Sir, please do not be afraid," said Klaus, speaking Greek, "you are not in any trouble. My name is Klaus Schreiber. Your nephew, Nikos Gantos, and our friend Mortis and I were roommates in college in Thessaloniki before the war. I know you have heard that we are leaving Greece, and I very much would like to speak with my old friends before I leave. I hope you can help me contact them."

At first Nikos' uncle was not sure what to say. He knew that Nikos was with the resistance and had also operated with the Greek-American unit against the Germans. And he knew that Nikos had developed a reputation as a deadly killer of Nazis. He was suspicious of some kind of trickery or trap. Could this young soldier be sincere, or perhaps was he sent here to lure Nikos to some location for capture or assassination? Not knowing how to immediately respond, he decided to be hospitable and ask the soldier to come into his home and offer him some coffee and sweets.

"Please forgive me for asking," he said to Klaus, "but can you give me any identification of your name?"

Klaus was not offended and instantly understood the man's concern. "Of course," he responded, as he displayed his official identification with his picture photo.

"Thank you," said the uncle. "I know Nikos spoke about you often when he was at the university. He

317

said that you and Mortis and he were very close, almost like brothers."

"That's true, Sir. We were. And that's why I want to see him before I leave and somehow forget about this terrible war we have all been caught in. I very much want to see Mortis, too."

The elderly man was quiet for a moment. "I'm afraid that cannot happen. Mortis was killed by someone in your army."

Klaus was silent, then spoke, "Killed! When? Where?"

"I'm not sure. I don't know all the details, but Nikos told me some time ago."

"I don't know what to say," said Klaus, still shocked by what he had just heard. "It's like I have lost a brother, I just don't know what to say."

The uncle, seeing the sadness in Klaus over the news about Mortis, seemed more open to accepting his story of wanting to see his old friend rather than having some plan to entrap him. "I can't tell you where Nikos is," he said, "because I really don't know. He moves around a great deal. But I think I can get a message to him. I don't think it's a good idea for him to be seen with you or for you to be seen with him. There is a small, out of the way, coffee shop called the Olympic Café just behind the old Olympic Stadium. Very few people go there in the evening on weekdays, and there are even fewer people in that neighborhood at night. The Café stays open until about midnight. I will ask Nikos to meet you there at 10:00 p.m. next Thursday. I can't guarantee he will either receive my message, or, even if he does, that he will come. But I will try."

Klaus put the cup of coffee down, rose from his chair, and shook the man's hand, "Thank you," he said, "that's all I can ask, and I will be there."

As word spread in Athens that the Germans were preparing to leave, a sense of joy and relief grew throughout the city. On the designated day of evacuation, the Greek crowd gathered in front of the Parliament building to witness the official ceremony. Nikos was among the crowd. He had spent the previous night at his uncle's home and had received the news of Klaus' visit and request to meet with him. But today, his thoughts were on this official departure of the army he had come to hate, an army that had killed thousands of Greeks and destroyed hundreds of villages and was now leaving the country in economic chaos. Watching with the crowd, he saw the German commander officially return the city to the mayor of Athens. Next, all eyes focused on the Parthenon where the German swastika flag was lowered and the Greek blue and white flag restored to its position. Finally, the large crowd became silent as a German soldier approached the Tomb of the Unknown Soldier, saluted, turned, and was replaced by a Greek *Evzone*. Cheers broke out among the crowd, strangers embraced strangers, and spontaneous outbursts of the Greek national anthem sounded everywhere. It seemed as though the long, terrible nightmare might finally be over.

Nikos was not eager to celebrate. He had seen too much suffering, pain, starvation, and wholesale murder from these Germans. All these official impressive ceremonies could not mask what devastation the Nazis had brought to his country. In his young life he had never really experienced deep hatred for anything or anybody, but he now felt such hatred for these Germans, whom he considered barbarians. The Germans were leaving, he thought, and that was good, but the violence and the killing they had fostered would not end. Greeks had been killing Greeks, and a civil war had already started. He wanted no part of this new war. He was tired of killing. He was frustrated because he did not know what he would do or where he would go when these Germans left. And he was an angry man. Angry at the Germans for what they had done, angry at the Greeks who had collaborated with them, angry at the Communists who were now determined to continue the bloodshed to achieve their utopian dreams. He walked slowly away from the loud, cheerful crowd at Syntagma, wondering whether or not he could or should go to the Café to meet Klaus Schreiber, who was now wearing the uniform of those he had come to hate.

Within two days Nikos felt somewhat better. His nerves had calmed, he had finally slept well, and his aunt's food always made him feel full and satisfied. He had thought about it a great deal and had decided that he would meet Klaus. He wasn't sure why he wanted to go, since he knew, because of what his sister, Eleni, had told him, that Klaus had been one of the Germans at the Kalavryta massacre. But something inside him seemed to be pushing him to attend the meeting and look into Klaus' eyes and speak with him.

At 9:55 p.m. on the following Thursday Nikos arrived at the Olympic Café. It was virtually empty; only one old man was sitting at a table reading a newspaper and slowly sipping ouzo. The café owner was washing dishes and glasses in the kitchen. The store was dark; the low voltage in the overhead lights gave the place a dreary feel. On the wall were pictures of the original modern Olympic game events that had been held in Greece in the 1890s in the stadium just outside the entrance to the café. Nikos came in and sat at a table in the corner of the room. At exactly 10:00 p.m. a soldier in full uniform walked through the door. He removed his helmet, and Nikos immediately recognized that it was Klaus. Seeing a virtually empty room, Klaus scanned the tables and saw a man sitting in the shadows at a table in the corner of the café. He slowly walked over and approached the table.

Seeing that it was Nikos, he stopped, said nothing, and then awkwardly held out his hand. Nikos looked at him and with a slight smile on his face reached out and shook Klaus' hand. Klaus instinctively wanted to embrace Nikos, but he did not.

"Niko," he finally said, "thank you for coming. It's good to see you. I very much wanted to see you before I left."

Nikos hesitated as the café owner approached them to take their order. Both men requested a cup of Greek coffee, a small, strong and thick brew that most likely had originally been introduced to Greece during the Turkish occupation decades ago. When the coffee arrived, Nikos responded, "It's been a long time Klaus, and much has happened. Much has happened between our countries, and I'm sure much has happened to both you and me as well. But I guess I needed to see you, too."

Klaus found Nikos' tone to be constrained, cool, and distant. "I know how you must feel about us, Niko, but we're not all like what you what you have read about."

"Klaus," responded Niko, "it's not what I've read about, it's what I have seen. I don't understand how you Germans can claim to be a civilized nation yet act like barbarians."

"War does strange and irrational things to people, Niko. Your people were killing us, too. None of it is good or right, Niko, none of it. But can we talk about something else? This war is almost over, all of us know that within a year, at most, my country will surrender. I'm thinking of the future, of resuming my studies. What about you? And Niko, I heard about Mortis. I can't tell you how bad I have felt about that. The three of us were so close, Niko, so close."

"Mortis was like a brother to me, Klaus. I loved him. I can never forget what they did to him. Never."

Klaus nervously attempted again to shift the conversation. "So what about the future, Niko? Will you return to the university?"

'I don't know. I'm not sure. My country is in ruins, and this civil war that has begun will drive us even deeper into chaos. But I just don't know. Someday, I guess, I'd like to go back to the university."

Klaus smiled. He looked so strong, so official in his Nazi uniform. "Maybe someday, when all this has cooled down, we could both go back to the university, maybe even room together."

Nikos smiled back. "I doubt that, Klaus, I really doubt that. You know, Klaus, the only thing I really like about you German Nazis is your uniforms. You really have the best uniforms."

Klaus was finding the conversation increasingly strange. Something had happened. This was not the same Nikos he had known, the Nikos who had been one of his best friends.

"Klaus," said Nikos, "It was good to see you. Someday when this crazy war is over, look me up. Maybe things will be different, maybe memories will have faded by then."

"I agree," responded Klaus. "Maybe this is too soon. I'd like that, Niko, I'd like to keep in contact. You never know, stranger things have happened. We could still end up at the university together."

"We could," said Nikos, "anything's possible. Let's call it a night, Klaus, I'll walk out with you."

The two men left the café and walked toward their cars. It was dark, the moon seemed to have disappeared. The two men shook hands, Klaus put his helmet on. Nikos stared at the uniform, the distinctive insignias, the special Nazi helmet, and the thought of what Eleni had told him about Kalavryta crowded his mind. As Klaus walked away, his back to Nikos, Nikos called out, "Klaus, one more thing."

Klaus turned, faced Nikos, and Nikos, holding his pistol in his hand, fired three shots to Klaus' temple, neck, and chest. He fell to the ground, blood splattered over his uniform and on the ground. Nikos walked over to the lifeless body, "That's for all of us, Klaus, for all of us."

EPILOGUE
ATHENS, GREECE
2011

CHAPTER SEVENTEEN

H E HAD AWAKENED FROM SLEEP around 5:30 a.m. It was not that he had to be up to go to work or to keep some appointment. He had stopped working long ago, and this day, like most of his days, was appointment free. But Nicholaos Gantos had never seemed to be able to break the habit of rising early. He told his neighbor that he didn't mind the fact that he couldn't sleep longer because, at ninety-one years of age, he was happy to get up at all and realize that he was still alive.

This morning he followed his normal routine: shower, shave, dress, and then sit and read for at least two hours. He read many kinds of books, and his house was filled with them. He especially enjoyed twentieth-century history and biography. He told people that he liked those subjects because he had lived most of those years, and he wanted to see if the writers and historians had gotten their story right. Usually, while he was reading, he had his breakfast that almost always consisted of coffee and one or two pieces of toast with butter along with a small helping of strawberries or bananas.

After reading, Nikos turned on his television set to see what the latest news was in Athens, Europe, and around the world. Today local coverage continued on the demonstrations occurring in front of the Parliament building which were protesting the government actions that would reduce pension benefits, cut public employment, and privatize previously government-owned assets. Another day of signs and marches, thought Nikos. He debated whether he would walk over to Syntagma again today just to pass the time and see what was developing.

Nikos' apartment in the Plaka section of Athens was small but comfortable. He had a small balcony to sit on and in the summer months he passed the time simply watching the tourists who walked through the area buying souvenirs of their trip to Greece. Inside the apartment were photographs, pictures of him and Vasili as children, others of his mother and father, a number of his wife and children, and still others of his wartime colleagues. There was a large photo of Nikos with Napoleon Zervas, another with members of the British Special Forces, and one he had always particularly liked of him and Vasili with the

Greek-American soldier, Stan Peterson. Nikos' house had, over the years, become a museum of past memories.

At one time he had thought of writing a book or his memoirs about his life, and until he was about sixty-five, he had diligently collected or secured newspaper clippings about the war years that he carefully placed and labeled in scrap books. He had collected so much material that he had filled seven scrapbooks. He decided that he would spend some time this morning looking at those scrapbooks again. For some reason, he had never gotten around to writing that book, and now he thought it was too late and probably nobody cared anyway.

Nikos sat in his favorite comfortable chair and began looking at page after page of the newspaper stories he had saved. He looked at a story and photo of the day the Nazis left Greece and a picture of the German soldier who had saluted the Tomb of the Unknown Soldier, and Nikos remembered exactly where he was standing as he witnessed that event. He turned some pages and saw clippings on the death of Mussolini and his mistress, Claretta Petacci. Italian anti-fascists had found Mussolini disguised, wearing the overcoat and helmet of a German soldier. They executed both Mussolini and Claretta and then, along with others, hung their bodies upside down in Milan for every Italian and the whole world to witness what an unglorious end had come to his life. Nikos starred at the photo, shook his head, and thought to himself, what a fool Mussolini had been and he finally got what he deserved. He then went on to look at stories reporting that Hitler and his mistress, Eva Braun, whom he had married at the eleventh hour, had committed suicide just days after Mussolini had met his fate. Never, Nikos thought to himself, could he understand how the German people could have followed him so blindly. But Hitler's fate was appropriate, too, Nikos thought.

Nikos keep turning the pages of the scrapbook looking at the clippings, which were now turning yellow from age. He stopped at a story and photo of Aris Velouchiotis. What a passionate, sadistic, crazy man, Nikos thought. His fate had been brutal, too. His enemies captured him and killed him, although some had said that he, too, had committed suicide. However his life ended, his enemies decapitated him and put his severed head on a stake and displayed it in the center of his home town. And then there was a picture and story of Nikos' old war leader, Napoleon Zervas, who had started a new political party after the war, was elected to Parliament, and later held a number of cabinet posts in the government. He had continued his anti-Communist crusades, but his reputation was harmed when charges were made against him that he had collaborated with the Nazis during

never believed those accusations,
...rvas had been smeared by political
...ad only seen and spoken to Zervas
...es after the war, and Zervas had died

...t turning the pages as postwar Greek
...ed to come alive again in the stories he
...ed. There were many news clippings of
...ar that had followed the end of the World
...os read the stories in the scrapbook. It was
...uation of the hardship and killings he had
...om the Nazis, only Greeks then were killing
...Greeks during this terrible time. Nikos shook
...ead from side to side, wondering how, after the
...zi horrors, his countrymen were so irrational so
... to continue this conflict and killing. Nikos then
...hought about his brother, Vasili, who had first
joined with Velouchiotis, then left him, and then decided that the guerilla leader's agenda was best for
Greece and rejoined him. He thought often about
his brother. Vasili had been killed during the Greek
civil war, and Nikos had missed him every day since.

Turning the page in the scrapbook, he came upon
stories of the military coup that had established a dictatorship in Greece in the 1960s. Another sad episode,
Nikos thought, but the country survived that, too.

The old man closed the scrapbook and sat quietly
thinking about his own life. He sometimes wondered

why, when so many others had died in the war and after, he was still here. After the Germans and Japanese surrendered, civil war was raging in Greece between those who wanted a Communist Greece and those who didn't. Nikos wanted no part of this internal bloodshed and had returned to Kalavryta to try to live a quiet, peaceful life of a farmer who raised pigs, sheep, and olives. He had become a self-taught butcher and had opened a small store selling meats and vegetables to people in the immediate region. At first he had thought about returning to school, but he had little money and the country was in chaos, so he opted to return to his village. At a wedding of a mutual friend he had met his wife, Marina, married, and lived happily with her and their two children. He was twenty-eight and Marina was twenty-five when they married. He had missed his wife every day since she had died in 2006 of cancer. While living in Kalavryta he had successfully been elected to Parliament with the New Democracy Party but had served only a short time. He was impatient with the self-serving and corruption he witnessed in all the Greek political parties, and he wanted no part of that life.

When Nikos' daughter married, she and her husband moved to Athens, and Nikos and Marina followed them there. And when his wife died, he remained in the city at the insistence of his daughter. His daughter, his grandchildren, and now his great-grandchildren visited him often, and he found great pleasure in being around them. They really were the only close people he had now. He kept thinking that almost everyone he had known as a child and even as a middle-aged man had died; they were all gone. It was a strange feeling, Nikos had said to his daughter, when you realize that virtually everyone you had known in your lifetime was gone.

He decided to leave his apartment and get some fresh air and exercise by walking. Taking his cane, he left the apartment and decided that he would, after all, walk again to the city center to observe the crowd of demonstrators. As he walked he looked at the various streets and buildings he had seen for so many years. Much had changed, but much was still the same. The city had exploded in population; now half the country's population lived in Athens and its suburbs. It was much too crowded, thought Nikos.

Approaching the park area in front of the Parliament building, he found a bench and sat down to observe the speeches, the placards, and the general activity and conversation. Probably, he thought to himself, he was likely the only person among the thousand or more who had gathered who had any real sense of what suffering, what violence, and what widespread killing and enormous sacrifice had been part of the country's not too distant history. Nikos felt satisfied that he and his generation had done their part to save Greece so that these people could openly and freely demonstrate. Again and again he told himself, this current economic crisis was real, it was important, and many were now suffering economically, but this was really nothing compared to what he had seen, had lived through, and had been forced to do to survive. Greece would somehow, some way, survive these economic problems, he was convinced of that. He couldn't do much to help this time; he was too old, his time had passed. But at another crucial time, he felt proud that he had done his part to serve and save his country. At that time, long ago, many had recognized and applauded his actions. His exploits had become almost legendary. Many wanted to honor him as a hero, but Nikos politely said no to that. He knew he was not a hero; he had seen too many others do incredibly heroic things. And as he slowly walked back to his apartment, holding his cane in his wrinkled hand, he felt tremendous pride in knowing it was not that he was a hero but that he had been fortunate enough to live at a time and in a place that was a country of heroes.

MICHAEL J. BAKALIS IS PRESIdent and CEO of American Quality Schools, a not-for-profit educational management organization. Formerly Illinois State Superintendent of Education and Deputy Undersecretary of Education in the U.S. Department of Education, he has taught at every educational level and has served on the faculties of Northern Illinois, Loyola (Chicago), and Northwestern Universities. He received his PhD in American history from Northwestern University. American Quality Schools operates elementary and high schools in the Midwest. His most recent other publications are *In Search of Yannelli: A Son's Journey to Know His Father* and *The Achilles Heel: A Citizen's Guide to Understanding and Closing the Black-White Achievement Gap in Our Schools.* Dr. Bakalis can be reached at mbakalis@aqs.org.